THE
BILLIONAIRE'S
PROMISE

The Winters Saga
Book Four

IVY LAYNE

GINGER QUILL PRESS, LLC

CONTENTS

Also by Ivy Layne

THE HEARTS OF SAWYERS BEND

Stolen Heart

Sweet Heart

Scheming Heart

Rebel Heart

Wicked Heart

THE UNTANGLED SERIES

Unraveled

Undone

Uncovered

THE WINTERS SAGA

The Billionaire's Secret Heart (Novella)

The Billionaire's Secret Love (Novella)

The Billionaire's Pet

The Billionaire's Promise

THE BILLIONAIRE CLUB

CHAPTER ONE
MAGNOLIA

T-MINUS TWO YEARS

I couldn't breathe.

He opened the door, and my breath was sucked from my lungs in one big whoosh.

If you'd been there, you'd understand. One second, I was standing in the hallway, waiting impatiently to be interviewed for a job I wasn't sure I wanted. The next second, the door was swinging open, and he was there, filling the door frame, six and a half feet of panty-melting hotness.

A towel was slung loosely around his waist, barely clinging to his lean hips. Drops of water slid down his broad, defined chest. He leaned against the door and looked down at me, his eyes scanning me from head to toe. Was it too late to run?

There was no way I could work for this man.

Vance Winters.

Heir to billions, renowned artist at the young age of twenty-eight, and secret angel investor in up and coming tech companies.

All of that was intimidating enough.

I hadn't taken into account the impact he would have in person. I'd seen pictures in the society section of the paper and in glossy magazines. They didn't scratch the surface.

First, he was tall. I'm right in the middle, neither tall nor short, and he towered over me, all of him sculpted muscle and smooth, golden skin decorated with elaborate, inky black tattoos.

From the way the towel dipped across his abs, showing every inch of the cut V of muscle between his hips, as well as a stark tan line, I knew the golden skin came from the sun. He must spend a lot of time outdoors.

I tried not to imagine him jogging without his shirt. Or swimming, that too-long, dark blond hair pulled back, powerful legs propelling him through the water.

I definitely didn't imagine tugging on the towel to get a better look at the white skin below the tan.

Absolutely not.

I blinked hard. What was wrong with me?

I had a boyfriend. He was a good guy, a med student, and we'd been together for years. He wasn't in Vance's league, but he was very attractive.

Brayden. I had to think of Brayden.

I was quiet, but not easily intimidated. Not usually. There was something about the way Vance lounged in the door, his blue eyes lazily hooded as they studied me. He threw me off balance.

Then he grinned and said, "Are you coming in?"

My knees went weak. That grin. Holy crap. With his blond hair, vivid blue eyes, and all those golden muscles, he reminded me of a Viking.

A debauched Viking with a killer grin.

I don't know where it came from, but in a crisp, cool

voice, I said, "I don't know. Are you going to get out of the way?"

Another grin, and a wink. Vance Winters was trouble. Fighting the weakness in my knees, I straightened my spine and followed him into his loft, ready to get this over with.

"Can you make coffee?" he asked, gesturing to his ultra-modern kitchen. "Consider it part of your interview."

Again, not sure where the attitude was coming from, I said, "Are you planning on getting dressed?"

He looked down at his lack of attire and shrugged. "Do you want me to?" His tone suggested I'd be crazy to cover up all that gorgeous. He was right.

Telling Vance Winters to put on clothes was a crime against nature. A man with a body like that should be naked all the time.

But I was there for a job interview. I wasn't looking to get laid. Brayden. I had Brayden. I wasn't into casual hookups anyway, even if I were single. Vance Winters was known for many things, and sleeping his way through Atlanta was one of them.

"Please," I said, as coolly and professionally detached as I could manage. Not waiting for his response, I turned to the kitchen to start a pot of coffee. I heard him leave and let out a breath I hadn't known I'd been holding.

What was I doing here? I didn't need the job. Well, I did, and I didn't.

I had money. My grandmother had left me well provided for. I wasn't wealthy, not like the Winters family, but I had a beautiful home—my grandmother's—and enough money to live on if I was careful.

Six months ago, I graduated from Emory with a degree in Business, after staying an extra semester to complete dual concentrations in Finance and Accounting. I'd planned on working for a year or two, then going for my MBA.

A month after I'd finished school, my grandmother had died.

I should have seen it coming. She'd been almost eighty, and for the last few months of her life, she'd been unusually tired. She'd refused to go to the doctor, saying she was fine.

She'd been wrong. Losing her had leeched every drop of vitality from my life. For as long as I could remember, my grandmother was the only adult I could depend on. She remembered my birthday. She gave me a home for summer vacations.

That first year in boarding school, eight years old and terrified of being alone in England, she'd called me every night, the time difference be damned.

Iris Henry had loved me like no one else, and then she'd died on me. I'd imagined I'd be able to return the favor one day, envisioned caring for her as she aged. Instead, I was rattling around in her house, alone, losing my bearings more and more with each day that passed.

I'd been drifting for months when I'd run into Rupert Stevens, an old bridge crony of my grandmother's. I'd known him since I'd been a child, and if Rupert wasn't family, he was the closest thing to it. It hadn't taken him long to size up my situation.

Two days after we spoke, his wife, Sloane, Vance's manager, had called me with a job offer. I knew if I didn't at least drag myself out of the house and go see Vance, Rupert would call in the cavalry.

I was having a hard enough time dealing with my grandmother's death. I didn't think I could take an intervention from her bridge club, no matter how well-meaning.

So, I was here, willing to let Vance Winters interview

me to see if I'd fit the role of his assistant. I hadn't been sure I wanted the job when I'd knocked on his door. Now, after seeing him in the towel, I thought my best option might be to tell him 'no thanks' and go home.

I remembered the ridges of his six pack and my mouth watered. I hadn't had sex for over a month. Brayden was never home lately, and when he was, he said he was exhausted.

I caught the scuff of a bare foot on hardwood and turned to see Vance prowling toward me, his magnificent body covered by a pair of jeans so old they were worn white at the knee and an equally threadbare t-shirt with the faded logo of a classic rock band.

All that luscious tanned skin was covered, only the trailing vines of a tattoo visible on his left arm. His streaky dark blond hair was wet and loose around his face, his vivid blue eyes dancing as they took in the full mug of coffee in my hands.

"That mine?" he asked, sliding onto a stool at the counter built into his kitchen island. I nodded and placed it in front of him. He took a sip and let out a low hum of approval. "Good coffee. You're hired."

"That fast?" I asked, raising an eyebrow as I took a sip of my own coffee. He was right. I did make good coffee. I'd worked as a barista in college, and I knew everything about coffee. It was my only addiction. "I haven't agreed to take the job."

"True. Do you want it?"

"I don't know what it is," I said. "Sloane said you needed help with your schedule and errands. I'm at loose ends right now, but I'm over-qualified if that's all you need."

Vance shook his head. "Sloane has no idea what I need.

But Rupert speaks highly of you. He said you have a business degree and a sharp mind."

"I do," I said.

His eyes narrowed on my face, and he said, "I was sorry to hear about your grandmother. I didn't know her, but my brother, Aiden, did."

I nodded and choked out, "Thank you."

I still wasn't used to the sharp stab of pain every time someone told me how sorry they were. I knew they meant it, but the kind platitudes were miles away from my own raw emotions and they always left me frustrated.

I was bereft. Furious she'd abandoned me, guilty for being angry—a jumbled mess of pain and hurt I couldn't quite hide from the world—hence my drifting through life.

Vance must have sensed my mood, because he broke eye contact and went on, "Sloane told you I need an assistant. That's accurate, but it doesn't really cover the scope of what I have in mind. Do you know what I do?"

"Some of it," I said, glad to be back on familiar ground. "I know you're a sculptor, working primarily in metal. Large pieces, mainly, a combination of your own inspiration and commissions. You also act as an investor on occasion, mostly for small tech companies, though last year, you branched out and went in with your brother and cousin on a nightclub."

"You do your research," he said. I sipped my coffee without responding. He went on, "I want help managing my life. I have a lot going on between my work and the investing and other things. I need someone who can keep track of mundane shit like my dry cleaning and dentist appointments, but who can also stay on top of my investments—vet proposals, keep an eye on the books, that kind of thing. You'd have to be flexible. Every day is different around here."

It sounded intriguing. I wanted to use my degree, but I couldn't see myself in an office, even though that had been my plan while I'd been in college.

I opened my mouth to ask more about the details when a toilet flushed on the other side of the loft. I sat up straighter. I'd thought we were alone. Vance slouched over his coffee and muttered, "Sorry about this."

A door shut, and a woman appeared, her micro mini and strappy top straight from a club. So was her big hair and smoky eye makeup. I'm sure she'd been stunning the night before. With smeared mascara under her bloodshot eyes and badly in need of a comb, she wasn't that appealing. I knew her type.

When she stumbled on her spike heels on the way to Vance, I looked away. She ignored me, didn't even bother to ask who I was or why I was there, her focus all on Vance.

She slipped her arms around his torso from behind, leaning forward to nip his earlobe, saying, "Vance, baby, come back to bed." She eyed me with vacant disdain. "Get rid of her. Or bring her with you. Whatever, it's cool with me."

Out of the corner of my eye, I saw her hand slide into Vance's lap. I swallowed and stood. I wasn't a prude, but this was just weird and uncomfortable. I had no interest in being the third wheel in another woman's awkward morning after.

As if he had a lot of practice—and I imagined he did—Vance twisted from her embrace and stood, turning the woman to face me.

"Not now. I have a full day. Ms. Henry will show you out."

I raised an eyebrow at him, caught between annoyance and reluctant amusement. Vance had balls, I'd give him that. Taking in his expectant look, I understood.

My job description would include managing his morning-afters. Ugh. If rumor was half accurate, this happened a lot. I thought about walking out. I didn't need this. I didn't much like his one-night stand, but I didn't want to humiliate her either.

My irritation let me see through the mask of Vance's beauty to the red lines dulling his eyes, the faint circles beneath. He was as hungover as she was.

Vance had the looks and talent of a god, but he was really just like every other party boy I knew. Thinking over my options, I got to my feet and took the confused woman's arm in a gentle grip, steering her to the door.

She glanced back over her shoulder at Vance, almost losing her balance in her high heels, and I got the feeling she was going to plead her case. I shook my head, nudging her through the door.

"Do you need me to call you a ride?" I asked gently. She snatched her arm from my hand and stalked to the stairs. Guess not. Locking the door behind her, I turned back to finish my interview.

"Thanks," Vance said from across the kitchen. He refilled his coffee and held out the pot. I shook my head. We had more to talk about before I decided if I was staying for a second cup.

"Does that happen often?" I asked, again in a crisp tone. I realized I sounded exactly like my boarding school headmistress, minus the posh English accent.

Vance shrugged. "Often enough," he said with unashamed honesty. "Why? Interested in taking her place?" His electric blue gaze caressed my body with indolent interest. "I don't usually mix business and the bedroom, but I could make an exception for you." He raised one eyebrow as if daring me. For a second, I thought about slapping him.

"Are you kidding?"

He shrugged. "Not really, but I'm getting the idea sex isn't in your job description."

"Sex is absolutely not part of my job description." I was both offended and flattered.

Yes, flattered.

I know, I know.

I should have given him a good smack and walked out. My only excuse is that no man who looked like Vance had ever hit on me. Granted, Vance's standards weren't that high, but still, the sex-deprived woman in me appreciated the offer.

There was no way I'd ever sleep with him, but it was nice to be asked.

"I figured you'd say that." Vance shrugged again, amusement glinting in his red-rimmed eyes. "It was worth a try. Now that we've gotten my obligatory pass out of the way, here's how I see this working. You'll show up by ten every day, evict any guests, make me breakfast, and get my lazy ass out of bed. Once I get rolling, we'll go over business, then I'll head down to my studio and you'll do whatever you've got on for the day."

"So you need a combination babysitter, errand girl, and business manager," I said, disarmed by his upfront explanation.

"Something like that," he admitted. "Interested?" He named a salary that wasn't outrageous, but it was more than generous.

I was tempted. It wasn't a long-term plan, but it would

get me out of the house and force me to move forward with my life. I couldn't keep going as I was.

"Can I bring my dog?" I asked. I'd gotten Scout a month after my grandmother had died, and I didn't want to leave him alone at home all day.

"What kind of dog?

"A mutt. A boxer-corgi mix." At the look on his face, I pulled my phone out of my pocket. It was impossible to describe Scout unless you could see his absurd cuteness for yourself.

He had the face, ears, and long, low body of a corgi, with the stance and fur of a boxer. He wasn't the brightest dog, but he was all love. We were a perfect fit. He'd needed a home, and I'd needed someone to hold on to.

Vance took my phone and flipped through the pictures of Scout, smiling down at my adorable dog. He stopped on a picture and held my phone up.

On it was a shot I'd taken of Brayden, backing up as Scout went for his bagel. Brayden didn't like dogs, and Scout returned his lack of affection.

"Who's this?" Vance asked. "He looks familiar."

"My boyfriend, Brayden." I took my phone back, turning off the screen and sliding it in my pocket.

"Brayden Michaels?" Vance asked, an incredulous look on his face.

"You know him? How?"

"School. I was in the same class as his older brother. Brayden's a twat."

Before I knew what I was doing, I stood. Brayden wasn't perfect, but he was mine, and I wasn't going to listen to this dissipated playboy put him down.

Picking up my keys and my purse, I said, "This isn't going to work, Mr. Winters. I'll see myself out."

"Wait," he said, shoving back his stool and coming to his feet. "Magnolia, don't leave."

Against, my better judgement, I stopped and whirled to face him. "I don't know that I want to work for you," I said bluntly. "You're rude and immature."

Vance shoved his hands in his back pockets, dragging his jeans down an inch to reveal a strip of taut golden skin.

I shouldn't be tempted. I didn't even like him. I dragged my eyes away, forcing myself to look at his face.

His blue eyes were shadowed when he said, "Yeah, I am. Rude, immature, sometimes a complete asshole. I'd be a pain in the ass to work for half the time."

"And the other half?" I asked.

"You'll get more hands-on experience with me than an entry-level job at a bigger company. My personal shit aside, I get first look at some very interesting investment opportunities, and you'd be involved at every level. You'd get one-on-one exposure to some of the biggest players in business, not just in Atlanta but across the country. When you're ready to move on, you'll have connections you'd never be able to make sitting in a cubicle. All you have to do is put up with me."

When he laid it out like that, how could I say no? Wondering if I was making a huge mistake, I held out my hand. Vance took it in his, his strong fingers closing around mine with possession. I tried to ignore the spark of heat as we touched.

"So you'll take the job?" Vance asked, holding onto my hand when I tried to tug it free. I gave a hard yank and took a step back.

"On a trial basis," I said in what I was starting to think of as my headmistress voice. "If you're too much of an asshole, I'm quitting, and I want a guarantee of six months' severance."

"Agreed," Vance said, grinning down at me. "But the severance is only payable if you leave because I'm an asshole."

"Does sexual harassment count as being an asshole?" I challenged. I'd admitted to myself that I was flattered by his offer, but if he kept it up, I'd walk out.

"It would, if I were planning on harassing you. I won't pull that shit. I'm an asshole, but I'm not a complete dick." He ruined it by leering at me and saying, "Anyway, when we finally sleep together, it'll be because you can't keep your hands off me."

"And that's strike one. Jury's out on whether you're a complete dick."

To my surprise, Vance laughed. "Cross my heart." With two fingers, he swiped a cross over his chest. "I have a twin sister who'd kick my ass if she thought I was harassing a woman who works for me. Give me a chance. I promise the job will be worth it."

"Fine. I'll start tomorrow." I turned on my heel and walked out. I'd had as much of Vance Winters as I could take for the day. His voice followed me into the hall.

"Ten A.M. Don't be late, Magnolia."

Like he would notice if I was. I'd bet my inheritance Vance would be passed out in bed when I showed up, with another nubile, hungover girl beside him. On the drive home, I tried to convince myself I'd done the right thing. It wasn't easy.

The truth was, my first instinct was spot on. Vance Winters was trouble—six feet of dangerously beautiful mayhem.

I should have taken one look and run in the other direction.

I should have told him to take his job offer and shove it up his tight, perfect ass.

But hindsight is 20/20. By the time I knew what was coming, it was already too late. For Vance, and for me.

CHAPTER TWO

MAGNOLIA

T-MINUS EIGHTEEN MONTHS

I let myself into the loft, Scout padding in behind me, not bothering to be quiet. It was 9:58 am, and if this morning was like every other, Vance would be passed out in bed.

It was even odds whether he'd be alone.

I headed straight for the coffee maker and got a pot going. Coffee was essential to getting Vance up in the morning.

Once I had the coffee brewing, I hit the fridge and pulled out the ingredients for my 'morning after' smoothie. Fruit, greens, and a few herbs to help his body detox, with some protein powder and MCT oil for energy.

The first time I made it, he complained, claiming he didn't drink kale. Now, he scowled at me if I didn't hand him one with his coffee.

Some mornings, the buzz of the industrial strength blender was enough to rouse him. I flipped it off and poured, listening for movement.

Nothing but the rustle of Scout settling into the dog bed Vance had bought him. He raised his head and glared at the blender, then at me. Like Vance, my dog was not into mornings.

Deciding I wasn't going to interrupt his sleep again, Scout let out a low grumble and set his head on his paws. The loft was silent. No movement from the bedroom, though I could see the door was open. Hmm.

It was going to be one of those mornings. I screwed the lid on his insulated cup and weighed my options. Some days, I went straight for the kill, but not today. Today, I was in too good a mood to be mean.

I pulled my phone from my pocket and turned on the wireless speaker on the counter, waiting for the two devices to connect. A quiet blip, and I was in business. Seconds later, the opening bars of *Walking on Sunshine* by Katrina and the Waves filled the loft.

And I mean *filled it*. All the way.

I saw—but didn't hear—Scout lift his head and shoot me another glare. My poor dog. He really didn't like mornings. This was Step Three in my wake-up plan.

Step One: Coffee. That one never worked, not unless Vance was still up from the night before.

Step Two: The blender. That one worked half the time, but when it did, Vance was particularly grumpy.

Step Three: Music.

My choice varied by the day. Today I was in a happy mood, so Katrina. Other days, he got Korn, Megadeath, or—if I was feeling evil—a boy band. Metal worked better than pop or the classics, even though it wasn't my personal favorite.

Most of the time, Step Three did the trick.

I carried his smoothie across the loft and peeked in the

bedroom. Damn. Two naked bodies were sprawled across the huge bed, spread out but not touching. A quick glance at her black hair told me the female body was probably Amy, a girl Vance hooked up with often but claimed not to be dating.

Vance lay on his stomach, his head pillowed on one arm, legs splayed, dark blond hair tangled around his face. I didn't even pretend I wasn't staring. Working for Vance had its upsides and downsides.

Dealing with the aftermath of his drinking was a downside. Ogling his body? Definitely an upside.

I wasn't interested in Vance. Not personally. Not like that. But there wasn't any harm in appreciating the way he was put together. Muscles everywhere. Everywhere.

My eyes lingered on his legs, tanned from the sun, strong yet sleek. And his ass. Yum. Seriously yum. Don't forget about the shoulders. Broad and thick with muscle. It wasn't just that he worked out, which he did. Every day.

Sculpting metal meant he spent a lot of time hauling around heavy equipment. His strength wasn't just from the gym. It was functional, and it showed. Even his scars were hot. And the tattoos. Covering most of one shoulder and running down his arm, the intricate designs were stark against his golden skin, dramatic and way too sexy.

I'd never been into body art, but the tattoos fit Vance, the ink as much a part of him as the scars from his work and his muscular build.

I gave myself another minute to watch him sleep, my heart hurting just a little at the sight of him so defenseless. Vance was a good boss, most of the time. He was a good guy most of the time, too.

I wished he were happier.

At first, I'd thought he was just another party boy, one

more guy in search of a good time. Maybe he was. Maybe I was reading him wrong. But the more I got to know him, the more certain I was that his drinking was more than that.

All of it—the drinking, the endless string of women— felt desperate, and he wasn't happy. Sometimes, when he didn't think anyone was looking, his eyes went dark and lost.

I never let on that I knew, but I wished I could fix what was eating at him. I didn't dare ask. Vance wasn't the kind of guy who talked about his feelings. Ever.

I knew enough to guess at what might be the cause. He was a Winters, a family notorious for scandal and tragedy. Vance and his siblings had lost their parents when he was just a child to a grisly murder-suicide.

His aunt and uncle had taken them in and raised them along with their own children until they, too, had been murdered when Vance was seventeen.

The whole thing was creepy and terrible. Awful. The Winters family was wealthy and powerful. Not *nice cars, big house, great job* wealthy. They were generations of billionaires running a company that made more money every year than many countries' GDPs.

You'd think it would be easy to be that rich. In some ways, it was. Vance never had to work a day in his life. He didn't have to worry about rent, or student loans, or car payments.

But all that money, all that power, couldn't bring back his dead parents. And when they'd died, their wealth had made them all targets. The media attention had been brutal.

I didn't remember his parents dying. I'd been in school in England by then, but I vividly recalled his aunt's and uncle's murders. The speculation had been wild and unending.

The remaining Winters still attracted attention on a

regular basis. I'd chased photographers away from Vance's building myself on more than one slow news day. I thought I understood why he drank so much, but it made me worry for him. I liked him, and I hated to see him so unhappy.

Not your business, I reminded myself. *You're here to do your job.* That Vance had become a friend as well as my employer didn't change anything. Shaking myself out of my daze, I went back to the kitchen, set Vance's smoothie down on the island, and proceeded to Step Four.

This was going to be fun.

I filled a tall glass with cold water and walked back to the bedroom, taking my time, the music still blasting through the loft. Vance hadn't moved an inch. Oh, well, he'd asked for it.

Standing beside him, I held the glass over his head and tilted it, spilling the icy water into his closed eyes for a second before trailing it down his spine. Usually, the first drop of water did the trick. On a bad day, like this one, I got all the way to that tight, perfect ass before he reacted.

When he moved, it was so fast I almost dropped the water. He flipped onto his back, one hand shooting out to snatch the glass from my grip, totally comfortable with his nudity.

He propped himself up on one arm and drained the water, his blue eyes on mine, sleepy and oddly intent.

I did *not* look at him. I didn't. So I definitely didn't notice his erection. Not like I hadn't seen it before. Vance was no stranger to morning wood. Since I woke him up and he slept naked, neither was I.

I'd learned exactly where to look to avoid getting an eyeful. And I did. Avoid it. It was hard, considering Vance had the biggest cock I'd ever seen.

Seriously. It's not like I'd seen a ton, but I knew he was above average. Well above average.

I wasn't tempted by him. Really, I wasn't. I knew him too well at this point to be enticed by the size of his dick. Vance was not boyfriend material.

And I had Brayden, who had a lot more to offer me than just a hot body and a huge penis. Not that Brayden had a huge penis. He didn't, which was part of the reason I went out of my way to avoid looking at Vance's cock.

I'd just signed up for a lifetime of average, and I didn't need to get used to the sight of super-size. Based on the way most of his women begged for another roll in his sheets, I assumed Vance knew what to do with his cock. Brayden . . . not so much.

Sex wasn't everything in a relationship.

It was the one area where Brayden fell short. And it was all Vance had to offer any woman. He didn't do fidelity. He couldn't even get out of bed on time, much less maintain a relationship.

My eyes were wide open about Vance Winters, which is why I kept my gaze on his and waited, patiently, for him to finish the water.

"You up?" I asked.

"You're in a chipper mood this morning," he said, his voice gravelly, rolling his eyes to the ceiling to indicate the music. I grinned at him.

"I am. Are you up?"

He gave a grunt, which I took to mean that he was.

"Do you want breakfast or just the smoothie?"

Vance winced. I knew what that meant and made a note to get out the Ibuprofen.

"Check," I said. "Just the smoothie. It's ready. Do you need me to get Amy up?"

To my relief, he shook his head. "We're good." He handed me back the water glass and swung his feet to the side of the bed, letting his head fall forward for a moment, his blond hair sliding into his face, hiding his eyes.

I was standing barely a foot away when he surged to his feet, his body so close I could feel the heat of him, the head of his hard cock brushing the back of my hand.

I jumped away, snatching my hand back as if scalded, my cheeks flushing and my skin suddenly too tight. I scowled at him, refusing to acknowledge my body's reaction to his.

It didn't help that he towered over me, surrounding me, his eyes as dark as midnight. Pulling out my headmistress voice, my best defense when he made me nervous, I said, "Put some clothes on."

My spine stiff, I marched out of the room, hoping he hadn't noticed my blush. Vance had never hit on me after that first day, but he loved to tease. If he saw how flustered I was, he'd probably refuse to get dressed or do something equally juvenile.

I pressed the empty, but still cold, water glass to my hot cheeks, willing my blush to fade. It was just naked Vance. No big deal.

So what if his cock had touched my hand?

It had been an accident, nothing more. It hadn't even been sexual. I put the glass in the dishwasher. The shower turned on.

Knowing Vance would have roused Amy before getting in the shower, I set the music to a more bearable volume level and put on one of my normal mixes. I loved Katrina, but the same song six times in a row was enough.

By the time Amy dragged herself from the bedroom,

dark circles like bruises beneath her eyes and her dark hair in a messy bun, I had her coffee ready in a to-go cup.

She gave me a thin smile. I'd never seen her when she wasn't hung over, but I imagined she was normally beautiful. Even the morning after, exhausted and half-sick, she was more than just pretty.

A flash of jealousy hit me as I handed her the coffee. She was everything I wasn't—thin, gorgeous, easygoing. She took the cup with a wry smile and said, "Thanks, Maggie. You make the best coffee." Taking a sip, she rolled her eyes to the ceiling in rapture. "The *best* coffee. Have a good one." Then she was gone.

"You too," I called out the door. She gave a wave, but she didn't stop. Easygoing. She was the only one who never asked Vance for more. I didn't know what she did in her real life.

I only saw her in these little snippets of time, at first, once or twice a month. Lately, more often. She and Vance seemed to want the same thing—a never-ending party followed by sex. If that was what made them happy, I wasn't going to judge.

Okay, maybe I was judging. Just a little. It was only that it didn't seem to be making either of them happy in the long run. Or maybe I was just assuming that a relationship would make them happy just because being in one made me happy.

But does it? Does it really make you happy? a tiny voice in my head whispered. I shut it off.

I *was* happy.

I was.

Today, more than any other day, I was blissfully happy. And anyone who said otherwise could shut the hell up.

The shower turned off. Now that Vance was awake, my

actual workday could start. I poured myself a mug of coffee and headed to my office, sending a quick glance at Scout. Passed out on his side, his back foot twitching, my silly little dog loved to sleep. I could relate.

I let myself into my office, a large room on the far side of the loft, opposite Vance's bedroom. It was actually Vance's office as well as mine, but he hated sitting at a desk.

He did most of his work on his laptop, usually on the couch or down in his studio. His desk and mine were a matching set, custom built from cedar in modern, spare lines that fit the look of the loft.

Vance's had a blotter, pen holder, and an in-box, all neatly arranged and undisturbed. Mine was covered in stacks of papers, notebooks, pens, sticky notes—anything and everything I might need in the course of a day.

I was efficient and effective, but I wasn't particularly neat. Not at my desk.

I flipped on my monitor and started on my email while I waited for Vance. He appeared in the door a few minutes later, fully clothed, his wet hair pulled back into a low pony-tail, drinking his smoothie.

His eyes were bloodshot with circles beneath. Not as bad as Amy's, but the sight of them bothered me.

"You drink too much," I said in greeting. He grunted at me. "It's not good for you," I muttered.

"No shit," he said.

"Maybe switch to beer," I suggested, knowing I was wasting my time.

"No thanks. Takes too long to get drunk on beer."

"You could try not getting drunk at all," I said tartly. Vance let out a bark of laughter and set the empty smoothie cup down.

"None of your business," he said, perching on the

corner of my desk and looking over my shoulder. "Nagging isn't in your job description."

I laughed. "Nagging *is* my job description."

"Fine, then you can only nag me about stuff I do during work hours."

"Whatever. Drink yourself to death if you want," I said, pushing back my chair and taking a sip of coffee. His eyes narrowed on mine in suspicion.

"Why are you so cheerful this morning?" he demanded. I took another sip of coffee and smiled, knowing the non-answer would annoy him.

"None of your business," I said.

"Come on, Magnolia, tell me," he cajoled. Vance was the only person who called me Magnolia. Before Vance, only my Grandmother had used my first name. Even my parents, as formal as they were, called me Maggie when they bothered to speak to me.

But Vance insisted he liked my full name and wouldn't use anything else. I didn't mind. I liked my name too.

"I don't know," I said, enjoying having the upper hand for a minute and oddly reluctant to share my big news.

"Tell me, or I put The Dead on repeat."

It was a potent threat. By the time I was thirteen, I'd heard the Grateful Dead's *Sugar Magnolia* more times than I could count. I loathed it. Not the first fifty times I heard it. At first, I liked the song, but by now, the opening bars were enough to make my teeth grind.

"Fine, if you're going to whine about it. Brayden and I are getting married. Happy?"

Vance's face went utterly blank. Devoid of emotion, his eyes flicked to my left hand, then to my face. I curled my naked hand into a ball and dropped it into my lap, out of sight.

In a flat voice, Vance said, "Where's the ring?"

"We're not getting a ring. Not yet. We're waiting until he finishes his residency."

"Because he's spending all that money on rent," Vance said, sarcasm heavy in his words. He knew very well that Brayden lived with me and I didn't make him pay rent. "Student loan bills?"

I ignored that. Vance also knew Brayden's family had paid his tuition to medical school.

"If you're going to be an ass—"

"When's the date?" Vance interrupted.

"What do you mean?" I asked. "We just got engaged last night."

"I don't need the exact day, just a general idea. Are you going to be a spring bride? Summer? I'm assuming you'll want time off for the honeymoon."

Deflated, I said, "We thought we'd wait until—"

"After his residency? Isn't that a year away?"

"Sixteen months," I admitted, my sparkly joy drained away under Vance's relentless questions.

I'd wanted a real proposal. I won't lie about that. The ring, Brayden down on one knee, the whole deal. I didn't need Vance to remind me it hadn't worked out that way.

But the proposal wasn't what was important. We were getting married. We had a whole lifetime together.

"You're not engaged," he announced, standing up, his tight shoulders now loose, the sympathetic smile on his face at odds with the hard expression in his eyes.

"I am," I insisted.

"You're not. When he gives you a ring and you set a date, then you're engaged."

"What do you know about it?" I demanded. "You're the

least romantic guy I know. You sleep with a different woman every night. You've never even had a girlfriend."

"What does that have to do with anything?" he shot back. "I still know how it's supposed to work. You give the girl a ring, get down on one knee, and do it somewhere special she'll be able to remember her whole life. Did he even give you flowers?"

I didn't bother to answer. I didn't need to. He saw the answer in my eyes. "What did he do, announce over pizza that you should get married when he finishes his residency?"

I looked into my coffee cup and nodded, my throat thick with unshed tears. At the time, even a few minutes ago, I'd been happy about it.

After hearing Vance rip it apart, I wanted to cry. When Vance crouched down beside me, one hand on my shoulder, I did, hot tears spilling over my cheeks.

"Tell him, no, Magnolia. He's not good enough for you. Not even close."

"I want to get married," I whispered, so quietly I might have been talking to myself. "I want a family."

Vance's hand squeezed tight. "I know you do, babe. But you can't make up for the past with the first asshole who comes along. Trust me. I know."

"So what, I should just drink away the pain like you do?" I said, knowing it was mean but unable to stop myself. Vance just shook his head and stood, giving my shoulder another squeeze before letting go. "No. You should dump that twat and get some therapy to help you deal with having neglectful assholes for parents."

"I'm the one who needs therapy?" I asked, incredulous through my tears. When it came to sad childhood stories, Vance had me beat by a mile.

"Hey, do as I say, not as I do." He winked at me and disappeared. I knew he was headed for the kitchen to get some coffee.

I also knew when he came back and sat at my desk to review the day's work, his coffee would smell of whiskey.

I wiped my face clean of tears and stared blindly at my laptop screen. I had no place to judge. Vance was probably right.

A therapist would tell me that I was rushing into marriage because my parents had dumped me in an English boarding school at the age of eight while they partied their way across Europe and had never really come back.

I'd seen them only a handful of times since then. My father, now loosely connected to the embassy in Belgium, had come home for my Grandmother's funeral and stayed only long enough to scowl over the reading of the will before heading back overseas.

Now that my Grandmother was gone, I was alone.

I wanted a family. I wanted children.

I'd watched my friends at school go home on the weekends, the way they'd run out to the car and throw themselves into their mothers' arms, the way their fathers would pull them into a hug and kiss the tops of their heads.

I'd wanted that. I couldn't change the past, but I could create the fantasy with my own family. I would. I just had to get married first.

I'd been with Brayden for four years. It wasn't like a ton of other guys were knocking down my door. This was my chance to change my life and I was taking it.

Vance could just shut the hell up about it.

He came back a few minutes later and pulled up his chair beside me. A cup of Irish coffee in one hand and a tablet in the other, he got down to business.

"The Cane-Webber proposal. Where are we with that?"

"I emailed you my analysis yesterday afternoon."

"Got it," he said, flicking his finger to scroll through my report. "I read it last night."

"So you know I think the market is oversaturated and they're over-leveraged."

"I agree. We'll let them reel in some other sucker. What about the security app?"

"That one is interesting," I said, pulling up the file on a proposal from a new tech company with some ideas for social media security. "I highlighted the key points I liked, as well as some questions I have."

"Your screen is bigger," he said, moving his chair closer. "Pull up your report, and we'll go through it. I agree, I'm intrigued by this one."

Heads almost close enough to touch, we studied my report and the proposal side by side, breaking it down until we could put together a game plan.

This was what I loved about working for Vance. He could be frustrating, rude, and annoying, but he was smart, and he valued my opinion.

I'd learned more in the last six months with him than I would have anywhere else.

Despite the crazy morning routine, I loved my job. Most of the time, we got along well. I'd even say we were good friends. We were close enough that I worried about him.

Clearly, he worried about me, too. The difference was, only one of us had anything to worry about. I'd be fine with Brayden. We'd get married, and everything would be good.

If Vance didn't get a handle on his drinking, he wouldn't be around to dance at our wedding.

CHAPTER THREE
MAGNOLIA

T-MINUS ONE YEAR

I was early to work, but I didn't go in to wake them up right away. Later, I'd regret that. But Amy had been there most nights for the last few weeks, and I was getting tired of being their morning wake-up call.

Vance's drinking had escalated. In the past month, it was rare to see him without a glass in his hand. The week before, he'd burned his leg badly while working.

We'd spent the afternoon in the emergency room, Vance silent and sullen with pain, me trembling in rage at his carelessness.

I hadn't spoken to him for two days. He'd been lucky the burn on his leg was the worst of it. Between the blow-torch and the huge pieces of metal he used in his sculptures, he could easily kill himself if he kept working while he was drunk.

Even his family was getting concerned. No, that's not accurate. They'd always been concerned. They just didn't nag. His cousin, Charlotte, rode his ass the hardest, along with his oldest cousin, Aiden.

Charlie and I had struck up a friendship. We were the same age, and it turned out we knew a lot of the same people despite my going to school overseas. She'd confessed that the family was worried, but they couldn't figure out what to do about it. I could relate.

I hated his drinking. Every time I smelled alcohol on him, it made me sick. Vance was impervious to nagging or suggestion. When I gave him a hard time about it, he either made a joke or changed the subject. He did the same to Charlie. Aiden, he shut out completely.

According to Charlie, only Vance's twin sister, Annalise, could get through to him, and she hadn't come home to Atlanta in almost two years. His older brother, Gage, was also absent, an Army Ranger serving in the Middle East.

His only immediate family was his younger brother, Tate, who was busy running two companies, one of which was a night club. Not the ideal choice to talk to Vance about his partying.

I still loved my job. I even loved Vance, in a way. Despite his drinking, we'd grown close. If I were being honest, I'd have to admit he was one of my closest friends. That's why it was killing me to see him like this.

I never would have thought it was possible, but lately, he was even losing his looks. His golden skin had a sallow tone, and he'd lost some of his muscle as his workouts had tapered off.

He was turning a corner with his drinking, and I didn't know how to haul him back.

I'd figure it out. We all would. I refused to think we'd lose him. But if there was a solution, I wasn't going to find it today. I'd had a fight with Brayden the night before, and I was feeling raw, annoyed at the world, and in need of solitude.

Instead of hitting the coffeemaker and the blender, I went straight for my office.

A half hour later, I heard stirring in the bedroom and got up to make some coffee. I didn't care if Vance and Amy wanted any, but I needed a cup. Ready to indulge myself, I got the coffee going and mixed up some hot cocoa and creamer for mine.

After being up half the night yelling at Brayden, I deserved some chocolate in my coffee. A good mocha could fix almost anything.

I couldn't get the fight out of my head. It had been so stupid, one of those fights you get into when you've been in a relationship for a long time. The kind that starts over something small and escalates until you're pulling up everything that's ever bothered you until, by the end, you have no idea why you're still fighting. Or why you're still together.

Brayden was in the last stage of his residency with a plastic surgeon and had suggested I think about getting some work done. I'd been a little upset.

Massive understatement.

First, I'm only twenty-three. And second, while I'm sensitive about my body shape, I'm not getting plastic surgery. I'd been planning on starting a workout program. Soon. Eventually.

While I'd been nagging Vance to stop drinking, he'd been nagging me to exercise more. He said sitting at a desk all day was bad for my heart. Maybe, but not as bad as drinking all day was for his liver.

While Vance wanted me to work out for my heart, Brayden was all about my ass. Mainly that it should be smaller. He said my breasts would shrink when I lost weight, but I could get that taken care of too. The women he mentioned as good role models were all super skinny, at least ten pounds underweight.

I was more like fifteen to twenty overweight. By my definition, not his. The thing is, I'd been basically the same size since the day we met. Just thinking of the argument had me adding another spoonful of cocoa to my coffee.

When I wouldn't agree to get surgery or go on a diet, he started on buying a vacation home at the beach. With my money.

My Grandmother left me provided for, but she'd also left me her house. While it was gorgeous and had been in my family for generations, it was also a money pit.

Between the house itself, the carriage house, and the grounds, it took a chunk of cash to keep everything running. Since I was never selling my family home, I needed to be smart about the way I spent my inheritance.

My Grandmother had put some money aside in trust for the house, and I'd transferred a portion of my inheritance over as well—another thing that pissed Brayden off.

Not that the fight was only him yelling at me. I had plenty to say about his long hours and his always weaseling out of helping with the bills.

I didn't have a mortgage, but there were still utilities, groceries, and a bunch of other expenses we should have been sharing. Technically, we did share them, but more often than not, he came up short on his half of the bills. I hadn't minded at first, but lately, it was starting to bug me.

Especially when he said he was saving for my ring. That excuse wasn't as comforting as it should have been.

I gulped at my homemade mocha, letting it scald the top of my mouth. Chocolate made almost everything better. A thump sounded from Vance's room, then the sound of glass breaking.

Swearing to myself, I put the mug on the counter and strode to the door of the bedroom.

I'd check on them, but I wasn't cleaning anything up. I'd put my foot down about that when one of Vance's one-night-stands had puked all over the bathroom. I was his business manager, not the clean-up crew.

As usual, Vance was passed out naked in bed, the sheet pushed to the floor. It was a measure of how cranky I was that I barely spared him a glance. The bathroom door was open halfway, the light on, the room silent.

I stopped, struck by the eerie quiet. I'd heard something break. Shouldn't the girl be cleaning it up? I didn't even know who Vance had slept with the night before. I wondered if he did.

Suddenly nervous, I pushed open the door. It moved less than a foot before it struck something and stopped. I called out, "Hello? Are you okay?"

No answer. Vance shifted in the bed behind me but didn't wake. My annoyance was turning to alarm. I edged closer to the bathroom and peeked around the door. What I saw made me dizzy with fear.

Amy lay on the floor, motionless, eyes open but unblinking, her arms splayed. A ceramic soap dish lay beside her, shattered. On her other side, I saw a leather folio with a zipper, hanging open, a burned spoon and a needle clearly visible.

Shit. Shit, Shit, Shit!

I pushed frantically at the door, shoving it open far enough to let me through. My heart pounding, I screamed, "Vance! Vance, wake up!"

Terrified of what I would find, I leaned in as close as I

could. Amy didn't react to my presence. I heard the faint rasp of her breathing, ragged and shallow, but there.

It took me too long to find her pulse, thready and faint. Her lips were tinged blue. So were her fingernails. Her pupils were pinpricks in her light blue eyes.

I thought I was going to throw up. I hadn't had any idea she even used drugs. Did Vance know? Was he using drugs too?

Terror seized my chest. Bile rose in my throat. Was he just passed out, or had he overdosed too? What if he was dying, and I'd walked right past him?

I left Amy and slipped from the bathroom.

"Vance," I shouted his name and pulled at his shoulder, trying to turn him over. He rolled to his back and spread out, one arm coming around me as I put my ear to his chest.

"Magnolia," he murmured, tightening his arm. I barely heard him over the strong thump of his heartbeat. Relief flooded through me as I shoved away from him.

"Wake the fuck up, you asshole," I shouted, shoving at him one more time. My phone was in the kitchen. Vance could wait.

I called 911 and was assured that they were on their way. After unlocking the street door so they could get in, I went back to Vance.

I was pissed. Scared, sad, and royally pissed.

Grabbing the nearest pillow, I whacked him in the face, yelling his name. If he didn't wake up soon, I was dumping a whole fucking pitcher of water on his head.

I grabbed his wrist and leaned back, pulling until his torso rose a few inches off the mattress. Vance was seriously heavy, even though he'd lost some muscle mass in the last few months. I let go, dropping him, tears pricking my eyes.

"Wake up," I shouted, jerking on his arm, half dragging his heavy body across the bed.

My heart pounded in my chest. Cold sweat dripped down my spine. Amy was dying in the bathroom, and Vance was passed out. I didn't know what to do.

There was nothing I could do for Amy. The 911 operator had told me to leave her where she was once she'd determined that Amy was in a safe location. I just had to pray she could hang on long enough for the paramedics to get to her.

But Vance was another story. I'd already been at the edge of my tolerance with his drinking, but now he was leaving me to deal with Amy by myself. I was sick of the men in my life leaving me to deal with their shit on my own.

Vance stretched his arms over his head, his fingers briefly holding on to the headboard before letting go. He curled on his side and rolled his head into his pillow, apparently settling in for another hour or two of sleep.

Forget that.

He was getting his drunk ass out of bed right now. Rage and fear warring inside me, I smacked him in the face with the pillow again. No response except for a quick wrinkle of his nose.

If I hadn't been so mad, it would've been cute.

I stormed into the kitchen and grabbed a vase of fresh-cut flowers off the island. Dumping the flowers on the granite countertop, I carried the vase into the bedroom and upended it in Vance's face.

That did the trick. Kind of. His eyes blinked open, bloodshot and unfocused. "What the fuck, Magnolia?" he groaned.

Fury bloomed in my chest. I snatched up the pillow I'd used before and whacked his wet face. Hard. Vance snatched the pillow from my hand and hurled it across the room.

"What the fuck? You don't have to be such a bitch."

I flinched. Vance and I had had some spirited disagreements, but he'd never, ever called me a name. The worst he'd ever said was *Sugar Magnolia*, because he knew it annoyed me.

Hearing him call me a bitch, after getting the same from my fiancé last night, tipped me over the edge.

Setting my hands on my hips, I adopted the chilliest version of my headmistress voice and said, "Get your drunk, lazy ass out of bed. Amy overdosed on drugs. She's dying in your bathroom. Paramedics are on the way. I suggest you put on some clothes and look like a semi-coherent human being before they get here."

Blood drained from Vance's face, and he jerked to his feet, his head swinging on his neck as he looked from the bathroom to me and back again.

Too furious to talk to him, I walked around the bed to the bathroom and sat on the closed toilet lid, holding Amy's cold hand in my own.

I prayed with every ounce of faith in my heart that she kept breathing until the paramedics got here. If she didn't make it, I wasn't going to let her die alone.

I saw movement at the open door. Vance leaned against the door frame, his face sheet white, bloodshot eyes wide and panicked. He'd managed to pull on a faded pair of jeans.

"Put on a shirt," I snapped.

I don't know why it mattered to me. Amy was more important than whether Vance was dressed or not. I assumed he'd be coming to the hospital with us, and I didn't want to have to wait while he got dressed.

Faintly, in the distance, I heard sirens. Hoping I was right, I gave Amy's hand a squeeze and said, "Hang on, help is almost here. Just hang on."

Her chest moved in tiny increments as she breathed. My eyes were fixed on the faint shift of her T-shirt over her ribs. As long as I kept seeing that small flutter of fabric, I knew she was still alive.

"Is she . . ." Vance trailed off. I didn't look at him. I couldn't look away from Amy.

"Will you please just go get dressed?" I said flatly. "The paramedics are almost here, I hope, and I'm assuming you'll want to follow us to the hospital. You can't do that without shoes or a shirt, so get fucking dressed. Now."

I was done with babying Vance. It was one thing to watch him drink and fuck his way through life. I didn't like it, but it was his life, not mine. But this, seeing a woman I liked hover near death, I couldn't take it anymore.

I didn't have time to think about what that meant. The door flew open, and the paramedics rushed in. Seeing them, I lowered Amy's hand to her lap and stepped out of the bathroom to give them space to work.

I couldn't see what they were doing. There were too many people in a small space, and I wasn't hovering because I didn't want to get in the way.

By the time they were strapping Amy down on a stretcher, Vance had emerged from the other bathroom looking panicked but clothed. He'd even taken the time to brush his hair and pull it back with a rubber band.

He watched with wide eyes as they moved Amy to the front door, headed for the elevator.

To me, he said, "Is she—"

I shook my head and went to get my purse. "She's hanging in there. We'll follow them to the hospital."

I poured my cooling mocha into a travel mug and filled one for Vance, desperately needing the caffeine. There was no point in rushing with the paramedics blocking the doorway.

I shoved a mug into Vance's hands, and we followed them out.

Sitting in the waiting room at the hospital was a new form of torture after the rushed fear of the past hour. Vance didn't have any contact information for Amy's family. Not even a roommate. All we could do was sit and wait. And wait.

We didn't speak. I had no idea what Vance was thinking. I wasn't sure what I was thinking either. I'd started my day pissed off at Brayden. And pissed at myself for putting up with him, if I was honest.

Finding Amy, the fear that she might die, the regret that I hadn't woken them earlier, and anger at Vance for letting his life get to this point in the first place—it was all tangled up inside me in an unruly knot of emotion.

I didn't want to talk to Vance. I wasn't sure what I would say, and I didn't want to regret it later. I had enough regrets as it was.

Finally, a doctor came out to tell us that Amy was stable. Vance went to talk to someone in administration, probably to make sure they knew the bills would be covered regardless of her insurance situation.

When he came back, he sat in the chair beside me, his eyes on the floor, and said, "I'm going to stay until they let me see her. You should go home. Take the day off. I'll call you later."

I nodded my head and stood up, my throat tight.

"Before you go," he said, "can I borrow your phone for a second? I left mine at the loft."

I nodded again and handed him my phone, relieved when I saw him pull up his cousin's number. Aiden must've answered right away.

"Hey, can you come down to the ER? I'm okay, but I've got a situation and I need your help."

I took my phone back when he was done. He still wouldn't meet my eyes. I was torn. Part of me wanted to run screaming from the whole mess. The other part didn't want to leave Vance on his own. I was furious with him, but I knew he was scared.

"Go home, Magnolia," he said. "Amy is going to be okay, and Aiden will be here in ten minutes. You shouldn't have had to deal with any of this. I just want you to go home."

My throat still tight with everything I hadn't said, with the tears I wouldn't let fall, I gave a brisk nod, picked my purse up off my seat, and left.

Vance didn't want me there. I didn't want to be there. I just didn't want to leave him on his own.

I ended up picking Scout up at Vance's loft and going home. I spent the rest of the day outside, weeding. I hated weeding, but it kept my mind off Vance and Amy and my fight with Brayden.

That night, just as I was sitting down to dinner alone in front of the TV, there was a knock at my front door. I was surprised to find Aiden Winters there, his suit rumpled and his brown eyes tired.

"Hi, Maggie. May I come in?"

"Of course," I said, stepping back to let him enter. Aiden followed me back to the kitchen.

"Can I get you anything?" I asked. "Beer? Wine? Tea?" I wouldn't normally offer Aiden Winters tea, but he looked like he could use a cup. He shook his head. Catching sight of my tray in front of the TV, he said, "I'm interrupting your dinner."

"It's okay."

"I wanted to update you on the situation," he said. I nodded, my chest tight as I braced for bad news. "Amy is doing okay. The doctor said it was close, but you found her in time. She wants to go into rehab, and Vance and I helped her get that set up."

I nodded again, sensing Aiden wasn't done. I was right.

"Vance," Aiden started, then stopped and swallowed hard. "Vance called me because he's decided he'd like to get some help. Once we were sure Amy was settled, we spent the rest of the afternoon looking for someplace that would be a good fit for him. We found a clinic in Colorado that specializes in addiction treatment with a combination of counseling and a lot of outdoor activity."

Sheer relief broke open the knot in my chest, setting free the tears that coursed down my cheeks. I was very sorry that Amy had come so close to dying. But if the result was that they were both going to get help, I was a little grateful, too.

"Tell me, honestly, was it Vance's idea, or yours?" I asked.

His voice rough with emotion, Aiden said, "It was his. Thank fucking God, it was his. I tried not to push. I didn't want him to feel like he couldn't talk to me when he needed help, but he always said everything was fine even though—"

"I know. I know." I scrubbed the heels of my hands against my eyes.

Vance was going to try to stop drinking. I wasn't going to fool myself into thinking he had an easy road ahead of him. He didn't drink for fun. He drank to escape the demons riding him.

If he wanted to stop, he was going to have to face those demons one way or another. But when Vance wanted something, he never gave up. If he'd decided to get sober, he would do it. I had to believe that.

I dragged in a shaky breath and looked at Aiden, whose dark eyes were suspiciously glossy. Aiden was reserved. The rest of his family called him uptight, but he wasn't cold. He loved his family more than anything.

If I was relieved, I couldn't begin to imagine how Aiden must feel knowing that Vance was at least willing to try to stop drinking.

"So," I asked, "how long will he be gone?"

"At least six weeks, possibly twice that," Aiden said. "I'm hoping he stays the full three months. He won't have much communication with the outside world, but if you're willing to, he asked me to ask you to continue working while he's gone."

"Of course I will. I'm not going to walk out on him. Not now." I'd been on the edge of doing that this morning, but everything had changed. If Vance was willing to try, I wouldn't abandon him.

"I told him you weren't going to quit. He feels awful about this morning—"

"It's over," I said, cutting Aiden off.

I didn't want to talk about everything that had happened that morning. I didn't want to think about it.

Vance's refusal to wake up. Amy's shallow breaths and blank eyes. The needle and the spoon.

I didn't want to think about any of it. It was over, everyone was alive, and they were both going to get help. That was all that was important.

"You shouldn't have been in that position," Aiden

41

insisted. "No one would blame you if you quit, and Vance knows it."

"If he's getting help," I said, "then I'm willing to let it go. I don't want to punish him for hitting bottom, Aiden. I just want him to get better."

"Me too, Maggie. For the first time in years, I think he might get there."

I walked Aiden out and locked the door behind him. It was going to be a long three months without Vance, but I'd wait as long as he needed me to. After months of worrying, I finally had hope for his future.

Chapter Four
Magnolia

T-MINUS SIX MONTHS

The door swung open before my key hit the lock. Vance stood there, shirtless, beads of sweat rolling down the golden planes of his chest, catching on the sparse blonde hairs before tracing out the lines of his eight-pack.

Holy Christ, the man needed to start wearing a shirt when he worked out. Loose athletic shorts clung to his lean hips, dipping down just enough to show the edge of his tan line.

In the three months since he'd been back from rehab, Vance had transformed. Gone was the dissolute playboy with the sallow skin and bloodshot eyes.

Before his drinking had gotten out of control, Vance had always been into fitness. Now that he was sober, he'd taken it to a new extreme.

I got it. He had to do something with the darkness that had driven him to alcohol. It was still there. He just channeled it into his art and his workouts.

The result was a studio filled with pieces and a body I couldn't tear my eyes from. I almost didn't notice the bag in his hands as I walked in and he closed the door behind me.

Vance pushed the bag toward me. "Here, take this and get changed. We have a meeting at noon."

I took the bag, noticing the label of a local sports gear shop in the Highlands. I didn't know what was in the bag, but it couldn't be good.

I wanted a cup of coffee, stat. I did not want a bag of sporting goods.

"What's this?" I asked, trying to push the bag back into Vance's hands. He stepped away and shook his head.

"You've been dodging me for a month," he said. "You're going running with me."

"No way," I said. "I don't run. I am not a runner. I have no interest in being a runner. Your fitness kick is great and all, but don't drag me along with you."

"Nope, not accepting excuses. I've got everything you need. Running clothes, brand-new shoes, and I even got a step tracker and set it up. You spend too much time sitting. It's not good for you."

"Vance, I'm a grown woman," I said, trying to hand him back the bag. "I don't need anyone to tell me what to do."

"I let you talk me into those kale shakes, didn't I? Even when I was still drinking? Do you have any idea how disgusting they tasted when I was hung over? But even then, I knew you were worried about me, so I drank them anyway. Every day."

"It's not the same," I protested, knowing it *was* the same, but I really didn't want to go running. Did I mention I hated running?

"It's exactly the same," Vance said. "You stopped going to yoga classes and you've been depressed. And you sit almost all day. You need to get some exercise, and since I get way too much, you're coming with me. Think of it as multitasking. We'll talk business while we run."

I burst out laughing at the idea that I'd be able to talk and run at the same time. Gasp for breath and run, maybe. Carry on a conversation about business? No way in hell.

Vance's blue eyes narrowed on me, and I knew it was useless to argue. Easier just to go running with him than to try to talk him out of it. The same determination that had carried him into sobriety was now focused on me. Crap. I knew him well enough to know I was wasting my time trying to resist.

"Fine," I said, "but I'm really getting sick of people telling me I'm fat."

I bit my tongue the second the words were out.

I hadn't meant to say that. I knew Vance didn't mean to hurt my feelings, but I was a little sensitive about the whole issue.

I didn't like to admit that the reason I stopped going to yoga was Brayden's reaction to seeing me in a tank top and yoga pants. After that, I couldn't stop thinking about the other women in class looking at my giant ass every time I bent over.

I tried to pretend I hadn't said a word and went to walk past Vance to change in the bathroom when he grabbed my arm.

"You are not fat, Magnolia. This is not about weight. This is about you coming with me so we can both get some exercise. That's all. Whatever that twat has been saying that's messing up your head, don't pin it on me."

Automatically, I said, "Don't call him a twat. It's coarse."

"Did he make some comment about you being anything

less than gorgeous?" Vance asked, his arms crossed over his chest.

I tried not to notice the way the position made his biceps bulge. I shrugged and tried to walk past him. He stepped in my path, blocking me.

"Magnolia, did he? Did he say something stupid and shitty that hurt your feelings?"

He already knew the answer. I wished he would stop pushing. Things weren't great with Brayden. I barely saw him lately, and when I did, he felt more like a roommate than a fiancé. That didn't mean I wanted to talk about it with Vance.

"Can we just let it go?" I asked, tugging my arm out of his grip. "I'll go change and we'll go for a run, but don't complain when I slow you down."

Thankfully, Vance dropped the subject. I escaped into the bathroom and changed into the clothes Vance had picked out. I should let him shop for me more often. He had great taste.

I pulled out gray leggings with pink and purple wavy vertical stripes that looked streamlined but whimsical. A matching pink and purple tank top went with the leggings, along with a pink jog bra that would keep my breasts from hitting my chin when we ran. Of course, everything fit, including the running shoes.

I wasn't too sure about the step tracker, but I fastened it on my wrist anyway. I didn't like the idea of anything monitoring my activity, but I did like apps and gadgets, so I was willing to give it a shot.

I pulled my hair up into a ponytail and left the bathroom, hoping Vance wasn't planning on running that far. If he was, he was destined for disappointment.

My eyes widened as I saw he had a leash on Scout. "Are we bringing the dog? I don't think he runs," I said.

That wasn't entirely accurate. Scout could run, and when he did, he was fast, but that was only for short distances or when it related to getting food.

Running for the sake of running? My dog was no more into that than I was.

I underestimated Scout's devotion to Vance. He trotted happily beside Vance as we headed for the elevator, looking like he went running every day and couldn't wait to hit the pavement.

"That pink looks good on you," Vance said, sounding offhand. His eyes, laser sharp, skimmed me from head to toe with a focus that made me want to squirm. "Pink doesn't always work on redheads, but it's perfect on you."

I flushed and looked away. "It's a little tight," I said, fidgeting. I hadn't worn anything like this since my last trip to yoga class, and I was self-conscious, especially standing next to Vance, who was six feet of chiseled muscle. He still wasn't wearing a shirt.

"It's not too tight," he said. "You look fucking fantastic. I don't know if I can run with a hard on."

"Sexual harassment, Mr. Winters," I said in my head-mistress voice. "Behave."

I'm not going to lie and say I didn't appreciate the compliment, but I didn't believe him. The running clothes fit me well, but they were still way too snug on my curvy frame.

"Just being honest." Vance's eyes flicked down to the front of his shorts, and mine couldn't help but follow.

Oh my God.

He wasn't kidding. The long, thick bar of his erection pressed against the flimsy fabric of his running shorts. My cheeks flamed, and my eyes shot to the ceiling of the elevator.

Could you fake an erection? I didn't think so, but I wasn't an expert on male anatomy. Did that mean he really did think I looked good?

Doesn't matter, I told myself. *Vance is out of your league, he's your boss, and you're engaged.*

I was flattered, but that was as far as it would ever go. I wasn't going to look at the front of his shorts again. Definitely not. Maybe once. I snuck a peek and flushed hot all over again.

"You're going to have to stay behind me. I don't want to watch that bobbing in your shorts while we're running." I was trying for my headmistress voice, but I didn't quite make it.

Instead of crisp, my words were husky.

Vance chuckled. "Okay, but if I'm running behind you, it's not exactly going to go away. Do you know what your ass looks like in those leggings?"

"Yes," I snapped. "Fat. It looks fat."

"If that's what you want to call it," Vance said, still laughing. "My dick disagrees."

I whirled and pointed my finger at him. "You behave, or I'm going right back upstairs and I'm not talking to you for the rest of the day."

Vance raised his hands in defense and gave me his most innocent smile, all charm and sweetness.

"I won't say another word."

He didn't, and after a while, I forgot about the too-tight clothes, my embarrassment, and his hard cock. At first, because we did talk business during the warm-up, and business was always a good distraction.

Then, once we started jogging, I couldn't think of

anything but my burning muscles and my oxygen-deprived lungs.

Why would anyone do this voluntarily? It was awful.

Vance took me through intervals of walking and jogging that he told me were the best way to start a running habit. My heart sank at that information. Clearly, he intended for us to do this on a regular basis. Dammit.

I survived the first run. I barely dragged my way through the second and third. I have to admit, once I got the step tracker set up and synced to my phone, I got a kick out of seeing all the miles I was logging. And I couldn't really complain about Vance paying me to work out with him.

In terms of his fitness, it was a waste of his time to run with me. I slowed him down and couldn't go very far, even after a few weeks, but it was his time to waste and it wasn't like I was holding back his program.

These days, he was up every day at dawn, either lifting weights or using the suspension system he'd installed in the roof garden. By the time I showed up in the morning—my start time was now nine—he'd already been working out for a few hours and was ready to wind down with a slow run.

I didn't want to admit it, but after we'd been running together for a few months, I looked forward to it. It wasn't just that Vance was an entertaining companion. I did, truly, feel better.

I don't think I lost any weight since running made me hungry. It also made my body feel good. I even started going back to yoga class. I had decided to agree with Vance.

My ass looked good, and anyone who didn't think so could go to hell.

Vance didn't tease me about the way that I looked after that first run, though I caught him eyeing me more than once with heat in his piercing blue gaze.

I didn't say anything.

I snuck a few glances here and there when I thought he wouldn't catch me. I couldn't help it. If he'd been hot before, now that he'd ditched the alcohol and replaced it with exercise, he was incendiary.

I could manage to keep my eyes off him when he was dressed and we were working, but the shirtless jogging was too much temptation.

I never flirted.

I absolutely never touched.

But I looked.

The muscles, the tattoos, the washboard abs. God damn. A saint would've looked her fill, and I was no saint.

Ironically, Brayden didn't like my new exercise habit. He was still pushing for plastic surgery, liposuction at the very least. Not going to happen. There were days, a lot of them, when I wasn't sure why we were still together.

Relationship inertia.

I wasn't in love with him. And I'd already realized I couldn't marry him. I was desperate for a family—I could be honest with myself about that—but I couldn't marry a man I didn't love. Especially when I wasn't even sure I liked him. But I couldn't seem to bring myself to do anything about it.

I thought about telling him it was over. Then I thought about how empty the house would be when he was gone.

I'd imagine what it would mean to be alone. Really, truly alone. I always ended up not doing anything. I was letting life carry me along, too scared to shake things up.

There's a problem with that. If you don't take control of your own life, eventually, someone will take it from you. Then you're stuck dealing with the fallout from the mess you let them create.

That was a lesson I'd have to learn the hard way.

Chapter Five

Magnolia

BLAST OFF

I wasn't getting out of bed. Ever. I was never, ever getting out of bed. Scratch that. I'd get out of bed to answer the door. I'd have my groceries delivered, and I could get up to let Scout outside.

Other than that, I was never getting out of bed. I was going to lay here, in my room, and eat ice cream for the rest of my life. Possibly while watching action movies. Explosions made everything better.

I know 'heartbroken girl eating ice cream' is a cliché, but I wasn't going to make it worse by watching sappy movies. Besides, I didn't think I could handle sappy movies, and I was done with crying. At least for the moment.

Pounding echoed up the stairs, interrupting my self-pity. I ignored it. I'd already texted in sick to work and then turned my phone off.

The pounding stopped, and I let out a breath of relief. Whoever it was would go away, and I could get back to my ice cream and the *Die Hard* trilogy.

Just when I thought I was off the hook, the pounding started again, louder than before and accompanied by shouting.

"Magnolia Henry, open this door right now, or I will break it down."

Vance. I should've known he wouldn't be put off by a text. I should have called, but I hadn't wanted to talk to him. I hadn't wanted to hear him say *I told you so.*

"If you don't let me in, I'll keep yelling and your neighbors are going to call the police," he threatened.

It was unlikely. My house sat on five acres, directly in the center, and while I could see my neighbor's rooflines, we weren't in shouting distance.

Though Vance was pretty loud. And I was in my pajamas and probably had chocolate ice cream smeared on my chin. I didn't want to entertain the police in my living room in this condition.

Sighing in annoyance, I dragged myself out of bed, picked up the pint of Hagen Das, and went downstairs, shoving a bite of ice cream in my mouth on the way.

Vance stumbled forward when I swung open the door, his hand raised and ready for another fit of pounding. His eyes widened at the sight of me, my hair in a messy knot on the top of my head, not a stitch of makeup, puffy red eyes and a pint of ice cream in my hand.

I made a sad sight, and I knew it. I just didn't care.

"What the fuck is wrong with you?" Vance demanded. "Are those your pajamas?"

I took another bite of ice cream and glared at him. Who was he to judge? At least I wore pajamas.

I looked down at the threadbare, pink- and white-striped broadcloth pajama set my grandmother had bought me when I was in college. They'd seen better days. The pink was faded, and all the bleach in the world wouldn't make the white stripes truly white again.

Was this why Brayden had left? I didn't have it in me to wonder.

"You don't look sick," Vance said. "You said you were sick."

"I lied," I said.

"Do you have coffee?" Vance asked, pushing past me to come in. "I tried making coffee, and it was terrible. If you're not coming into work, at least make me coffee."

"Can't you take care of yourself for one day while I have an emotional breakdown?"

"No," he said. "Is that what this is? An emotional breakdown?"

I gestured to myself with the ice cream spoon, splattering drops of chocolate on the front of my pajama top. "Can't you tell?"

Vance shook his head. "You tell me you're having an emotional breakdown, and you think that's going to make me leave? You've stuck with me through all of my shit. All those times you dealt with me drunk and hung over. Amy's overdose. Amy and me getting back together and breaking up again. You stuck with me when I went to rehab. You were waiting for me when I got out, and you kept my whole life together while I was gone. Now you're having a tough time, and you think I'm going to leave you here to eat ice cream and cry on your own? What did that twat do now?"

I burst into tears.

"Babe, don't cry. Don't cry. He's not worth it." I felt him take the ice cream and spoon out of my hands.

One strong arm wrapped around my shoulders, and Vance led me to my kitchen, seating me on a stool at my island. I heard water running in the sink, then a cold, wet towel pressed against my hot face.

I took it from him and tried to wipe away the tears. And the snot. My nose always ran when I cried. When I had myself under control and my face cleaned up, Vance asked again, "What did he do?"

I let out a shuddering breath and said, "He dumped me. Two days before Valentine's Day, and he dumped me."

"Well, hallelujah," Vance said with an oddly determined grin.

"I hate you," I said.

"No, you don't. You hate him. He's an asshole. I'm your best friend. And he never deserved you, Magnolia. Ever. He was never good enough for you. The only person who didn't know that was you. You should've kicked him out years ago. I'm sorry that you're hurt. I hate seeing you unhappy. But that asshole leaving you is the best thing for you, and you know it."

I didn't say anything. Vance was right. I should've kicked Brayden out a long time ago. He was an asshole, and I did deserve better.

I shrugged, and Vance scowled at me.

"Are you going to make coffee? Because you know if you let me do it, it's going to be shit."

I pushed back the stool and went to the coffeemaker. I did want coffee, and if I let Vance make it, it would be disgusting. He could cook. He was actually pretty good in the kitchen, but every time he tried to make coffee, it was either too weak, burned, or as thick as mud.

"I'm taking you out," Vance said. I stared at the slowly filling coffee maker in disbelief.

"No," I said. "I'm not going out. I'm getting back in bed with my coffee and my ice cream and watching *Die Harder*.

I'm taking the day off work, and I don't care what you have to say about it."

"No, you're not."

"You're not the boss of me," I said.

I wished for my headmistress voice—that one always seemed to work on Vance—but instead, I ended up sounding like a disgruntled toddler.

Vance crossed his arms over his chest and raised one eyebrow, looking like the debauched Viking I'd first thought him, charming and dangerous.

"I am exactly the boss of you," he said. "And today is a workday. As soon as I get a cup of coffee in you, you're going to go upstairs, take a shower, get dressed, and then do what I tell you to for the rest of the day."

Suspicious, I narrowed my eyes at him. "What are you going to tell me to do?"

"We're going to brunch. You're going to drink a lot of mimosas, then we'll go to the movies, and then you'll go to bed early so you can wake up and be at work on time tomorrow."

I poured us both mugs of coffee, handing Vance his. It was too hot, but I didn't care about burning my tongue. I needed the caffeine.

"I don't want to go to brunch, and I don't want to get drunk. Anyway, you don't drink," I said.

Vance blew on his coffee. "I didn't say I was going to drink. I hate mimosas. But you love them." He shuddered at the thought. "I'm going to keep you company. You can spend the morning telling me all about what a dickhead the twat is, and I'll agree with you because he is a dickhead and I've always hated him. Then you'll feel much better. That's how this works. Do you want me to call Charlie? She hates the twat as much as I do."

"You need to stop calling him that," I said.

"Why? You're not still defending his honor, are you?"

"No, but it's vulgar. I hate that word."

"I don't really like it either, but it fits him so perfectly I just can't help myself," Vance said.

"Try," I insisted.

"If I promise not to call the dickhead a twat for the rest of the day, will you come out with me?"

Still channeling my inner toddler, I rolled my eyes. Not yet ready to agree to his plan, I asked,

"Why do you hate him so much? You already hated him when we met."

Vance sighed. "You know I went to school with Brayden and his older brother, right?"

I nodded, sipping my coffee.

"The brother is okay, but Brayden was always a whiner and a bully. One year, he stole the charity fund his class was raising for Habitat for Humanity. It was a lot of money. Thousands of dollars. And he pinned it on another kid, one of the scholarship students. He almost got the guy kicked out of school."

"Why didn't you ever tell me this?" I asked, shocked. Vance shrugged.

"Honestly, I wasn't sure you'd believe me."

"Did he get kicked out of school?" I asked.

"Kind of. He missed the rest of the school year, but he was allowed to come back." Vance raised one hand and rubbed his fingers and thumb together in the universal sign for money.

What a surprise, Brayden letting his parents bail him out of trouble.

"I'm such an idiot. I should have kicked him out a long time ago," I said.

"No comment. Now go get ready while I call Charlie."

"Charlie can't come with us. It's a weekday, and she's working."

"Charlie runs her own department," Vance said. "She can let her assistant handle things for one day. God knows, she works enough. She hates her job, and she needs a day off."

His comment distracted me from my own misery. "You picked up on that too, huh?" I asked.

"Ever since she finished school and started working for the company full time, she's been miserable. But she won't admit it. Too stubborn to give up, like some other people I know."

He gave me that raised eyebrow again, as if I didn't already know he was talking about me. There was nothing wrong with being stubborn. Or tenacious.

Sometimes, it's hard to know when you need to stick with something and when it's time to cut your losses. I knew Charlie wasn't enjoying her work, but I didn't give her a hard time about it for the same reason she never gave me a hard time about my relationship with Brayden.

In the end, we had to make our own mistakes.

"Fine, I'll go out. But I want it on record that I'm doing this under protest. I liked my ice cream and John McLane plan better."

"You'll have more fun with me," Vance said, confiscating the pint of ice cream before I could take it back upstairs. I managed to hang on to my coffee and finished drinking it after I got out of the shower.

I wanted to spend the day in my pajamas, but if Vance was taking me out for brunch somewhere they served mimosas, I was going to put a little effort into my appearance.

I put my wet hair up, starting with two long braids and winding them around into a loosely structured bun. I'd put on makeup and pick out something decent to wear, but I was not about to spend forty minutes blow drying my hair.

All the makeup in the world couldn't hide the signs of crying, at least not the makeup I had at my disposal, but I did the best I could with eyedrops and cucumber gel.

I thought about wearing a dress. Brunch always felt dressy to me. But I didn't want to. Showering and putting on makeup were enough of a concession. Every dumped woman has a right to wallow in ice cream and movies and occasional bouts of tears.

If I was getting dragged out of the house, I was doing it in my most comfortable clothes. Though I wasn't going to wear my jammies. And after taking a good look at the set I'd just stripped off, maybe it was time to do a little shopping.

I'm not going to say that Brayden being a cheating dick-head was my fault, but it's possible I could've tried a little harder in the lingerie department. Then again, it would have been wasted on him. Pulling on my favorite pair of jeans and my favorite t-shirt, I headed for the stairs.

Vance met me at the front door, my purse in hand. "Come on, let's go. Charlie is going to meet us there."

I followed him out the door, stopping only to lock it behind me. Vance didn't say much on the way to the restaurant. I'd expected him to either grill me on the details or jump right into insulting Brayden, but he did neither.

He opened the car door for me and then took my hand in his as we drove down my driveway. The simple kindness brought tears to my eyes. He was a good friend. I should've remembered that. I wasn't alone without Brayden. I had Vance. I had Charlie. And other friends besides them.

I hadn't needed to hang on to my crappy boyfriend.

Still, I felt lost. I'd been the other half of a couple for so long. Even though I knew I was better off on my own, Brayden had dumped me and moved out so quickly I couldn't quite get my head around the idea of being single.

Vance parked in front of the restaurant and led me past the hostess station to a table on the terrace, where Charlie was already waiting for us with a mimosa in front of my empty seat.

"I shouldn't say this, considering the present company, but drink," she said, pushing the champagne glass toward me.

I did. I'd said I didn't want to drink, and that I didn't want any mimosas, but the second I saw that tall chilled glass, smelled the fresh orange juice and the dry tang of champagne, I realized I'd been wrong.

I did want a mimosa. I wanted several mimosas. And French toast. With hash browns. And bacon.

I drained half my glass in one long sip.

"Do you know what you want to order?" Charlie asked, tucking her sleek auburn hair behind her ear. She wore a sharp black suit, perfectly tailored, with a plum colored blouse and a matching scarf.

Charlie was beautiful, but she didn't seem to know it. I thought about her question. I'd been here before, and I was pretty sure about the French toast, hash browns, and bacon.

"I do, why?" I asked.

"Because I want to hear about what happened with that rat bastard and why you didn't call me," she said.

"Oh, okay."

"Tell," Vance commanded. Charlie looked at him.

"You don't know either?" she asked.

"I was waiting for you," he explained.

I let out a sigh. "He's been cheating on me for the last

year." I drained the rest of my mimosa and pushed the glass to the edge of the table so the waitress knew to refill it when she came back. "With the daughter of the surgeon who owns the practice where he was interning and is now employed. Now that he's officially a junior member of the practice, he dumped me to move in with her."

"What a fucking asshole," Vance said.

"Are you serious?" Charlie asked. Charlie was a sweetheart, but she was tough as hell in her own way. She looked pissed. "Which practice is it?"

I shook my head. "No, Charlie, no. He's a huge jerk, but we're not going to do anything."

"Why not?" Vance asked. "He deserves some retribution. He's been taking advantage of you, now you find out he's been cheating on you, and you're just going to let him walk away?"

I was. I tried to explain. "I'm not going to do anything because if I do something, he's going to think it's because I'm so brokenhearted I can't live without him. I'm not going to give him the satisfaction."

"I can see that," Charlie said. "Still, I don't like letting him get away with this."

"He left his golf clubs," I offered. "I'm pretty sure he hasn't figured that out yet, and he's going to come back for them."

"What did you do?" Vance asked.

"I thought about throwing them away, but they're worth a lot of money and it seems like a waste. Did you know it was garbage day this morning? It turns out my garbage man is a golfer. Now he has a really nice set of custom-made golf clubs. He was very appreciative."

"I bet he was," Vance said, laughing. "Did he leave anything else? Anything we can light on fire?"

"No." I hit him lightly on the shoulder with my menu. "No," I said more seriously. "He was very thorough. I think he'd been quietly moving his stuff out for a while because when he left, he only had a duffel bag, but there's nothing of his in the house, and we'd been living together for two years."

As I said the words, tears flooded my eyes again. Two years. We'd lived together for two years and had been dating for four.

What had I been thinking?

How could I have stuck with him for so long, this man who could just walk out on me, cheat on me?

Why had I put up with him?

And what did it say about me that I was so upset he'd left?

Chapter Six
Vance

I was going to kill that fucking twat. Fucking kill him.

Don't get me wrong. I was thrilled he'd walked out on Magnolia.

The woman had very few faults, but her refusal to throw in the towel on Brayden Michaels was one of them. He'd been freeloading off her for years, cutting her down and treating her like crap.

Loyalty was usually a good quality. God knows, I'd been the beneficiary of Magnolia's stubborn variety of loyalty when I hadn't deserved it either. The difference was, I'd realized I was an asshole.

I'd changed. I deserved that loyalty now.

Brayden had broken her heart. She'd said she didn't want us to do anything to him. Watching her sip her third mimosa and pick at her French toast, it was all I could do not to track the fucking dickhead down and beat him to a pulp.

My Magnolia should be happy. I loved seeing her when she was happy, those blue eyes bright, her full pink lips curved into a smile. Brayden was a dickhead, but the worst of his crimes, in my opinion, was convincing Magnolia that she was unattractive.

There was only so much I could do to change her mind. I couldn't, for example, strip off her clothes, lay her out on my bed, and kiss every inch of her creamy skin until she was screaming in orgasm. I couldn't hold her, and touch her, and fuck her until she couldn't walk.

It wasn't just that I was her boss. I pulled the boss-card when I needed to, but we both knew she was more my partner than my employee.

Once I'd realized how valuable she was, I'd even started cutting her in on some of the deals we worked together. So, it wasn't the job that was the problem.

But in the past two years, Magnolia had become my closest friend, the one person I relied on more than any other. If I'd made a move on her while she was engaged, Magnolia would've walked.

It would have killed her to do it, but she never would have cheated on Brayden.

Now, I had to figure out how I was going to play this. Option number one—get her drunk on mimosas, bring her home, and fuck her silly—was appealing, but not smart.

I knew my girl. Right now, she was second-guessing every choice she'd ever made, wondering how she could have been so stupid as to stay with Brayden for so long.

The last thing she needed was to be seduced into another decision she might end up regretting. That would send her running in the opposite direction.

I was going to have to be patient. I was not a big fan of patience. I saw what I wanted, and I went after it. I never gave up, and I never failed.

I'm not perfect. I've had my share of fuck-ups along the way. More than my share.

I was not going to fuck this up. Now that I finally had a shot at Magnolia, I was going to do it right.

Magnolia giggled at something Charlie said and wiped a tear off her cheek. I couldn't tell if it was a tear from laughing too hard or from crying.

At the sight of the puffy pink skin beneath her eyes, I wanted to leave the table, find the twat, and rip out his spine. I'd already promised we wouldn't do anything to him, and we wouldn't. Exactly. Okay, that's a lie.

As soon as I had Magnolia tucked away for the night, I was calling Evers. Evers Sinclair was my oldest friend. Our families had grown up together, and he—along with his brothers—ran one of the premier security companies in the country.

While I was more inclined to find Brayden and beat the shit out of him, Evers was well-schooled in the art of sneakiness. And he adored Magnolia. He would be thrilled she was shed of that loser and more than happy to plot some secret revenge.

Yes, it's as petty as it sounds. I didn't care. He hurt Magnolia, had been hurting her for years, and now he was going to pay for it.

I thought about the things Evers could do—mysterious parking tickets, fucking with his phone—the list was long, and all of it would be entertaining.

Then I thought about Magnolia finding out. Hmm. She'd be pissed if she knew we were messing with the twat, no matter how much he deserved it.

Damn it. As much as I wanted to get revenge for Magnolia, I set aside the idea.

I wouldn't call Evers. I'd behave myself. But if that dick-head loser ever gave me an excuse, I was going to beat the shit out of him.

Charlie's phone beeped, and she looked down, her laughing face falling into a frown.

"What's wrong?" Magnolia asked, draining the last of her mimosa. I gestured to the waitress to refill it. Magnolia was a little tipsy, but not tipsy enough.

Charlie shook her head and tapped out a message on her phone. "Just work. You'd think I could leave for a few hours."

"You practically live there," I said. "You know, have you thought about—"

"Don't," Charlie said, pinning me with her ocean blue eyes.

Charlotte was perfect in almost all things—perfect grades, perfect clothes, perfect hair, perfect in the board room, perfect at a cocktail party—so seemingly perfect that most people missed her core of steely determination. She had all the patience in the world with the people she loved and none with herself.

"Charlie," Magnolia started to say, but Charlie cut her off with a sharp shake of her head.

"No. Today is about you. We're not talking about me."

She stood, tucking her phone into her purse and pulling out her car keys. "I'm so sorry, Maggie, but I have to go." She leaned down and pulled Magnolia into a tight hug, whispering something into her ear that brought tears to Magnolia's eyes.

I heard Magnolia whisper back, *Love you, Charlie*, before Charlie stood up, smoothing her suit jacket and turning her attention to me.

"Take care of her," she ordered. "Fun, but not too much more alcohol or she'll be miserable tomorrow."

I saluted Charlie and sent Magnolia a wink. "Yes, ma'am," I said.

Magnolia let out a cute little harrumph.

"You know, I'm sitting right here, and I can take care of myself."

"Not today, you can't," Charlie called over her shoulder as she walked out of the restaurant to her car. Magnolia let out a sigh as the waitress arrived with another mimosa.

She took a sip and said, "I shouldn't drink anymore. I don't want to feel like crap tomorrow."

"I've got a plan," I assured her. "You're having a few more mimosas, we're going to the movies, then I'm cooking you dinner, and you're going to bed early. By the time you wake up in the morning, you'll feel fine. I promise."

Magnolia's eyes skated away from mine, and I caught the sheen of tears. She was thinking about going home to that empty house, about waking up alone.

I was going to make that asshole pay for doing this to her.

I'd never so much as kissed Magnolia, but she was mine. She was mine in a way no woman had ever been mine. I knew her, in some ways better than I knew myself.

It was going to take time for her to get over Brayden's betrayal. I would be there every step of the way, and when she was ready, I would claim her. Finally.

For now, the agenda was mimosas, movies, dinner, and a good night's sleep. It was a good plan. It would have been better if I'd managed to stick with it. But Magnolia was just too much temptation.

We got through the mimosas part just fine. Magnolia was a happy drunk, even reeling from a breakup, and she happily followed me to the movies and settled in beside me to watch the latest action thriller, even holding my hand when I reached for hers in the dark.

I didn't want the day to end. After the movie, we

stopped by the store to pick up groceries, and I took her back to her house to make her some food—her favorite, Linguine Pomodoro with extra shaved parmesan. I could make it in my sleep.

She kept me company in the kitchen, drinking the water I poured her while I chopped tomatoes and basil. It was so easy and natural. I was almost convinced we were together, that she was already over Brayden. That I'd already made my move, and she was mine.

A dangerous line of thinking. Too dangerous. I'd started out cautious, but after a day with Magnolia, I was feeling confident. Reckless.

We ate dinner side by side on the couch, watching *Die Harder*.

I loved that she liked action movies. The champagne plus the pasta eventually got the best of her, and she slumped into my side, her eyelids drooping. I should have let her fall asleep right there and snuck out.

I let her drift off beside me for a few minutes. The apple scent of her shampoo enveloped me, familiar from all those days working together at her desk and somehow exotic in the dark room.

An explosion on the screen woke her, and she sat up, blinking and pushing her hair off her face.

"I think I need to go pass out," she said. "Sorry. You can hang out and watch the end of the movie if you want."

"No, I'm good. I've seen it."

"I'll walk you out," she said, straightening the couch pillows while I found my shoes. She followed me to the front door, her eyes sleepy and unfocused.

"Are you going to be okay?" I asked. "I can stay, sleep on the couch."

Magnolia shook her head. "I'm fine. I have to get used to it," she said.

"Yeah, but you don't have to start tonight."

"No, I'm okay. I promise."

I wasn't convinced. I knew I needed to go, but I didn't want to leave her. Facing her, I cupped her cheeks in my palms and met her eyes. "You're going to be okay, Magnolia. You're so much better off without him. I promise you."

Her eyes filled, tears glazing the blue with a watery film. Those tears were my downfall. I hated to see Magnolia cry. It killed me. I did the exact thing I'd sworn not to do.

I kissed her.

I knew it was a mistake. I knew it. The moment her lips touched mine, soft and warm, I no longer cared.

The little gasp she made went straight to my cock.

I ran my tongue along her lower lip and groaned. Fuck, she was sweet. I'd imagined kissing Magnolia for two years. The reality, even this brief taste of her, blew every fantasy right out of the water.

Before my common sense had the chance to kick in, I tilted her head and deepened the kiss, sealing my mouth over hers, taking everything I could get.

At first, she kissed me back, her tongue sliding along mine, her body leaning into me. When she took a step closer, fitting her soft curves against me, I almost lost my mind.

My cock was screaming, *yes*, but my brain was sounding the alarm.

Too fast. Way too soon.

Unfortunately, my brain didn't get the message through in time. Magnolia wrenched herself away and stared at me, her eyes wide with horror. She pressed the back of her hand against kiss-swollen lips, her shoulders heaving as her breath came hard and fast.

"Why did you do that?" she asked, crossing her arms over her chest, her posture so defensive she might as well have been carrying a sign that said, *Stay Back*.

"I wanted to."

Bad answer.

Magnolia's expressive eyes shut me out, turning opaque and hard.

"Don't ever do that again," she said.

"Magnolia—" I started. She cut me off.

"No. We'll pretend it didn't happen. It's not a big deal. Just forget about it."

My mind raced, searching for the right thing to say that would erase the last few minutes. I'd meant to kiss her, but not yet.

I needed an excuse. A reason. Anything was better than, *I wanted to*. I was supposed to be charming, for fuck's sake.

I ran out of time.

While I was still searching for words, Magnolia swung the door shut in my face, softening her rejection with a quiet, "I'll see you tomorrow."

The one time I cared about a woman, and I'd already fucked it up. Now I had to figure out how to fix things before she came up with an excuse to shut me out forever.

CHAPTER SEVEN
VANCE

ONE MONTH LATER

Magnolia was true to her word. I made a single attempt to mention our kiss the next day, and she shut me down, saying only, "We're not talking about it. It never happened."

I let it go. It didn't fit my plan to start something with Magnolia when she'd just lost her fiancé. I'd been giving her time, occupying myself by switching between plans for our first date and fantasies of what she'd look like naked.

I had to be sneaky about the date. I couldn't just ask her out. She'd say no. I was going to have to take her by surprise. My current favorite plan was to invent a business trip. We had a few investment opportunities that could require travel.

I had a feeling it would be easier to change things between us if I could break the pattern of our daily lives. Little did I know how true that would be.

I was forced to stick with fantasy and plans for the moment. I had a show coming up in a few weeks, and between that and some problems with a project we'd invested in, we'd been putting out fires right and left over the past few days.

Things had been so crazy we'd missed lunch. I'd stopped for groceries on the way home from a meeting and was hoping I could talk Magnolia into letting me cook for her at my loft.

I called it my 'loft', but really, I own the whole building. On a short block of mixed-use development in Midtown Atlanta, the building had been an auto shop and a supply warehouse, then vacant before I'd snapped it up and renovated the entire structure to suit exactly what I wanted.

The first floor was my studio and garage, the second floor my living space, and the roof was a custom-designed garden. My gym equipment was split between the studio and the rooftop.

It was modern and open, with huge windows on the second level and garage bays on the first that let in fresh air when my work got too hot.

The building had one other thing I required. Privacy. Sinclair Security had designed my system, and it included both a sophisticated alarm and video surveillance.

I was a Winters. That meant I had to deal with a certain amount of media attention. It didn't help that I hadn't lived a quiet lifestyle for most of my twenties.

So it wasn't entirely a surprise to turn the corner onto my block and find a strange woman lurking outside my front door. I drove past the building and slowed to turn into the alley that led back to my private garage.

Magnolia hit the button on the remote that opened the gate. Both of us noticed the stranger mark our entrance.

"I don't see a camera," Magnolia commented. Neither had I, but the woman had been carrying something.

"Don't worry about it," I said. "If she's a pap, she missed her shot. And if she wants something else, she'll ring the bell, and we can tell her to get lost."

Magnolia's brow furrowed, but she didn't say anything. She didn't like media scrutiny any more than I did, but she was used to it by now. Everyone knew she worked with me, and they didn't bother her more than the usual. I pulled my Range Rover into the garage and parked.

"I'll grab the groceries," I said.

"I can help," Magnolia offered. I shook my head, not hiding my grin.

"I've got it, Sugar." Magnolia graced me with an absolutely brilliant scowl. I wasn't much into pet names. I never bothered with them for the women I was sleeping with. Everybody called Charlotte *Charlie*, so that didn't count.

When I did call Magnolia something other than her name, it was usually *Babe*. She thought that was a generic term I used with every woman. She hadn't realized that she was the only female I've ever considered worth a pet name, even something as common as *Babe*.

When I wanted to get a rise out of her, I always called her *Sugar*—a reference to the Grateful Dead song she so despised.

I didn't use it very often. She would have beaten me senseless if I had, but every once in a while, I couldn't resist. Thanks to my teasing, she ignored me as we left the garage and crossed my studio to the freight elevator.

The chimes from the front bell were already ringing when we exited the elevator on the second floor. Maybe we should've checked the door while we were down there, but I'd been hoping it wouldn't be necessary. No such luck.

Magnolia went to the keypad beside the elevator while I

headed for the kitchen to put down the groceries. She tapped the button to activate the camera at the door.

The screen flashed on to show a young woman with long, dark hair and a washed-out complexion, her expression annoyed. Something about her was vaguely familiar.

Pressing the speaker button, Magnolia said, "Can I help you?" in her best British headmistress voice. She refused to admit she had a faint British accent from her years spent living in England, but when she used that starchy tone, it came out. It was intimidating as hell, even when she used it on me.

The woman at the door said, "I'm looking for Vance Winters. I'm Stephanie Albert, Amy's sister. I need to talk to Vance."

Magnolia looked at me. "Fuck," I swore under my breath. "Tell her I'll be right down."

Magnolia came with me, refusing to let me handle Amy's sister on my own, out of curiosity or protectiveness. Probably both. I hadn't seen Amy in a while. Close to a year.

We'd tried getting back together after we both went to rehab, but sobriety revealed that we had absolutely nothing in common. She'd been doing okay last time I'd seen her.

Still, a sense of foreboding filled me as I unlocked my front door and opened it.

Stephanie Albert looked like a faded version of Amy. The same petite fairy-like frame, dark hair, blue eyes, and pale skin. But where Amy's hair was inky black, her eyes sapphire blue, Stephanie's hair was dark brown, her eyes a watery shade and less attractive than her sister's.

We'd only met once, and I barely remembered it. Mostly since I'd been drunk at the time.

"Stephanie, it's good to see you," I lied. "What can I do for you?"

Stephanie leaned down to pick something up off the ground. "I need to talk to you," she said. "I have your daughter, and you need to take her."

I blinked and shook my head as if I could somehow clear my vision and ears at the same time. As if I could erase the sight of Stephanie Albert holding a baby carrier.

What the fuck? My daughter? Since when did I have a daughter?

She was probably expecting me to say something. I had no words.

I had zero words.

All I could do was stare at the sleeping infant in the baby carrier. She was tiny, with a chunky scrunched up little face and a trail of drool coming from her rosebud lips.

For the first time in months, I desperately wanted to drink. Beside me, a throat cleared. In her best crisply British tone, the accent more than faint, Magnolia said, "Why don't you come in, Stephanie? It seems we need to have a conversation."

Mute, I held the door open to admit my unwanted guests, following behind as Magnolia led Stephanie back to the elevator. We rode up in silence.

The second the elevator doors opened, I stalked out, heading for the kitchen. I could not have a drink. I was not going to have a drink. I'd been sober for well over a year, and I wasn't going to fuck it up now.

Ignoring the three females following me, I poured a glass of cold water and drank the entire thing. It wasn't whiskey, but somehow, it seemed to clear my head.

Magnolia led Stephanie to the kitchen, where she set the baby carrier on the island. Crossing the room to stand behind me, Magnolia looped her arm through mine and turned her attention back to Amy's sister.

"I'm assuming you're implying this is Amy's child?" Magnolia asked in her starchy best. Stephanie's back went ramrod straight, and her eyes narrowed.

"Of course it is. She's not mine. I never slept with that man-whore."

Her words hit, then skidded off me. I've been called worse. And I didn't care what Amy's sister thought of me. Magnolia ignored the insult.

"If this is Amy and Vance's child, then where is Amy? It seems more sensible for Vance to deal with—"

"Amy's dead," Stephanie said in a flat, empty voice.

The strength drained from my muscles. I braced my palms on the island to hold myself up, my head dropping forward, my eyes staring blindly at the countertop.

Dead? I wished I were more surprised. I didn't need to hear the answer when Magnolia whispered, "How? What happened?"

It could've been an accident. She could've gotten sick. But I knew that wasn't what had killed Amy. I squeezed my eyes tightly shut and gritted my teeth when Stephanie said, "She overdosed," in that same flat, empty voice.

"Oh, God. I'm so sorry," Magnolia said, her voice thick with tears. "When? How long ago?"

She tucked her body into mine, pushing her shoulder under my arm and wrapping her arm around me, sliding her hand under my shirt so that her palm rested on the bare skin of my back.

I leaned into her, grateful for the anchor of her touch when everything I knew was suddenly spinning out of my grasp.

"Why didn't she tell me?" I asked, still staring at the

countertop, my voice low and ragged.

"I wanted her to," Stephanie said. "She said she wasn't ready. I think she wanted to be sure she could stay sober."

"Was she? Sober? The last time we were together, she said she was clean."

I had to force the words out. I wasn't surprised Amy was dead, but fuck, the thought of it hurt.

"She was. She was clean the whole pregnancy. She relapsed right after Rosie was born. Just once. Then she stayed clean for a few months until last week—" Stephanie broke off with a choking sound.

"So, what do we do now?" Magnolia asked gently. "Since you're here, I'm assuming that you want Vance to play a role in his daughter's life."

"He's on the birth certificate. He's her father, and he needs to take her. I love Rosie, and I loved my sister, but I can't do this. I can barely support myself. I can't take care of a baby."

Slowly, Magnolia said, "I don't want to make this more difficult, but just because Vance is on the birth certificate, it doesn't mean he's the father. I assume you want more than just for Vance to take the child?"

Stephanie straightened, and in a hard voice, she said, "I want fifty grand, and you can have the baby."

"What the fuck?" I said.

She'd flipped from grieving sister to extortionist in a breath. Magnolia was right. Just because they said I was the father, it didn't make it true.

Amy was a fun girl. We had some good times together, but she wasn't exactly a nun. I wasn't the only guy she slept with on a semi-regular basis back in the day. Fortunately, Magnolia was thinking, even if I wasn't.

"Obviously, we'll have to do a blood test before there's

any discussion of payment. If she *is* Vance's daughter, and he agrees to take custody, you'll have to sign papers agreeing as well. He's not going to be open to blackmail."

Stephanie's shoulders sagged. "Look, I'm not trying to be a bitch here. It's just that I'm a waitress, and I'm trying to go to school. I blew more than half of my savings on hospital bills for Amy, and the funeral pretty much wiped me out. I can't afford to take care of Rosie, and I can't pay next semester's tuition. This isn't my problem. You got her pregnant, and she left me with the baby. I don't deserve to have my whole life fucked up because of it."

"I understand," Magnolia said in a crisply dismissive tone. "I need you to excuse us for a moment." She nudged me in the ribs to get my attention. I grunted in response. "Vance, I'd like to talk to you in the office."

Obedient for once, I followed her into the office, saying nothing until she shut the door. My mind spun. Amy was dead. I was a father. I couldn't get a handle on it all.

I braced for Magnolia to cut into me. Instead, she said, "Sit down. You look like you're about to pass out."

I sat, resting my elbows on my knees and letting my head hang as I stared at the floor.

"I don't think she's lying," Magnolia said, her voice barely above a whisper. The office had a door, but the walls didn't extend all the way to the ceiling. I nodded, responding in the same low tone.

"I don't think she's lying either," I said. "Fuck. How the fuck did this happen?"

Magnolia leaned against the desk and surprised me with a wry laugh. "Considering how many times I've woken you up with a naked woman in your bed, I'm pretty sure I don't need to explain how this happened."

"Bite me, Sugar."

"I don't think so," she said tartly. "Look, I'm going to call Dr. Whitmore's office. The first thing we need to do is determine that she's your daughter. If she is, what do you want to do?"

"What you mean, what do I want to do? If she's my daughter, I want her. She's mine. It's bad enough that her mother died. No way in fucking hell will I walk out on her."

Magnolia's eyes filled with tears. One fell over her lashes to skate down her cheek before she lifted her hands and pressed the heels of her palms to her eyes.

Sucking in and blowing out a quick breath, she said, "Okay, good. So, that's settled. I'll call Dave Price and get him to put together papers so Stephanie can relinquish any rights, assuming the blood test comes back showing that you're the father."

"I'll call Dave," I said. "But I'd appreciate it if you could get on the line with Dr. Whitmore's office and have them agree to rush the blood test. If that little girl is my daughter, I want to get this wrapped up as soon as possible."

Magnolia nodded and walked out of our office. I picked up the phone and dialed my attorney. While I was waiting, Magnolia came back in, pulled out her own phone, and got on the line with the doctor's office.

There were downsides to being a Winters. Most people didn't see them. They saw the money and thought we had it all.

The truth was, a lot of it sucked. Dead parents, dead aunt and uncle, and the media ripping us apart on a regular basis before we could even walk. But at times like this, being a Winters made life so much less complicated.

The tests to show paternity could be done in hours. Dave was already drawing up the legal work. If that little girl was mine, we'd know it by morning.

CHAPTER EIGHT

VANCE

Stephanie left with the baby shortly after we made our calls, heading straight for the doctor's office.

Rosalie.

Amy had named her daughter—our daughter—Rosalie. I wondered if she'd had that little pink rosebud of a mouth when she'd been born. I'd only seen her sleeping, but she looked like a Rosalie.

I was in shock and totally fucked. I knew nothing about babies. Less than nothing. I'd never even held a baby, and assuming the test came out like I thought it would, tomorrow, I would be the sole caretaker of a three and a half month old.

How the fuck was I supposed to do that?

It bothered me, watching Stephanie leave with Rosalie. Stupid. I didn't even know that she was my daughter. The idea that she could be was absurd, and all too possible. Part of me wanted to snatch the baby carrier from Stephanie and boot her out the door, locking it behind her.

How fucking dare she? How dare she call me a man-whore when she was here to extort money in exchange for my child?

The more rational part of my brain reminded me that if she was telling the truth, she was my child's aunt, the only living reminder of Rosalie's dead mother. I had plenty of money. If Stephanie needed some help after taking care of my daughter, of course I'd help her.

I wasn't a big fan of the rational side of my brain at the moment. I was pissed and freaked the fuck out.

Magnolia fell back on her typical efficient organization in the face of our crisis. Yes, *our* crisis. She didn't know it yet, but no fucking way was Magnolia leaving me to deal with this on my own.

I may have had my life under control again—my career, my investments, my sobriety—but I had no clue what to do with a baby. I might deserve to be abandoned with an infant, but Rosalie needed a competent adult taking care of her. Since she was stuck with me, it was all hands on deck.

We ended up cooking dinner at Magnolia's house after a quick stop at the lab to give blood for the paternity test. It was after hours, but they promised we'd have the results first thing in the morning.

Evers showed up at Magnolia's door halfway through dinner. I'd called him on the way home to ask him to look into Amy's death.

I was sure Stephanie wouldn't lie about something like that, but I learned the hard way that when people started asking for money, especially tens of thousands of dollars, you had to be suspicious.

I was well aware this could all be a big lie. Amy could very well still be alive, and Rosalie might not even be her child.

People did some shitty things when they needed money. When you had a ton of it, you were a target.

This was not the first time a woman had claimed I'd fathered her child. It was the first time I believed it might be true.

Magnolia got a plate of stir-fry together for Evers, and he joined us at the table.

"Did you find out anything?" I asked. Magnolia set her fork on her plate and watched Evers. I did the same.

He finished chewing and swallowed, then he shook his head and said, "I'm sorry, man. We don't know about the baby yet, obviously, but Amy Albert overdosed five days ago. From the information I got, she'd been clean for a few months, then she fell off the wagon and miscalculated the dose."

Magnolia let out a gust of breath. My eyes watered. I felt wet heat on my cheeks and realized I was crying.

God dammit.

I hadn't realized how much I'd been hoping that Stephanie was a con artist. Amy and I hadn't been in love. At our very best, we'd been two broken people in a fucked-up friendship based on sex and getting wasted.

But she was a good person, and I cared about her. She'd cared about me.

Her first overdose, the one she'd survived thanks to Magnolia, had been the beginning of the best part of my life.

I owed her for that. It crushed me that she'd never know the same freedom, that she hadn't been able to escape the tentacles of her addiction. I wasn't fool enough to think that I was home free, that I'd ever be home free, but I'd gotten this far.

It killed to know one mistake had stolen Amy's life. I

wiped my cheeks with the back of my hand and heard Magnolia say, "What about the baby?"

"The blood test will give us the truth," Evers said. "But she did put Vance on the birth certificate, which legally makes all of this much easier. I talked to Dave, and he's got a copy of the certificate. It also helps that she gave birth here in Atlanta. Easier to get ahold of the records. She gave birth on November twenty-fifth, which means she would've gotten pregnant around last February. That line up?"

"Yeah, it does," I said, remembering the weekend Amy had shown up and we'd given a stab at getting back together.

It hadn't lasted. We were not a good fit when we were sober. We'd used condoms, but everyone knew they didn't always work. Ironically, but very luckily, she'd gotten pregnant when we were sober.

I shuddered to think about how half-assed my condom use had been when I'd been drinking. It was a miracle I was clean, all things considered.

"What about Amy's family?" Magnolia asked. I answered before Evers could.

"Amy and Stephanie were tight, but they've been estranged from their parents for years. I doubt they have any interest in Rosalie, and from some of the shit Amy told me, she would not want her daughter growing up in their house even if I was willing to give her up."

"And you're not?" Evers asked, one eyebrow raised.

I scowled at him. He should know me better than to ask such a stupid question.

"Of course not, asshole. How could you ask me that? You think I would walk away from my own child? Fuck, even if she turns out not to be mine, I might pay Stephanie off and get her to sign the papers anyway."

"What?" Evers said in confusion. I shrugged and gritted my teeth before I answered.

"Look, Stephanie doesn't want her niece. She's made that abundantly clear. Amy's dead. The parents? From some of the things Amy told me, these are people who should not be raising goldfish, much less children. They're the reason Amy ended up the way she did. The last thing she would want is for her daughter to wind up with them. The kid could end up in the system. That's a shitty memorial to Amy's life."

"I get where you're coming from, but you have to think this through, Vance," Evers said. "It's not like taking in a puppy. This is a child. You'd be a parent. That's a whole new level of responsibility. Are you're saying you're willing to step up even if she's not yours?"

"We don't need to worry about that yet," I said. "If Stephanie is telling the truth about Amy, she's probably telling the truth about Rosalie, too. There's no way I'd ever turn my back on my own kid. If she's not mine, I promise I'll think it through before I do anything rash."

I went back to my stir-fry, not interested in discussing the issue any further. I was already reeling from the news about Amy and Rosalie. I didn't need to get into a fight with my oldest friend on top of it.

Evers left after dinner with a warning to be smart and a promise to keep digging. I wasn't sure what else there was to dig up, but if there were anything, Evers would find it.

Magnolia and I barely spoke for the rest of the evening, both of us caught up in our thoughts. We did the dinner dishes and watched a movie, neither of us paying any attention to the action on the screen.

A few times, I caught the glimmer of tears on Magnolia's cheeks. My eyes were dry, but my heart was heavy in my chest.

Amy's death was such a fucking waste. I tried not to think about that little girl in the baby carrier. Whether or not she was mine, she'd lost her mother. Nothing I did could fix that.

I spent the night in Magnolia's guest room. I didn't want to leave her alone, and I didn't want to be alone myself. We were both still reeling from learning about Amy, and the next day felt like it was bearing down on us far too quickly.

I woke the next morning to find Magnolia in the kitchen, making coffee. She wore her favorite pair of jeans, the pair that made her ass look fantastic, and a knit sweater with a cowl neckline that teased at cleavage but showed nothing.

She probably had no idea how hot she looked. She almost caught me leering before my brain kicked into gear and the events of the day before rushed back.

Even though it wasn't quite seven o'clock, I grabbed my phone. No messages. Of course not. The lab wouldn't be open until eight, and Stephanie wasn't due back at the loft until ten.

I was just going to have to be patient in the meantime. I hated being patient. I wanted everything resolved right now.

Was she my kid or not?

If she wasn't, was I going to walk away and leave her with a woman who was willing to sell her?

Coffee. I needed coffee, stat. I needed to clear my fucking head.

"Drink your coffee," I said when Magnolia had poured us both a mug full. "We're going for a run."

Magnolia shook her head. "Vance, seriously. I really don't feel like running today."

"Yeah, neither do I, but what else are we going to do? We've got hours before we know anything. Even if we go to work, are you going to be able to pay attention to emails and contracts?"

Magnolia didn't answer. She just stared at me over the rim of her coffee cup. Finally, she took a gulp, set the cup down on the counter, and said, "I'll go change."

I had a gym bag in my car, just in case. Yes, I have an obsessive and addictive personality. Sometimes, it just hits me out of nowhere, the fierce longing for a drink. For something, anything, that will ease the hard edges, that will shut off the fucking nightmares I can't shake at almost thirty years old.

I'm done with drinking. I'm done with that shit. Even if I hadn't been done with it before, knowing that Amy was dead, alcohol was never going to be the answer for me again.

Giving it up didn't kill the need. Working out and sculpting helped channel it. Every once in a while, the craving for a drink took me off guard. For that, I kept my running gear in the car.

No matter where I was, I could throw on my gear and run until I'd burned it out of me and the only thing I wanted to drink was ice cold water.

I drank half my coffee, grabbed my gear, and got dressed in time to meet Magnolia at the front door. We started walking, warming our muscles up, falling into the familiar rhythm. Sometimes, we talked when we warmed up. Now that Magnolia was used to it, we even occasionally talked while we jogged.

Not today.

Neither of us felt much like talking with the specter of

Amy's death and her child's unknown fate hanging over our heads. An hour later, we were back, splitting up at the top of the stairs. Magnolia headed for her shower, and I headed for the shower in the guest room.

Stephanie was waiting for us, Rosalie in her carrier, when we got to the loft.

The infant was sleeping again, this time in a pink cotton one-piece thing with a matching hat on her head, a pink blanket with brown teddy bears wrapped around her.

If all she did was sleep, the baby thing wouldn't be too bad. Unfortunately, I'd heard enough about exhausted parents to know I knew absolutely nothing about what I was getting into.

Magnolia made more coffee when we got upstairs, and she pulled out a box of muffins I hadn't known were in the pantry. She hadn't baked them, but they were probably okay.

I ate two, my eyes flicking between the sleeping Rosalie and my silent phone. Magnolia picked the cranberries out of her muffin but didn't eat it.

Stephanie paced in front of the plate glass windows overlooking midtown, stopping once to ask, "Is it okay if I smoke?"

"No," Magnolia and I snapped back in unison.

I knew jack-shit about taking care of kids, but I was pretty sure you weren't supposed to smoke in front of them. Shit. I just wanted to know what we were dealing with.

At ten twenty-seven, my phone rang.

A short conversation, impossibly short, considering the magnitude of the information communicated, and my entire life shifted on its axis.

I was a father. Rosalie was mine. I had a little girl.

How the fuck was I going to manage this?

I didn't say anything. Magnolia and Stephanie watched me with anxious eyes as I set my phone beside my empty coffee cup and left the room. I returned a moment later with a check in one hand and a sheaf of papers in the other.

As I'd expected, Stephanie reached for the check first.

I raised it above her head and said, "Wait."

"She's yours, right? That's what they said, right?" Stephanie bounced on her toes and tried to grab the check from my hand.

"Calm the fuck down. Yes, that's what they said. You'll get your money, but you're going to have to sign some papers first."

"Fine, whatever," she said, her eyes glued to the check. "What do you want me to sign?"

I spread the papers across the island, showing them to her as I spoke. "We don't really need these considering the blood test proved I'm her father and Amy put me on the birth certificate, but assuming Amy didn't have a will—" I paused, and Stephanie shook her head. "Then this just verifies that as her next of kin, you agree with my having sole custody of Rosalie. If you decide you want to see her, I have no problem with that. You're her family. But by signing this, you relinquish the right to sue for custody in the future."

"Fine, that's fine." Stephanie picked up the pen and began to sign everywhere I indicated.

I looked at Rosalie, still sleeping in her baby carrier, a little pink pacifier between her lips, and wondered how Stephanie could be so willing to ditch her niece and run.

Oh, yeah, the check. The shit people would do for money.

Five minutes later, Stephanie was gone, a check in her pocket, without Rosalie.

So far, my daughter showed no signs of waking up

anytime soon. I had the odd feeling that I'd been left with a grenade, and Stephanie had walked out the door with the pin.

As long as Rosalie was sleeping, I had this under control. I could be quiet and not wake her up. But eventually, she was going to need something from me. Food, a clean diaper, something. Stephanie had left a diaper bag beside the carrier.

As quietly as I could, suddenly terrified to set off the ticking bomb that was my new daughter, I picked up the diaper bag and headed for the office, grabbing Magnolia on my way.

"What?" Magnolia asked, looking over her shoulder as if worried to leave the baby.

"She's fine as long as she sleeping, but we have to figure out what the hell we're going to do with her," I said in a hushed voice. "I'm assuming there's stuff we need in this bag, like what the hell she eats and what kind of diapers we're supposed to buy."

"Oh, good thinking." Magnolia sat at her desk and helped me unpack the bag. Then, as if my words were still sinking in, she sat up straight and dropped a plastic bottle next to a pile of papers. "What do you mean, *we?*" she demanded.

"Do you think I'm going to do this by myself?" I asked.

Was she crazy?

"Vance," Magnolia protested, "I'm not a nanny. I don't know anything about kids. How am I supposed to help you?"

"I'm not asking you to be her nanny," I said, all of a sudden terrified Magnolia might walk out and leave me alone with Rosalie. "I know that's not your job. I'm asking as your friend, please fucking help me. Please. At least until I get on my feet with this. I can't do this by myself."

"What do you expect me to do?" she asked, her eyebrows knit together in confusion. I shrugged helplessly.

"Just help me. From now on, you're working twenty-four seven. I'll double your salary. I'll give you whatever you want. Just . . . just stay with us until we get this figured out. Please."

"You want me to move in with you? And Rosalie?" Magnolia looked doubtful. I thought about it. My loft was not ideal for a baby. The space was huge, but I'd only designed it with two bedrooms, mine and the one we were currently using as an office.

I couldn't ask Magnolia to work twenty-four seven and then sleep on the couch. Sadly, she wouldn't be sleeping with me. Now was not the time to shake up our relationship.

"No," I said, the answer suddenly clear. "We'll move in with you. You've got plenty of room, and the yard is much better for Scout."

I could see her thinking, running over the options and evaluating the risks. I was asking a lot. I knew that, but I was desperate.

I was not ready to be a father.

I'd only gotten my own shit together in the last year. But it didn't look like I had a choice. Rosalie and I were stuck with each other, and I knew in my gut that if Magnolia was with us, everything would be okay.

Finally, she said, "You guys can move in with me, and we can go back and forth to the loft during the day. You do realize that means we'll have to get double of almost every-thing, right? Two cribs, two changing tables, two of all the stuff we don't even know we need yet."

I grinned in relief. "Who cares? I'm loaded. We've got a lot of problems right now, but money isn't one of them."

"We need a list," Magnolia said. She pulled over a notebook and grabbed a pen. At the top, she wrote Crib x2. After that, she wrote Formula, Monitor, Diapers. "What kind of diapers are in that bag?" she asked.

I finished unpacking the bag onto the desk and looked at the diapers. They had cartoon characters on them and the number two. Magnolia wrote it down.

"I have no idea what else we need," she said. "Did Stephanie leave clothes?"

"There's one change of clothes in this bag," I said. "That's it. We have a plastic bottle, one change of clothes, a half-empty package of wipes, a can of formula, four diapers, some dirty rags, and a baby."

I hung my head and scrubbed my fingers through my hair. "Fuck. We really have no fucking clue what we're doing. How could she leave Rosalie with us when she knows we have no idea what we're doing? We don't even have a car seat," I said in a near shout.

"Shh," Magnolia said. "Don't wake her up. The thing she's in is a car seat, I think. The bottom part straps into the car. That's why it looks bigger today than it did yesterday. But we're going to have to figure out how to get it in the car. I don't even know where the store is to buy all the baby stuff."

She got up and left the room. A minute later, she was back with her phone in hand.

"Okay, I found the baby store, and the directions for installing the car seat thing are on the side of the base. We can probably figure that out, but we're going to end up waking Rosalie up."

She looked terrified at the thought.

I was pretty sure the expression on her face was a mirror of my own.

Sleeping baby, no problem. I could handle Rosalie when she was asleep, could marvel over her rosebud mouth and soft cheeks.

That didn't mean I was ready to face my daughter when her eyes were open.

CHAPTER NINE

MAGNOLIA

We woke up Rosalie when we tried to put the car seat in the back of the Range Rover. She screamed for a solid five minutes while we drove around trying to find the big box store packed to the rafters with baby stuff. I'd probably passed it a thousand times and never even noticed it was there. I had a feeling I'd be visiting it often.

By the time we got Rosalie back out of the car, her carrier strapped into a shopping cart made to hold it, we both felt like bumbling idiots.

A family of five passed us in the parking lot, their infant twins cozily arranged in their shopping cart with a toddler walking beside them, all smiling and laughing as if they hadn't a care in the world. Clearly, they'd figured this out.

"She's screaming," Vance said, watching Rosalie, his vivid blue eyes a little panicked. "What are we supposed to do?"

I looked down at Vance's daughter, her sweet little face bright red, eyes squeezed shut, rosebud mouth wide open and screeching her rage at the world.

Or, possibly, rage at her incompetent caretakers. What Vance and I knew about babies wouldn't fill a postcard, and Stephanie had taken off the second she had her check in hand.

"Okay so she's not tired," I said, basing that assumption on the hours she'd napped. "So I'd guess that leaves hungry or she needs a diaper change."

I eyed Rosalie doubtfully, hoping it was option number one. I'd never changed a diaper in my entire life, and I wasn't quite ready to start.

Not in a parking lot.

Vance opened the back of the Range Rover and set the baby carrier inside, the diaper bag beside it.

Fortunately, Stephanie had left an already mixed bottle of formula in the bag, along with a canister of the weird smelling powder she'd used to mix it up.

She'd mentioned that Amy had been nursing, and the formula was a new addition to Rosalie's life. She also mentioned that it was causing some stomach distress.

I did *not* want to know what that meant. I had a bad feeling stomach distress in a four-month-old was not good.

For a guy who didn't know what he was doing, Vance figured out the bottle pretty quickly. He got the seal off and the nipple screwed on, handing it to me to hold while he carefully unbuckled Rosalie and picked her up for the first time.

His eyes soft with wonder, Vance tucked her into his arm like a football, cradling her against his chest, her head propped up on his bicep, and held his other hand out for the bottle. Wordless, I handed it to him.

As if he'd been doing it forever, he popped the nipple into her screaming mouth. At the first touch, she tried to turn her face away, too furious to realize what was going on.

Vance gave the bottle a little shake, and a drop of formula hit Rosie's tongue. That was all it took. Her mouth closed around it, and she began to suck with a vigor that was both reassuring and alarming.

"Hey, there," Vance said as his daughter's eyes focused on his face. "You were just hungry. It's okay, Rosie. I get cranky when I'm hungry too."

There was a good chance my ovaries were about to explode. Vance was hot enough on his own. He would've been hot wearing a trash bag. In faded jeans, a T-shirt stretched tight around his biceps, and Rosalie's little baby head resting against the dark lines of his tattoos, he was too much.

When you added in the look on his face, he brought tears to my eyes—tears and a raging case of panty-melting lust.

This was going to be a nightmare.

Vance was even more off-limits than ever. Since the day we'd met, up until a month before, I'd been with Brayden. Vance had been eye candy, then a close friend, and always my employer.

He was not a romantic prospect. Ever. Not even now that I was single. The kiss I refused to discuss was proof enough that I was vulnerable to him. It didn't matter how swoon-worthy he was.

I tore my eyes away from the sight of Vance adoring his daughter and rummaged through the diaper bag, pulling out a plastic lined pad, a package of baby wipes, and a diaper.

I had no idea when Stephanie had last changed Rosalie, but I knew we hadn't dared to see what was underneath her pink onesie.

Rosalie drained the bottle, and Vance tried to burp her by leaning her against his shoulder and patting her back.

Nothing happened. Hmm. We could figure out burping later.

First, we had to get her changed. Together, we lay her on the changing pad and confronted the dreaded diaper.

I don't want to talk about it. Let's just say that Rosie was capable of creating a mess that smelled like it had died a week ago. Yuck.

It's safe to say we used way too many baby wipes and complained excessively. I found a diaper disposal bag, sealed away the toxic waste bomb, and threw it out on our way into the store.

By that time, Rosie was fussing again, and we had no clue what to do about it. She'd been fed, she'd been changed, and she wasn't tired. I was out of options, and so was Vance.

We pushed the cart down the aisles of the store, trying to ignore Rosie screaming inside her carrier. We had no idea exactly what we needed. Vance's answer to that problem was to buy everything.

I mean *everything*.

A nursing pillow—to hold her on while we bottle-fed her—and bottles, nipples, formula, diaper cream, diapers, wipes, a baby bathtub, baby bath gel, and lotion. We pretty much cleaned out the first-aid aisle, Rosalie wailing all the while.

That was only the first third of the store.

By the time we hit the back of the store, I'd gone in search of a second cart. I returned to find Vance standing in front of the baby carriers.

Was he going to *wear* the baby?

He answered that question pretty quickly, opening a box with an olive-green baby carrier. Of course, he chose the most expensive one there, though I have to admit it looked pretty comfortable, though a little more hippie than Vance's usual style.

I checked the directions while he unpacked it. Between the two of us, we got it strapped around his waist and over one shoulder. Carefully, I unsnapped Rosalie from the car seat and picked her up.

She immediately stopped crying, blinking up at me with blue eyes identical to her father's.

"Oh," I said. "Hi."

She smiled at me. I've heard people say babies can't smile, but they were wrong because Rosie smiled at me. "She just wanted someone to pick her up," I said.

"Hand over my kid," Vance said, and I turned to tuck her against his chest, pulling the other shoulder strap of the carrier into place and securing it behind Vance's back. Rosalie squirmed against his chest, gave him a long, measuring look, then settled her head against his T-shirt and promptly fell asleep.

"I feel like we just brokered world peace," Vance whispered. "Did we get to the book section yet? We need books about babies."

"We're getting there," I said. "But at least we figured out the formula, the diapers, and one way to make her stop crying."

Vance cradled her bottom in his strong hand, holding her secure even though the carrier was more than enough to keep her safe.

I have to admit, I was surprised at how well he was taking all of this.

Vance was a good man. I knew that already, despite some of his earlier behavior. Still, I would've expected a bit more resistance to having a baby suddenly disrupt his life.

Maybe, once the shock had worn off, he'd be resentful.

Watching him walk through each aisle of the baby store, his daughter nestled against his chest, I doubted it.

He couldn't stop touching her. Stroking a finger down her soft cheek, pink and flushed with sleep and the warmth of his body. Tucking her wisps of black hair, so like her mother's, behind her shell of an ear.

He evaluated each purchase seriously. It took us thirty minutes to choose a baby monitor before he ended up just grabbing the top-of-the-line video option, muttering under his breath, "This is just for now. I'll get Evers to wire everything up. One monitor isn't enough."

I shook my head. I was going to have to keep an eye on him. At the rate we were going, Vance was going to buy the whole city for his daughter, and she couldn't even sit up by herself. I didn't think.

By the time we read all the books we'd thrown in the cart, I was sure I'd know exactly what stage of development she was supposed to be in.

I didn't miss the glances Vance got from the other women in the store. I couldn't help the stab of jealousy. It was ridiculous. He was my boss, not my boyfriend. But I knew what he looked like; tall, broad-shouldered, his Viking's face, the roguish blond ponytail, the muscles and tattoos, tenderly cradling an infant.

I would've bet every pair of panties in the store was wet at the sight.

By the time we were done, we had two associates trailing us and six shopping carts. There was no way we could fit all of that in the Range Rover, but for an absurd additional fee, the store was willing to deliver on the spot. It took almost two hours to drop half of our loot off at the loft and then the other half at my house.

A part of me was deeply uneasy at playing house with

Vance and the baby in my own home. Logistically, it made sense.

If I was going to help Vance with Rosalie twenty-four seven, the loft would not work. We needed privacy. I needed privacy, and the loft was too open. Not only was my house huge, but I had the perfect setup to handle both Vance and Rosalie.

My bedroom, the bedroom I'd claimed as an eight-year-old on summer vacation from my English boarding school, was tucked in the back of the house, over the kitchen. I'd stayed there after my grandmother died, unable to face changing bedrooms, despite Brayden's complaints that we were wasting a perfectly good master suite.

A few months before, I'd finally cleaned out my grand-mother's bedroom, donating what I didn't want to keep and packing away what I did. It had been painful, and I'd resented every second of it.

I was still angry that she'd died on me. Sometimes, I think grief is the least rational emotion. Now, with Vance and Rosie moving in, I was grateful the task was behind me.

The master suite consisted of six rooms in total—sepa-rate his and hers bedrooms, a connecting sitting room with a fireplace, a couch, and an enormous bay window that looked out over the gardens, plus a dressing room-slash-closet for each bedroom and an expansive shared bathroom.

The two deliverymen from the baby store set up the crib in the sitting room while I moved my things from my bedroom to my grandmother's.

It was easier than I expected. When I'd cleaned out her room, I'd redecorated. Not enough to erase her presence—her favorite quilt was still on the bed, family pictures on the dresser—but I'd switched out one of the armchairs and some of the paintings.

Just enough so that I didn't expect my grandmother to come walking back in.

I finished up and entered the sitting room to see the crib fully assembled, the mattress covered with a pink sheet, and a mobile with dancing teddy bears spinning cheerfully overhead.

Vance and Rosalie were nowhere to be seen. I found them in the bedroom that had been my grandfather's, Vance stretched out on the king-size bed, Rosie tucked in beside him, her head resting on his chest as he read to her from *What to Expect the First Year*.

At the sight of me, she squirmed restlessly, her rosebud of a mouth working, lips pursing and falling open.

She was hungry. I thought that was it. It had been a while since we'd fed her, and her little mouth was making the exact motions as when she had her bottle earlier.

"I think she's hungry," I said. "I'm going to go try to figure out the bottle thing. I'll be back."

Chapter Ten

Magnolia

I felt like an explorer venturing into the jungle, hoping to return with berries and nuts. Just because we'd bought everything in the store related to feeding a baby, didn't mean I had any idea what to do with it. I had a vague notion that you mixed the formula with something—water?—and put it in the bottle.

I read the side of the formula canister. Then I read it again. It only took a few minutes to boil water in the electric kettle and wait for it to cool enough for Rosie. I mixed in the right amount of powdered mix, wrinkling my nose at the smell. It didn't smell awful, but it wasn't appetizing either. As long as Rosie was willing to eat it, that was all that mattered.

Vance met me in the kitchen just as I was headed upstairs, a squalling Rosie in his arms.

"Here, take her for second?" he asked, passing Rosie to me.

I didn't get a chance to protest. Vance dropped her into my arms and was gone. Rosie screeched louder when I squeezed her too tightly, but she was squirming like mad. I was juggling the bottle, plus the baby, and I didn't want to drop anything. I got us into the small sitting room off the kitchen, sat in the armchair, and tried to arrange her on my lap. When Vance had done it, it looked so easy and natural. With Rosie wiggling and the bottle falling over, I was mostly frustrated and a little freaked out.

I grabbed the couch pillow to prop her up and popped the bottle nipple in her mouth, watching in delight as she went to town. I felt an absurd sense of triumph. I'd figured out she was hungry, made her food, and now she was eating.

Yay me.

I only had to do this about a thousand more times. Surely, it got easier. This was only the first day.

I'd always wanted kids, wanted a family, but I'd never been one of those people who was instinctively good with children.

Vance was. Not that his life intersected with small humans very often, but I'd seen him with kids before, and he was always easygoing and comfortable, which in turn set them at ease.

I, on the other hand, got nervous I wasn't doing the right thing and then felt awkward and out of sorts. I'd agreed to help Vance with Rosie, at least for the foreseeable future, so I was going to have to get over it.

I wanted to. Looking down at Rosie's face, a barely formed combination of her parents, with Amy's black hair and pale skin and Vance's vivid blue eyes, I was already half in love with her. She'd lost her mother. As troubled as Amy had been, she'd also been sweet, and funny, and kind.

I don't know if she would've been a good mother. It's hard to say since she was also an addict. If she'd kept doing drugs, she would've made little Rosie's life difficult, to say the least.

I thought that if Amy had been clean, she could've been a great mom. I hated the idea that Rosie was so tiny and had already lost so much.

She had me, for as long as she and Vance needed me.

As soon as Rosie finished the bottle, I propped her up on my shoulder and promptly learned what burp cloths were for when she vomited half the formula into my shirt. And on the chair. And in my hair.

Vance and I switched places. He popped her into a swinging chair while he tried to clean up the chair and I headed upstairs for a shower. I returned to find Vance in the middle of cooking dinner, Rosie crying in her swinging chair.

"What's wrong?" I asked.

Vance stirred the sizzling vegetables on the stove and said, shaking his head, "I have no idea. Seriously. I tried to give her another bottle. She's not hungry. I tried picking her up. I tried putting her in the floor gym. I checked her diaper. I am fucking clueless."

So was I. Vance had already exhausted all the options I could think of. Leaving her in the swing didn't seem to be working, and the sound of her scream was drilling through my brain. The sight of the tears on her pink cheeks hurt my heart. I picked her up and bounced her on my hip.

Her crying stopped, and I felt like I'd won the lottery. For about a second.

The moment the bouncing stopped, the wailing started up again. Dammit. I switched her to the other hip and bounced her again.

She stopped crying. For another second.

Five minutes of bouncing her from one hip to the other, and my arms were aching. She wasn't that heavy, but the position was awkward and it only stopped her crying for moments at a time.

Vance stayed in the kitchen, working on dinner and eyeing us warily, probably afraid I was going to ask for his help.

Finally, I looked down at Rosie's face and saw her mouth working again. Maybe this time, she was hungry. "Vance, can you make a bottle, or take Rosalie so I can do it?"

"Yeah, one sec." He was sliding dinner onto our plates when the phone rang.

"Don't answer that," I called out. I didn't care who it was. They could wait until we plugged Rosalie's mouth with a bottle.

She was adorable, and I was half in love with her, but the sound of her scream was a bloody nightmare, and she showed no signs of stopping. The bottle was my only hope.

The phone stopped ringing, then started again.

"Don't answer it," I warned.

"I'm not. I'm making her bottle," Vance said, staring at the kettle, willing it to boil.

We should have bought the ready-made formula. Or prepped bottles ahead of time. Anything so we weren't standing around with a starving, screaming baby and no food.

The phone started to ring again. Vance checked the screen and picked it up. I tried to shoot a death glare at him, but I must have missed. Maybe Rosie's screaming was causing interference. God knows, she was loud enough.

"This had better be an emergency," Vance growled into the phone, holding it between his ear and his shoulder as he tried to mix formula. Whoever was on the line said something. Vance answered, "I'm at home, and I can't talk right now, okay?"

Damn right, he couldn't. Rosie screamed louder, wiggling in my arms and pulling on the ends of my hair. I needed that bottle. Now. "Vance," I said, trying to get his attention without yelling in Rosalie's ear. He ignored me and spoke into the phone.

"It's a long story. I have to go. I'll call you tomorrow."

Rosie dripped a string of drool and snot on my arm, her sobbing face red and distraught. I'd had enough. I didn't care who was on the phone. I needed that bottle. Now. Covering Rosie's little ears, I yelled, "Vance Winters, you put down that phone and get that bottle over here right now, or so help me, I will *end* you. Do you hear me?"

Vance said something else into the phone and dropped it onto the counter. "I've got it. Here." He shoved the bottle at me, and I snatched it, juggling Rosie in my arms with the nursing pillow. She didn't wait for me to get her arranged but tried to get the nipple in her mouth as soon as she saw the bottle. Our girl was starving.

I got her settled, and my heart rate slowed as she snuggled into my arms and went to work on her bottle. She was a little demon when she was hungry, but once her tummy was happy, she was too cute. I cleaned her tear-streaked face while she ate and managed to burp her without getting puked on.

Victory.

Vance had purchased a bassinet we could roll around the house. Rosalie fell asleep after her bottle and stayed that way as I put her into the bassinet and sat down to my cold dinner.

We ate with single-minded attention. We hadn't been that hungry at breakfast, both of us too nervous about the test results, and then we had been way too busy with shopping and moving and Rosalie to think about lunch.

We'd fed the baby but forgotten to feed ourselves. Vance was a good cook, but I would've eaten anything to quiet the gnawing in my stomach.

Sitting back, I looked at Vance and said, "I'm exhausted."

"Yeah. So am I."

"If she eats every few hours—"

"We're going to be up all night," Vance finished for me.

"How do people do this?" I asked.

"We're going to find out," Vance said. He sat back in his chair and studied me, his blue eyes serious and warm. "I owe you for this. Big time. Bigger than anything."

I shook my head. Vance didn't owe me anything.

"No, I do," he said. "I couldn't do this without you, Magnolia. If I were on my own, I'd be scared shitless right now."

"You're not? Because I am," I said, only half-kidding.

"I am," he admitted. "Of course I am. But we can do this. I know we can do this. If you stick with me, I know we can handle everything, anything. I just want you to know what it means to me to have you with me."

I shifted in my seat, suddenly uncomfortable. Avoiding Vance's eyes, I got up and started to clear the table.

"I mean it, Magnolia."

"I'm not going anywhere, Vance," I said.

I didn't know exactly what he was getting at. He sounded like a friend thanking another friend, but it also sounded like he was trying to say something more. I didn't know if that was the truth or just wishful thinking on my part.

We were friends. He was also my boss, but that wasn't the conflict of interest as it might have been in a different situation. I liked working for Vance.

I liked being in on the deals and helping organize the

business aspects of his art career, but I could take care of myself if I decided I needed to pursue a new direction, professionally speaking. No, the boss-employee aspect of our relationship wasn't complicated.

But friendship . . . friendship was all complication. You weren't supposed to lust after your friends. It was easier when I had Brayden as a shield, asshole and awful fiancée though he was. Now that I was single, there was nothing between us, nothing keeping us apart.

Back when he was drinking and sleeping with half the women in town, I could tell myself I didn't want to be one more notch on his bedpost. But the last woman I knew for a fact he'd slept with had been Amy, probably the night Rosalie was conceived. I doubt he'd been completely celibate since then, but he had definitely been far more circumspect in his sex life.

Now I had no reason at all to tell myself I didn't want him. Only the looming specter of heartbreak far worse than anything Brayden had dealt me. If I let myself get involved with Vance, I'd be setting myself up for a huge fall.

I'm not going to read anything into this, I told myself. *I'm helping a friend, that's all.*

I kept telling myself that for the rest of the night. The very long night. Brief periods of sleep interrupted by Rosie's crying and a seemingly endless stream of bottles.

Next on my shopping list? A mini fridge for the sitting room and a bottle warmer. No more mixing formula in the middle of the night.

As I fell asleep, again, the faded light of dawn creeping through my curtains, I wondered how long it was going to take to get used to dealing with an infant.

I had a feeling that by the time I got my bearings, things would change and I'd have to start all over again.

Chapter Eleven

Magnolia

I was going to kill Vance. I was pretty sure the judge would rule it as justifiable homicide. He left me alone with Rosalie, the coward. Okay, we both had work to do, and Vance's timeline *was* more urgent than my own. The centerpiece of his upcoming show, an enormous sculpture twice as tall as he was, was still not finished.

It looked finished to me. It looked finished to Sloane, his agent and the owner of the gallery hosting the show, but Vance insisted it wasn't done. Sloane had ordered him to have it completed by the end of the day.

Not that Vance paid any mind to Sloane's orders. We were used to that. She tried to boss him around. Vance ignored her. She ordered me to get results. Vance ignored me. Sloane yelled at me.

Then the whole cycle repeated all over again. She'd already called me three times.

I was ignoring her.

I wasn't answering the phone. Not yet. Sloane wanted to talk about the layout for the brochures for Vance's show, and they weren't finished. At this rate, they were never going to be finished. On a normal day, I had a pretty full schedule. It was flexible, but I still had to get the work done.

I did not have an open slot on my to-do list for a four-month-old. Apparently, infants were a full-time job unto themselves. With Vance downstairs, armed with a blow torch, I was on my own, just me and Rosalie.

For a while, I thought I had it made. Rosie was happily lying on her back in the floor gym we'd picked out for her, batting at the toys, bells, and rattles overhead, making cute baby sounds, and even falling asleep for a blissfully quiet half hour.

Sitting at my desk, a mug of steaming coffee at my side, the sleeping Rosie on the floor, I thought I could do this. I could take care of Rosie and get my work done.

Then she woke up. A diaper change, a bottle—mostly spit up on me—and endless tracks around the loft with me bouncing her and singing to her and begging her.

I was ready to scream.

Or cry.

We'd gotten another one of those musical swing chairs for the loft and had even put it together, but Rosalie was not a fan. To be honest, neither was I. It came with eleven different songs, and every one was annoying.

What she liked best was being held tightly against my chest while I spun in a circle and sang to her. I was glad I'd found something that stopped her crying, but much like bouncing her on my hip, I couldn't spin in circles all day.

I tried tucking her into my arms like a football, as Vance did, and offering the bottle again.

No luck. Rosie didn't like this position with me, maybe because my arms were a third the size of Vance's. Maybe she just preferred her daddy.

I could sympathize. I tended to prefer her daddy too. Even when I wanted to kill him.

I thought about storming downstairs and demanding he put away the blowtorch and take Rosie, but I didn't. For one, he needed to finish the sculpture. And two, I could handle a four-month-old.

Well, I wasn't doing such a great job with it so far, but I was determined. Rosalie had two people in the world she could depend on, Vance and me.

It was ironic that the party boy who never gave a thought to commitment or family was a natural with the baby, while I'd dreamed of having a family for years and I was completely at sea when faced with tiny Rosalie.

I put Rosie back in the floor gym for a minute, ignoring her brain melting screeches, and rummaged through the empty boxes and bags littering the loft for the nursing pillow I was sure we'd purchased. While I wasn't nursing Rosie, the pillow helped me to prop her up in my lap at exactly the right angle to give her a bottle.

I never would've made it through the night before if I hadn't had it, but I'd left that pillow at home, sure I could find the one we'd bought for Vance's loft. I finally located it, shoved underneath the rolling bassinet in the kitchen, and I got Rosie in position to eat.

It took some singing and rocking to calm her down enough to get interested in the bottle, but once she started on the bottle, she ate happily enough and fell asleep.

Sleep. There was nothing as lovely as a sleeping baby. I had piles of work on my desk and brochures to lay out, but I sat in the armchair holding Rosie, watching her sleep. She was so tiny and so beautiful, especially when she wasn't shattering my eardrums or throwing up in my hair.

My heart squeezed. She wasn't mine. I would have to

learn to live with that. She was Vance's, and someday, there would be another woman who would be Rosie's mom.

Not me. I was Vance's friend. I worked for him, but that was it.

I would be Aunt Magnolia. That was okay. *It was.* It would have to be. Hoping for anything more would be foolish. I'd been left enough in my life.

Now that Brayden was out of the picture, I was done with risking my heart. This life I had was good enough as it was. Maybe I didn't need a family. What if I had married Brayden and we'd had children, and *then* I found out he'd been cheating on me? How much worse would that have been?

As it was, he'd hurt my pride more than my heart. My whole life, I'd wanted a family to make up for the one that had dumped me in boarding school and left, but maybe I was wrong. Maybe this—being Aunt Magnolia—was good enough. I couldn't lose her because she wasn't mine, and neither was Vance.

At that depressing thought, I stood, carefully, hoping I could tuck Rosie into her bassinet and get a little more work done before her nap was over. I'd only taken a few steps when the phone rang. I'd long ago silenced the ringer on my own phone. I'd forgotten about the landline to the loft office.

Dammit. As quickly as I could, I put Rosie in the bassinet and snatched up the phone before it could ring again.

"Yes?" I asked, trying to sound professional instead of annoyed.

"Why aren't you answering your phone?"

Sloane.

Of course.

Her shrill voice cut across the phone line, drilling into my head more painfully than the worst of Rosie's screams.

"We're on a deadline, Maggie. Or did you forget the show? I did not hire you to play around over there. I need those brochures, and I needed them yesterday."

"You didn't hire me, Sloane," I said with exaggerated patience.

Sloane liked to take credit for my job with Vance. She might have provided the connection between Vance and myself, but that was it.

I'd learned over the last two years that Sloane took any excuse she could to insert herself into Vance's life. She had a reputation for collecting her artists in more ways than one.

I knew Vance had never slept with her—he'd admitted that her pursuit creeped him out—but Sloane refused to give up.

Vance would have found another gallery, but he liked Rupert and didn't want to explain his reasons if he fired Sloane. Besides, she was rude, annoying, and regularly sexually harassed him, but she was very good at selling art.

Vance didn't have the patience to take over promoting his work, so he stuck with Sloane, ignoring her rudeness and dodging her come-ons.

"Where are the brochures?" she demanded. "They need to go to the printer this afternoon."

"I'm aware of that, Sloane," I said with a sigh. "They're almost done. I'll have them this afternoon, or at the worst, tomorrow morning. You're just going to have to be patient."

"I don't do patient, Maggie. You know that. Get me the brochures, or I'll have to come over there. Put Vance on the phone."

"Vance is in his studio, Sloane."

"He'd better be finishing that piece."

"He is. He said it would be done by tomorrow."

"It was supposed to be done two weeks ago," she grumbled.

She wasn't wrong, but Vance didn't care. Neither did I. Not really. This wasn't our first show, and this wasn't the first time I'd been caught between the two of them—Sloane with her schedule and Vance determined to get the work right.

I paced across the office, trying to figure out what to say to get Sloane off my back, when I stubbed my toe on the chair, sending it rolling across the floor and into the side of my desk. Metal hit wood with a crash, and my heart sank.

A second later, Rosie started to cry.

Crap.

So far, almost no one knew about Rosalie, just Vance's doctor and his attorney. He hadn't decided what he wanted to say, and I did not want to be the one to spill the beans.

Especially not to Sloane, who was as proficient a gossip as she was an art dealer.

"What. Is. That?" she screeched.

Double crap.

"Sloane, I have to go," I said. "I'll get you the brochures ASAP, I promise."

"Is that a baby? Is there a baby over there?"

"Sloane, don't worry about it. I have to go."

"Why is there a baby over there, Maggie? Answer me, or I'll close the gallery and come see what's going on for myself."

Oh, no. No, no, no.

That was not a good idea. I was contemplating snatching up Rosie and running for the hills. Rosie cried louder, and I ignored Sloane's questions for a second to peek into the bassinet.

Triple crap.

She'd spit up in her crib and all over herself, and the stink of a loaded diaper wafted up to greet me. I knew I should've burped her after that bottle, but she'd been so sweetly asleep that I couldn't bear to risk waking her.

Now I really did have to go.

At the moment, I had two responsibilities in my life— my job and Rosie. There was no question which was more important. The job could wait.

Since I was absolutely positive my boss would agree that his daughter was more important than designing brochures, I decided the easiest way to get rid of Sloane was a lie. I was not a good liar, but I had to risk it.

"Sloane, I'm sorry. I have to go. I'm helping a friend out by babysitting. It's her baby, she's crying, and I have to figure out what's wrong."

"You don't have time for babysitting, Maggie. You have a job to do, and if you don't want to get fired, you'd better get your ass back to your desk and—"

I missed the rest of Sloane's threat. She did not have the power to fire me. I hung up the phone and went to Rosie. Ugh. Everything within a foot of her needed to be washed.

It turned out little Rosalie loved taking baths. She was a slippery little bug, and even with the plastic bathtub set in the sink, I was half terrified she was going to slip and hit her head or get too much water in her eyes.

But I managed to get her cleaned up, freshly diapered, and in a new onesie. We won't talk about the mess in the kitchen or the fact that my clothes were soaking wet. I was focused on the clean, dry, happy baby.

I was fastening the last snap when the elevator rumbled and Vance entered the loft.

"What happened to you?" He asked, the words concerned, but laughter danced in his eyes.

I made a face and looked down at myself. I'd started the day reasonably put together. I'd put my hair up, so at least that was still okay, but my navy dress was a disaster, wet down the front, speckled with baby powder and smeared on the shoulder with formula and drool.

I hadn't thought to pack a change of clothes. We had diapers and extra outfits for Rosie. I had spare running clothes at the loft, but that was it. It looked like it was leggings and a tank top for the rest of my workday.

Annoyed that Rosie was clean and happy just in time for me to hand her off, I deposited her in Vance's arms and left the room to change.

When I came back, I said, "Did you get it done? Sloane just called, and she's on the warpath. By the way, she heard Rosie crying and I told her I was babysitting for a friend. I didn't think you were ready to tell everyone about Rosalie."

"Not yet," Vance agreed, rubbing his nose against Rosie's. "I need to think about what we're going to say. But I got the piece done. Can you call Sloane and tell her someone can come pick it up?"

I shook my head. "Not right now. If I don't finish the layout for those brochures, she's going to chew me a new one. Again. I've had enough of being yelled at today, thank you very much. Rosie is the only one who's allowed to scream at me."

Vance's eyes narrowed. "What did Sloane say? I told her to watch the way she talks to you."

"I appreciate the thought, Vance, but she talks that way to everyone except for you. She's just a bitch. I can handle her. But you need to take Rosie for at least two hours so I can get these brochures done, or Sloane is going to come over here, and neither of us wants that."

"No," Vance agreed. "Hold her for just a sec while I change, and then we'll get out of your hair."

I took Rosie, and she settled into my arms, laying her head against my shoulder and drooling on my collarbone. She smelled of lavender and lemons. I almost didn't want to give her back when Vance emerged from his bedroom in a long-sleeved T-shirt and a pair of athletic shorts.

"Where are you going? Are you taking her down to the gym?"

"Up on the roof," he said, rummaging through the bags on the couch and coming up with an adorable pink fleece-lined sweater and matching hat. "It's almost sixty degrees and sunny. We both need some fresh air."

I didn't argue, just helped him get her bundled up. We were probably being overprotective. It wasn't that cold out.

I wondered if I should go up there with them, then I remembered I had work to finish. I liked my job, but I'd rather be outside in the sun with Vance and Rosalie.

Vance tucked Rosalie against his shoulder and scooped up the baby bouncy in his other hand before disappearing into the elevator.

I settled myself back at my desk and dove into my project. The loft was too quiet without Rosie and Vance.

It was hard to believe that an hour before, I'd wanted nothing so much as peace and quiet.

Now that I had it, I wanted Vance and Rosie to come back.

CHAPTER TWELVE
VANCE

This whole situation was fucking with my head. Bad.

I can't describe the punch of emotion at coming into the room to find Magnolia and Rosie, seeing the proud look on Magnolia's face and my baby girl clean and happy. It got to me, the way the neat and efficient woman I knew had dropped everything to take care of my daughter.

And Rosie . . . I can't even begin to process what I felt when I walked into a room and saw her.

I was not ready to have a kid. Kids weren't even on my radar. I didn't know anyone who had kids. I figured eventually, I'd have a kid.

Possibly.

I had no idea how to be a dad, but I was going to figure it out. I had to. All Rosie had was me. And Magnolia.

I set Rosie into her bouncy and started my workout on the suspension system I'd installed on the rooftop deck, letting my mind wander.

I knew I wanted Rosalie. I was already head over heels in love with her. But her timing sucked. I'd planned everything carefully, and Rosie had dropped in the middle like a bomb.

I'd been giving Magnolia time to get over Brayden, planning to make my move. Now that was all fucked up. I couldn't make a move on her now. She'd think it was about Rosie.

I'd roped her into helping me with Rosie out of desperation. I won't lie, I was terrified at the thought of Magnolia going home and leaving me alone with a four-month-old baby.

With Magnolia, I knew I could handle it. Between the two of us, we could do anything. On my own? I didn't even want to contemplate that.

No fucking way.

Magnolia was a soft touch. She wouldn't abandon me. But now that I'd talked her into helping me take care of Rosie, it made my plan to seduce her so much more complicated.

As much as I hated the idea, I was going to have to wait.

I was tired of waiting.

Ever since I'd sobered up, I'd wanted to get my hands all over Magnolia. Wanted to claim her as my own.

That was a big fucking lie.

I'd wanted her since the first moment I'd seen her. Back then, it had been more lechery than anything else. You couldn't look at Magnolia and not want to fuck her. Pale blue eyes, thick red hair, soft, creamy skin, and fucking curves that blew my mind.

I told her I was forcing her to take up jogging for her health, and yeah, that was part of it, but seriously—her ass in a pair of leggings? I'd fucking run behind that all day.

I'd fallen for her so gradually that I never saw it happening. At first, it had been about her body, though I'd never dared to make a pass after our first interview.

She wouldn't have stood for that shit, and I wasn't willing to risk running her off. That didn't mean I didn't enjoy looking at her.

Her mind was next. I loved the way her brain worked, the way she would analyze proposals, her thought process in line with mine but different enough that she saw opportunities and obstacles I missed.

It got so I didn't like to make any major decisions without her insights. Aiden was right. She was wasted on me, but every time he mentioned trying to hire her away, I threatened to kill him. I wasn't willing to give her up.

I didn't realize I wanted a relationship with her until I was in rehab. I didn't trust it at the time. I was learning how to live life all over again, and when I thought about safety, about comfort, about what I dreamed in the deepest part of my heart, the answer was always Magnolia Henry.

It wasn't the right time back then. I had a lot to prove— to myself, to my family, and to Magnolia. She'd stuck with me through everything, and I needed to show her that I was worth it.

I also needed her to get rid of her dickhead fiancé. I'd been working on that when he dumped her. What an asshole.

But I'd had a plan. I was going to give Magnolia a few weeks to get over the twat, and then I was going to declare my intentions and sweep her off her feet. I'd even planned our first date—the restaurant, the flowers.

Now all that was out the window. We were stuck with a twenty-four-hour chaperone, and I was going to have to be very careful with Magnolia.

I tried to think my way through the problem as I went

through my familiar workout, and I came up with nothing. All my usual approaches to seducing a woman didn't work with a four-month-old hanging around, and it was way too soon to think about a babysitter.

I was barely competent to take care of my own daughter. I wasn't in any position to pawn her off on someone else.

I thought briefly about hiring a nanny. Half the kids I'd grown up with had been raised by nannies. We'd had one, too. Not when my parents were still alive, but once we moved in with Aunt Olivia and Uncle Hugh, and Olivia had needed an extra hand.

I might need to find someone, eventually. Not yet. I wanted to get to know my daughter, just the two of us, before bringing a stranger into the mix. Magnolia didn't count.

As far as I was concerned, she was Rosie's family too. She just didn't know it yet.

"Magnolia said you were up here." I heard the familiar voice across the roof and looked up.

Shit.

My cousins, Jacob and Holden.

Dammit.

Holden had been trying to call me the day before, but I'd ignored his calls. I shouldn't have been surprised Jacob had tracked me down after I'd hung up on him the night before, but I hadn't figured out what I was going to say about Rosie.

Looked like I was out of time. I untangled myself from the suspension straps and stood to find Jacob beside Rosie's bouncy, observing her smiling face with a serious expression.

"Is this what I think it is?" he asked.

"Depends what you think it is," I said, stalling for time.

"Is she yours?" Holden asked. "Don't tell me you're babysitting."

"Not exactly," I said. "And yes, she's mine."

Jacob's silver eyes fixed on me, cold and hard. "Are you sure? You don't want to get taken for a ride—"

"I'm sure," I said, cutting him off. "We rushed the blood test yesterday. This is Rosalie. Rosie. She's my daughter."

"No shit? She's pretty cute, man." Holden crouched down beside the bouncy and offered Rosie his finger in hello. She grabbed it and yanked, pulling it into her mouth to chew. "So, where did she come from?"

"Is her mother coming back?" Jacob asked. I shook my head.

"Her mother's dead," I said, gritting my teeth against the stab in my heart.

Amy was dead. I'd hoped, almost believed, that she was going to make it. Looking at Rosie and knowing Amy was going to miss everything in her daughter's life, and that her daughter would never know her, made it so much worse.

"Shit, I'm sorry," Holden said, looking up at me. "That sucks."

"Yeah, long story," I said.

I didn't want to get into it. I wasn't ready to talk about my history with Amy. Rosie was enough to explain.

"So what are you two doing here?" I asked. "Just being nosy?"

Jacob shrugged and grinned. "Basically. What's Magnolia's role in all this?"

Trust Jacob to ask the tough questions. He never let anything slide by.

"She agreed to help me with Rosie. I have no fucking clue what I'm doing. Neither does Magnolia, but she's a good sport."

"This makes things complicated," Jacob commented.

I knew what he was getting at. He and Aiden had been on my ass forever about Magnolia.

"I've got this, Jacob," I said, lying.

I didn't have it. I had no idea what I was going to do now that Rosie had thrown a wrench into my plans, but the last thing I wanted was Jacob's help.

Then again, he'd managed to get himself a smart, beautiful woman who adored him. Maybe I shouldn't be so quick to reject his input. I thought about it for a second, then threw that idea away.

I didn't need Jacob's help.

I'd figure things out with Magnolia in my own time, in my own way.

CHAPTER THIRTEEN
MAGNOLIA

J acob and Holden stayed for dinner at the loft. Rosie was asleep, and we couldn't bear to risk waking her up by strapping her into the carrier and driving her home. She'd be awake soon enough.

Holden ran out for pizza, and we had a relaxing meal except for the weighted glances Jacob kept throwing at Vance. Vance was ignoring him, and I couldn't tell what was going on.

Whatever.

I had more on my mind than the Winters boys.

I'd managed to get the brochure layout done and emailed off to Sloane, so at least she was off my back. I'd face the rest of my workload tomorrow. Once Vance's show was behind us, we could all relax.

Rosie woke up just as we were putting her in the car, starving and with a newly wet diaper. We'd already locked up Vance's building and loaded Scout into the back of the Range Rover. Poor Rosie had to suffer for fifteen minutes until we could get back to the house.

Vance offered to handle the diaper and the bottle while

I took Scout for a quick walk in the backyard. He'd been inside all day, mostly ignored, as Rosie demanded all of our attention.

I almost missed it, my hand going automatically to the knob on the kitchen door, my eyes on Scout beside me. The door was slightly ajar, the deadbolt mostly disengaged.

The house was old, and some of the doors and windows were tricky. This door had to be pushed all the way shut, then pulled out a fraction of an inch for the deadbolt to fully engage.

I always locked it correctly out of habit, but if Vance had let Scout in that morning, maybe he hadn't. I couldn't remember which of us had handled Scout after breakfast. The day felt as if it had been a million years long, that morning a lifetime ago.

"Vance, did you let Scout in this morning?" I asked, turning the door knob in my hand. It moved easily. Not only was the deadbolt open, but the lock on the handle wasn't engaged.

"I think so," he said from the other room. "Why?"

"The door isn't closed all the way." I shrugged and swung it open.

It wasn't a big deal. This wasn't a high crime area, and it didn't look like anything had been disturbed in the house, but I didn't want bugs getting in.

Every time I forgot and left the back door open while I was outside, I ended up finding a spider in my living room. Yuck.

Vance came back in the room, carrying a mostly naked Rosie. "The door was open?" he asked.

"It's not a big deal," I said. "It's an old house, and sometimes, the latch doesn't close properly. We just have to remember to shut it all the way after we let Scout back in."

"Are you sure we didn't? I don't remember leaving the door open."

"This morning was nuts, Vance. I'm surprised we all managed to put on our shoes. It's not a big deal. Just try to remember."

He was still staring at the door when I slipped outside with Scout, an old tennis ball in my hand. My dog was pretty lazy, aside from jogging with Vance, but he chased the ball for a few minutes before he got bored and nudged the back door, looking for his dinner.

If only babies were as easy as dogs.

I remembered the last time Scout had gotten into the trash can and thrown up all over the kitchen floor. Nope, still easier than a baby.

I was glad we'd already had dinner because I was too tired to cook. I was not too tired for ice cream.

Grabbing a pint of cookies and cream from the freezer, along with a spoon, I went in search of Vance and Rosie. I found them in the family room, Vance half reclined on the couch, Rosie tucked into his arm and happily feasting on her bottle. I sat on the other side of the couch and opened the ice cream.

"Hey," Vance said, raising an eyebrow at me and eyeing my spoon loaded with ice cream.

"You want my ice cream?" I asked. He nodded, giving me his sweetest look. With anything else, it might have worked, but this was really good ice cream and it had been a very long day.

I was also completely useless at saying *no* to Vance Winters.

I scooched closer on the couch and dipped the spoon into the ice cream, lifting it to his mouth. I hadn't been thinking, or I would've been ready.

His tongue flicked out, scooping the ice cream off the spoon, his eyes on mine, hot and blue. I shivered.

I took the spoon back and dipped it into the pint. Sliding it across my own tongue, knowing the cold metal had just been in Vance's mouth, was unbearably intimate.

Did he know I was thinking about that kiss? I pretended like I didn't remember. It was easier that way. I'd been drinking and too much of a coward to deal with the aftermath of kissing Vance.

It had been a bit more than just a kiss to me. A lot more than just a kiss, but I refused to go there.

We're sharing ice cream, I told myself. *It's not intimate. It's just dessert.* Then why didn't I get him his own spoon? Because he couldn't feed himself while he was feeding Rosalie.

That was my excuse for scooping out another bite of cookies and cream and raising it to Vance's mouth.

A blush rose to my cheeks as I watched his lips close around the metal and his tongue flick across the bowl, making sure he got every drop of ice cream before releasing the spoon.

I wanted to pretend he didn't affect me, but the redness in my cheeks made me a liar.

I should have put the ice cream away, but I didn't. We ate almost half the pint like that, Vance silent, his eyes on me, my cheeks pink with embarrassment.

Not embarrassment. I had to be honest with myself if I wasn't going to be honest with Vance. I wasn't embarrassed. I was turned on.

Rosie finished her bottle, and Vance turned his attention to the tricky task of burping her without getting thrown up on. He was better at it than I was. I escaped, returning the ice cream to the kitchen.

"Would you put the game on?" Vance called out on his way upstairs. "She's half-asleep. I'm just going to lay her down."

I did, flipping through the channels until I found the basketball game I thought he was talking about. Sports weren't my thing. I thought about going up to my room, pretending I was too tired to stay up any longer. It wasn't a lie.

I was exhausted, but it was still early. Too early to go to bed.

I was going to have to learn to deal with Vance. He hadn't been flirting with me. He'd been eating ice cream. I was the one who was reading too much into it. We were just going to watch a game, and that was it.

I made the mistake of sitting down in the middle of the couch. I wasn't used to sharing it, and that was where I normally sat, with my feet up on the coffee table. Vance came back and sat down beside me, wrapping his arm around my shoulder and pulling me into his chest.

Alarm bells went off in my head.

If sharing a spoon with him felt too intimate, this was way off the charts. But his arm was warm and solid around me, his heart thumped under my ear, and his fingers trailed through loose strands of my hair, the gentle tugging lulling me into submission.

I stayed where I was, curled into Vance, my eyelids drooping. Above me, he said in a low, laughing voice, "I put all the girls to sleep."

"Rosie's out?" I murmured.

"Like a light. She'll be up again as soon as she's hungry, but for now, she's asleep."

"Thank God," I said, letting my eyes drift shut.

I didn't care about watching basketball. I just wanted to

stay exactly where I was. I drifted off, lulled by the sound of Vance's strong heartbeat and the distant noise of the game on the TV.

I don't know how long I was asleep. My eyes opened when Vance leaned forward with the remote and shut off the TV.

"The game over?" I asked, not really caring.

"Mmmhmm," Vance said, stroking my hair off my face.

"K," I said, intending to get up. I was slowly waking up, but I was too comfortable to do anything about it. I'd move in a minute. Stalling, I asked, "What time is it?"

"It's late. Past your bedtime." Vance was half-joking. He knew I wasn't a night owl.

"Rosie still asleep?" I asked. His body was warm and solid against mine, his arm still holding me close. He smelled so good, clean and male. I wished I could curl up right there and go back to sleep.

Vance didn't answer.

"What time *is* it?" I asked again.

"Late," he said, tossing the remote on the couch beside him. He turned, shifting me from his chest to lay back into the cushions.

His body rose over mine, his face so close all I could see clearly were his eyes, dark and intent.

"I know it's too soon," he whispered, "but I can't wait anymore. I've been waiting for you forever."

I didn't know what he was talking about. I didn't have time to figure it out. It was exactly like the first time he'd kissed me.

My brain shut off and my body roared to life. My hands came up, pulling his face into mine, my fingers burying themselves in his hair, pulling it loose so it fell around us, smelling of the woods and Vance. His tongue stroked the seam of my lips, and I opened my mouth, all caution gone.

Kissing Vance was a terrible idea. I knew that. I'd already decided that.

I didn't care. I wanted this. I wanted the weight of his body pressing me into the cushions and his arm wrapped around my back, lifting me up, tilting my hips so my legs fell apart to make room for him.

I wanted the thick bar of his erection against the heat between my legs. His mouth moving on mine. His tongue tangling with my own.

I let out a whimper. Fingers slid under my shirt, under my bra—a bra he'd somehow unfastened while I'd been wrapped up in his kiss.

Before I knew it, both shirt and bra were pushed up to my shoulders, my breasts bared. Vance pulled his mouth from mine and sat back, his eyes gleaming as he studied me.

He started to say something, then he gave a quick shake of his head and slid backward down the couch so his mouth was lined up with my nipples.

His hands were strong, his long fingers cupping and molding my breasts as his lips and tongue tasted and teased, switching from one side to the other until I was mindless, writhing beneath him, my legs wrapped around him, my eyes staring blindly at the ceiling as I whispered his name.

"Vance."

I should stop him. Stop myself. We weren't supposed to be half naked on my couch, kissing.

Why weren't we supposed to be kissing?

My brain was at war, one side telling me to get up, to leave, that we were crossing a line. I wasn't drunk. I couldn't lie about this in the morning.

The other side of me wondered how fast I could strip

off the rest of my clothes and his, desperate to know what it would feel like to have that long, thick cock inside me. I hadn't had anything inside me in months.

I didn't care about the complications. I just wanted Vance.

He rose up from between my legs, dipped his fingers beneath the waistband of my leggings, and stripped them off. The less rational side of my brain gave a resounding cheer.

Yes! Naked with Vance. I'd been waiting forever to be naked with Vance.

The thinking part of me was drowning. I wanted this. Every part of my body was hot and needy and ready. I'd wanted this man since the second I saw him, and if he was tired of waiting, so was I. His fingers skated up my inner thigh, stopping just at the crease of my hip.

So close, yet not nearly close enough.

His mouth took mine again, distracting me, stopping me from begging.

I wanted.

His fingertip found my clit and swirled in a firm circle.

Holy fucking God.

Sensation splintered through my body, the pleasure almost too intense to bear. My neck arched, and I tore my mouth from his to gasp, my heart pounding in my chest, breath tight in my lungs.

His finger pressed inside, and he whispered, "Fuck, baby, fuck. You feel so good."

I groaned. I'd lost the power of speech. If I could've said anything, I would have agreed with him. Not about me.

But God damn, his fingers were perfect.

Heaven. I couldn't begin to imagine what his cock would feel like. A second finger joined the first and pumped in and out, in and out, the heel of his palm pressing on my clit.

I rocked against him, my hips thrusting up to take more, my breath hitching in my lungs.

"Fuck, Magnolia, I have to go get a condom. Don't fucking move. I'll be right back. Don't fucking move."

He was gone in a blink, leaving me alone, my flushed skin suddenly cold without his body against mine.

Without Vance, I was acutely aware of how wet I was between my legs. And how naked. I sat up, my leggings and underwear tangled around one foot.

What was I thinking?

Was I about to have sex with Vance?

No. No, no, no.

Hadn't I already decided this was a bad idea? A terrible idea. Didn't I have a million reasons I couldn't sleep with Vance?

One kiss and I'd lost my mind.

No more kissing.

His feet thumped on the stairs. I jerked up to stand, panicked.

We couldn't do this. It was going to change everything, and I was going to end up with my heart completely shattered.

I yanked my tank top back down and leaned over, struggling to get my bare foot back in my leggings before Vance returned to the living room. He came through the door just in time to see me hopping on one foot, wiggling the stretchy fabric over my hips.

He still had his shorts on, but they did little to hide the length of his erection.

My knees wobbled at the thought of what I was denying myself. Heat and need pulsed between my legs.

Inwardly, I swore, cursing myself for being such a fucking idiot.

"Magnolia," Vance said, condom in hand, his eyes shadowed. "Don't leave. We don't have to do this if you're not ready, but don't leave. Don't run out on me again."

So he knew I was lying when I said I didn't remember our first kiss. Vance was too smart to fall for that bullshit.

Damn it.

I didn't want to have this conversation.

I couldn't look him in the eyes when I said, "We can't do this. I'm so sorry. I should've stopped it sooner. I shouldn't have kissed you, but we can't do this."

Vance's hand dropped to his side. "Why? Why not?"

"Why not?" I asked, my voice tight and a little hysterical. "Why not? For a million reasons."

"Give me one," he said.

"Because I just broke up with my fiancé," I said.

Vance crossed his arms over his chest and set his jaw. "A month ago. You broke up with the dickhead a month ago. Give me a better reason."

"Because it's confusing," I said. "I can't play house with you and Rosie and then start sleeping with you. I can't be casual. I don't want to end up getting hurt, okay?"

"Who says I want this to be casual?" Vance demanded. "How could you think I would want anything with you to be casual?"

"Because I've never seen you do anything else. What do you expect me to think? You never say anything about having feelings for me, other than comments about liking the way my ass looks, and then you just kiss me, and then we're almost having sex. How am I supposed to think it's anything but casual? I'm just convenient. And you know what? I'm tired of being convenient. That's all I've ever been. Convenient. I want more than that."

"So do I, God dammit," Vance shouted.

I stared at him, confused. He sounded sincere, but it just didn't add up. He'd had plenty of time to say something, anything, about wanting a relationship. Even to ask me out on a date.

He'd kissed me a month ago, and he hadn't said a word about wanting more.

Now, he was exhausted, in no frame of mind to go find a hookup, and we ended up naked on my couch?

I didn't want to think Vance was lying, but I couldn't afford to believe he was telling me the truth. I had to look out for myself.

"I'm sorry," I said, looking at the ground as I rushed past him and up the stairs.

CHAPTER FOURTEEN
VANCE

Magnolia was stonewalling me. It had been two weeks since I'd kissed her, and she was resolutely pretending nothing had happened. Exactly like the last time we'd kissed.

Not like I hadn't fucked it up on my own.

I'd known it was too soon. I'd known Rosalie made everything infinitely more complicated and that I had to be careful.

Cautious.

But there was something about Magnolia when she was half-asleep that completely destroyed my resolve.

Awake, she was brisk and efficient and brilliant. I respected the hell out of her. Her brain was as much a turn-on as her body.

Magnolia was tough. She was a survivor. I respected the hell out of that too. All of these facets of her personality added up to a woman who captivated me, but who was also more than a little intimidating.

Yes, intimidating.

I know what you're thinking. I'm Vance Winters. How can any woman intimidate me?

But that's the thing. Magnolia was the first woman, the only woman, who ever really mattered. I'm man enough to admit that scared the shit out of me.

I couldn't afford to fuck things up with her. She'd been hurt enough by her parents and by Brayden. She was still struggling with the loss of her grandmother.

And I wasn't exactly a prize. On paper, maybe. Rich, successful, good-looking, fantastic in bed.

I was also a recovering alcoholic who wasn't even two years sober, now a single father, and I had no fucking clue how to have a relationship or deal with a woman I cared about.

Magnolia wanted stability. She wanted a family. I didn't know if I could offer her that.

The family, sure. Now that Rosalie had shown up, I was pretty much a ready-made family package. But the rest of it?

I had no clue how to be the other half of a couple. I definitely didn't know how to be a father. Every day since Rosalie had shown up was a new adventure. So far, we were doing okay, but that didn't mean I had any idea what I was doing.

Magnolia was stonewalling me, and I was letting her. I'd known it was too soon to kiss her again. I'd known, and I'd done it anyway.

When she was awake, Magnolia had her defenses up, a constant reminder that I had to be careful and patient.

But Magnolia asleep? Her eyes soft and warm, her creamy cheeks flushed pink, those full lips half open, her voice a low murmur . . . I'd lost my head. My feelings for the waking Magnolia were complicated.

Important and real, but complicated. My reaction to sleeping Magnolia was primitive and demanding.

One look at her blue eyes half-lidded and drowsy, and I wanted to scoop her up, throw her over my shoulder, and take her to bed, where I could spend hours showing her all the ways I'd dreamed of touching her, of making her come.

Two weeks since our last kiss, and I was done with waiting. I'd been watching, waiting for her to work up the courage to say something, for her to face what was between us.

I'd finally realized she would run forever if I let her.

I was going to make a move. So far, I was playing it by ear, waiting for my moment. If it didn't come soon, I'd *make* it happen. I was down in my studio, putting the finishing touches on a few pieces while Rosalie slept in my bedroom and Magnolia worked in the office.

I had a monitor in the studio now, so I'd know if Rosie woke up and Magnolia needed a hand. I didn't have a lot left to do for the show. At this point, most of the prep work was on Sloane and Magnolia.

I'd been messing around over the past few days, making toys for Rosie out of scraps in my workshop. I'd never done anything on such a small scale before, and it was challenging trying to imagine what would catch her attention.

I'd had accolades showered on my work ever since Sloane had taken over managing my career, but nothing matched seeing my daughter grab a toy I'd made and shove it in her mouth with glee.

The books said it was too early for her to be teething, but I was starting to wonder because the cool metal of the toys on her little red gums seemed to soothe her when she got fussy.

The front doorbell rang. I rolled my stool over to the

desk, hitting a button on the monitor to pull up the security camera.

Sloane stood at the door in a black suit, her dark hair pulled back from her angular face, her expression in its perpetual arrangement of annoyance and disdain. Since I was closer to the door, I clicked the button for the microphone and said, "Be right there."

By the time I got to the door, Sloane's face had rearranged itself into a smile. She was a lot of things, an excellent manager among them, but she wasn't subtle. I often wondered why Rupert put up with her. It was well known that she slept with most of her artists, but he didn't seem to care.

"Vance," she cooed, leaning in to kiss my cheeks, first one side then the other, an affectation that had always annoyed me. Her perfume was heavy, and the neckline of her blouse beneath the suit jacket was low enough to skirt the edge of good taste. I stepped back to let her in.

"Sloane," I said, stepping out of her reach, "What can I do for you?"

"Nothing, darling. I've got everything I need from you for the show. I'm here to speak with your assistant. Where is she? She's not answering her phone."

We'd been avoiding this confrontation, but I couldn't think of a good way to get rid of Sloane before she saw Rosalie. If the secret was about to get out, I might as well do it all at once, I decided.

Leading Sloane to the freight elevator, I said, "Sloane, I don't know how many times I've told you. Magnolia is not my assistant. She's my business manager. Big difference."

Sloane tossed her head and shrugged as if to say, *whatever, Vance.* She knew better than to speak the words out loud.

We entered the main level of the loft to find it silent and empty. Magnolia must have heard the elevator doors open because she greeted us at the door to her office. Her expression was polite and composed, but I knew my girl.

I could see annoyance and nerves simmering in those clear blue eyes. I winked at her, knowing it would aggravate her enough to chase off the nerves. When she scowled at me, pressing her pink lips together, I couldn't help but grin back.

Deciding to ignore me, she looked at Sloane and said, "Sloane, what are you doing here?"

"I needed to talk to you about the publicity we've set up for the show, and you're not answering your phone."

"Why didn't you just email me?" Magnolia said.

"Because I didn't want to type it all out. I wanted to talk to you. Why aren't you answering your phone?" Sloane's voice was shrill at the best of times. When she was annoyed, it could cut through glass.

I knew why Magnolia wasn't answering her phone. She'd turned it off when Rosalie fell asleep. We'd gotten in the habit of turning off all the phones when Rosalie was napping.

No interruption was worth waking the baby. We'd both read the entire stack of books we'd gotten from the baby store, so we were well aware that the conventional wisdom was to expose the sleeping baby to all sorts of noises so they'd sleep through them.

Clearly, those people had never lived with a four-month-old. I loved Rosie. I'd never imagined it was possible to fall so completely head over heels for a tiny human being who couldn't even talk to me. That said, she was a hell of a lot easier to handle when she was sleeping.

Every time she passed out, we were so fucking grateful

that the idea of letting anything wake her up was unimaginable.

And here was Sloane, working herself up to a hissy fit. No fucking way. Before I could say anything, Magnolia cut in.

In a low voice, she said, "Keep your voice down, Sloane. Come into the office, and we can go over whatever you want to talk about."

"Don't tell me to keep my voice down," Sloane snapped back, enunciating each word so precisely they shot from her mouth like bullets. "You were brought in to keep his business in line. That's the only reason you're here, and if you can't do that job, you're welcome to leave."

I expected Magnolia to lose her temper. She usually kept a handle on her emotions, but we hadn't been getting a lot of sleep and Sloane could be hard to take on a good day.

Instead, she shook her head and looked at me, raising one eyebrow.

"Can she fire me?" Magnolia asked, already knowing the answer. It was not the first time we'd had this conversation.

It looked like Magnolia was prepared to be amused, but I was done with it.

"She can't," I said, "and she damn well knows it."

"Vance." Sloane turned her back on Magnolia in an attempt to cut her out of the conversation. She placed one long-fingered hand on my chest. Her red-tipped fingernails reminded me of claws. Again, I wondered why Rupert put up with her.

"Sloane," I countered, removing her hand from my chest and taking a step back. "If you can't learn to treat Magnolia with respect, we're going to have to reevaluate our working relationship. Do you understand me?"

I kept my voice level and low, but there was no

mistaking my intent. Sloane's eyes widened in disbelief. She stepped back, her eyes shooting between us.

"You're sleeping with her," she screeched, pointing her finger at me and then at Magnolia.

A tiny sneeze sounded from the bedroom, followed by another, then a third. Why was Rosie sneezing? Was she allergic to something? Sick? She'd seemed fine when we put her down. A second later, a high-pitched wail cut through the tension.

Before I could stop her, Magnolia disappeared into the bedroom. She came back with Rosie in her arms. My daughter's wisps of black hair were standing straight up, her blue eyes tear-filled. She'd been asleep for two hours.

Two blissful, productive hours. I put out my arms, and Magnolia handed me Rosie after dropping a kiss on her red nose. Rosie sneezed again.

"She's hungry," Magnolia said, heading straight for the kitchen to mix up a bottle.

"Thanks, Babe," I said, nuzzling Rosie's cheek with my lips and whispering meaningless murmurs of comfort.

Her little hands closed over my ears, her tears dripping on my cheeks. I was still getting used to how tiny she was.

"Excuse me? What the fuck is this?"

"Watch the language around my daughter, Sloane," I admonished, surprised at how much I sounded like Magnolia when she was doing her British headmistress imitation.

Sloane took a step back, her eyes pinging between Rosie, me, and Magnolia in the kitchen. I knew it would be funny later, but just then, all I wanted was for her to leave.

I loved feeding Rosie. I loved the way she cuddled into me. She was still so mysterious, so difficult to predict, and the sense of accomplishment I got from feeding her when she was hungry kept me going all the times when she started crying and wouldn't stop.

An empty stomach was a problem I could solve.

Magnolia was almost done with the bottle. I shifted Rosie in my arms and pinned Sloane with a look.

"As you can see, we're busy. If you need to work with Magnolia on something to do with the show, you can go in her office if you can keep your voice down. If Magnolia tells me you were anything other than professional, we're going to have a difficult conversation. Get me?"

"Are you sleeping with her? Whose baby is that? What the fuck is going on, Vance?"

"Sloane, this is the only time we're going to talk about this. Yes, Magnolia and I are together. However, it's none of your business. This is Rosalie," I said, angling the baby so Sloane could get a good look at her. "She's my daughter. I have full custody of her now, so she's going to be in my life. None of this is your concern. If you can't stick to business when you talk to Magnolia or me, I will fire you and find another agent and another gallery."

"You can't fire me," Sloane said.

"I can do whatever I want," I said. "Let me explain my priorities, so we're clear. Rosalie comes first. Then Magnolia. Then my family. My work, business, all the rest of it, is an afterthought. Do you get that? Don't fuck with my family."

Magnolia came back with the bottle, her steps hesitant, her eyes on Rosalie. Ignoring both Sloane and myself, she put the bottle down on the side table and pulled Rosie from my arms. "Is her nose running because she was crying? Does she feel warm to you?"

Magnolia leaned into my side, offering up Rosie's flushed cheek. I laid my fingers on her pink skin. She felt warm, but she always felt warm when she woke up from a nap.

I wrapped my hand around the back of her neck, remembering that the doctor had said that was a more reliable gauge of her temperature.

Shit. She did feel warm.

"Should we take her to the doctor?" I asked, anxiety spiraling in my gut. She was too tiny to be sick. Logic told me kids got sick. But this was *my* kid. I was supposed to protect her, not let her get sick.

"Let's feed her first. Maybe it's nothing. Maybe it's allergies."

It was early in the year for allergies, but I didn't want to argue. We were both grasping. Magnolia handed me Rosie and turned to face Sloane.

"I can give you half an hour. What do you need to talk about?"

Sloane ignored her to stare at me in wide-eyed astonishment. "Are you serious? You've suddenly got a baby, and now you're fucking Magnolia? What is she now, the nanny?"

I wrapped my arm around Magnolia, pulling her into my side. Under her breath, she hissed, "Vance, what are you doing?"

In answer, I kissed her temple and tightened my arm. Her lush curves felt so perfect pressed into me that I had to wrestle my attention back to Sloane.

"Sloane, I'm not going to say it again. I have more important things to worry about than your temper tantrums. I'm with Magnolia, end of story. It has nothing to do with you, and if you give her a hard time about it, you're fired."

"We have a contract," she said, glaring at Magnolia.

"Read it," I said. "If I don't like how this is working out, I can walk with thirty days' written notice. Think about that before you open your mouth again."

Sloane took a deep breath, started to speak, then pressed her thin lips together, still glaring at Magnolia.

Ignoring her, I dropped my head to murmur in Magnolia's ear. "If you really have to talk to her, leave the office door open, okay?"

"Okay, but what the hell, Vance?"

Her beautiful blue eyes swirled with confusion and frustration. This wasn't the right way to escalate our relationship. But I was realizing there was no right way.

There was never going to be a perfect moment. I could either wait forever or I could take charge.

Magnolia was going to run, and I was going to chase her. That was our reality, and I was finally ready to deal with it.

I couldn't resist grazing her rounded cheekbone with my lips, loving the way her skin flushed under the gentle touch.

"Just telling Sloane how it is," I whispered.

"But, we're not—" she stammered, trying to step back. I held her tightly against my side, not ready to let her go.

"Semantics," I said. "Not right this second, but we will be. No point in pretending otherwise."

I dropped a kiss on the tip of her nose and let her go. Rosie was squirming in my arms, ready for her bottle. Her breathing sounded funny in my ears, as if her nose were congested.

Shit.

I really, really didn't want her to be sick. Not until she could talk to me and tell me what was wrong. She was too little. Too fragile.

I watched Magnolia disappear into the office with Sloane, leaving the door wide open as I'd told her to. I couldn't hear the specifics of their conversation, but I heard the tone.

It was level and polite enough to satisfy me. I hadn't been bluffing with Sloane. She was a bitch, but I'd kept her on all these years because she was good at her job, she sold my work, and in the process, she handled the shit I didn't want to.

I enjoyed business, investing. I loved creating things with metal and fire. I did not like selling art. I hated the parties and the bad wine and the people fawning over me as if sucking up would get them anything.

Sloane handled all of that. Neither Magnolia nor I had any interest in taking over the management of my art career.

Now that Rosie had entered our lives, we didn't have the time, either. I'd put up with Sloane for the sake of convenience, but if she said anything to hurt Magnolia's feelings, she was fired.

Sloane left without a word to me almost exactly a half-hour from the moment she'd entered Magnolia's office. By that time, I'd almost forgotten she was there.

Rosie had finished her bottle, but it had taken some coaxing. Her appetite was off, her cheeks were flushed, and her nose was a snot faucet. My baby girl was sick.

Magnolia must have known, because she left her office and went straight to the bathroom, where we'd stored the kit of baby first aid crap.

She came out with the high-tech infrared thermometer I'd picked out, and after scanning the directions, she turned it on, hit a few buttons, and held it gently yet firmly against Rosie's forehead. Five seconds later, it beeped, and the screen turned red. 101.4

"I'm taking her to the doctor," I said.

"I'll call and let them know we're on the way."

I won't lie. I was relieved Magnolia was coming with me. I could handle Rosie on my own, but I was not feeling all that confident in my fathering skills now that I'd realized I had a sick baby on my hands.

I needed Magnolia. Between the two of us, we could handle anything.

I wasn't sure of much lately, but I was sure about that.

CHAPTER FIFTEEN
VANCE

The doctor didn't laugh at us. Not exactly, but I could tell he wanted to. Rosie had a cold. The doctor listened to her heart, her lungs, checked her temperature, and pronounced her a normal, healthy four-month-old who'd caught a cold.

He gave us instructions about her fever and her breathing and what to do about all the snot before sending us on our way.

I should've been relieved to hear that everything was normal. The doctor was good. The best. I was a Winters. We always had the best. Still, Rosie had gotten worse since she'd woken from her nap.

A nagging worry prodded me. What if he was wrong? What if he'd missed something? What if it wasn't a cold? What if it was pneumonia?

I pushed my anxiety away.

This wasn't me.

I didn't worry.

But I'd never had anyone completely dependent on my judgment before. I hated seeing Rosie so miserable. She looked at me from watery blue eyes identical to my own, and I imagined I saw accusation there.

I was her father. I should be able to fix everything. Why wasn't I fixing this?

Blowing off work for the rest of the day, we went back to Magnolia's after picking up the dog and a few supplies at the loft. We were both too worried about Rosie to focus on business.

"Can you hand me the thermometer?" Magnolia asked. Pacing the small sitting room off the kitchen, she held Rosie against her chest, rubbing her back in gentle circles.

"You just took her temp, Babe. The doctor told us not to worry," I said, giving her the thermometer. It was easy to tell Magnolia not to worry but harder to take my own advice.

I didn't want her to know how freaked out I was. I was supposed to be the strong one.

Wasn't I? I didn't feel strong.

I was helpless and frustrated and grateful Magnolia was there to worry with me.

"What is it?" I asked when the thermometer beeped.

"99.1," she said, relief evident in her voice.

"Good. Better. Let me take her, and I'll change her. Maybe she can get some sleep. She's off her nap schedule."

I took Rosie and headed upstairs. Diapers and feedings no longer scared me. This cold was new, but I felt like I'd changed a thousand diapers and made even more bottles in the past few weeks.

I held Rosie tucked into my arm as I gave her the bottle, relieved to see her eating, even if she didn't seem as into her formula as usual.

From the sitting room in the master suite, I had a full view of the expansive grounds behind the house. Rolling green lawn sprawled between artfully placed trees and free-form flower beds. While the front of the house was formal, the private spaces looked like the setting for a fairy tale, cultivated and beautiful, but with a thread of wild beneath.

Just like Magnolia.

She was out there with Scout, throwing a tennis ball for her dog over and over.

She'd changed clothes when we'd come home. She dressed more formally during the work day, but I'd realized that my girl liked to be casual when she wasn't working. One more thing her dickhead of an ex had given her shit about.

He'd wanted her dressed to the nines around the clock. How could he have been so stupid?

Watching Magnolia playing with Scout, her dark red hair streaming behind her as she ran after the ball, her full ass and round tits sexy as hell in her faded jeans and worn t-shirt, I couldn't understand how he'd let her go.

How could anyone miss how beautiful she was?

All afternoon, I'd been waiting for Magnolia to blast me for telling Sloane we were together. I hadn't said we were fucking, but I hadn't denied it either. I'd gone out of my way to make it clear that Magnolia was mine. I'd expected her to confront me as soon as Sloane left.

If it weren't for Rosie, she probably would have. Now that her temper had cooled, she'd reverted to form.

Typical Magnolia.

Ignore, deny, and pretend there's nothing to talk about. That wasn't going to work this time. I could wear her down. I *would* wear her down. She belonged with me. We both knew it.

I was finished with giving her space. If she didn't want to talk about it, that was fine. I'd said we were together, and I'd meant it. We were already closer than most couples, especially now that we were living together. There was only one thing missing.

Magnolia hadn't had sex in over a month. At least. Probably more. I had a feeling the dickhead hadn't done his part in the bedroom. I hadn't slept with another woman since before they'd broken up.

I was holding out for Magnolia. She was the only woman I wanted.

We'd both feel a hell of a lot better once I got her naked.

Watching her bend over to pick up the tennis ball, her luscious ass in full view, I hoped I'd be able to manage it soon.

I was working on the worst case of blue balls I'd had since I'd learned what my dick was for. I'd been patient long enough. So had Magnolia. She just didn't know it yet.

Rosie fell asleep after her bottle. Her cheeks still felt too warm, but not as hot as earlier. I burped her carefully, trying not to wake her. It drove Magnolia nuts that I could manage to burp Rosie while she was sleeping.

I always told Magnolia it was my skill with women, but the truth was that I had no idea how I did it. Much like the rest of being a dad, I was working on instinct, doing the best I could.

I checked the monitor to make sure it was on and went downstairs to find Magnolia fiddling with the lock on the back door.

"Was it open again?" I asked.

"Yeah. I thought I checked it before we left this morning and it was shut, but when I went to let Scout out, the deadbolt wasn't closed all the way. It's weird."

"Who has the keys?" I asked, suddenly suspicious.

"No one," Magnolia said, shaking her head. "It was only Brayden and me, and I took his keys when he left."

"But you never had the locks changed?" I said.

"I'm sure it's nothing. I just need to call a locksmith and get this fixed. It's been sticky forever."

"I'm calling Evers," I said. "You need better security here. I don't know why I didn't have it upgraded earlier. I assumed your grandmother would have had a better system on the house. You barely have an alarm."

Magnolia put her hands on her hips and faced me, color high in her cheeks. "I don't need you to upgrade my security, Vance. I can take care of myself. Contrary to what you told Sloane, we are not together. You don't get to take charge of my life."

I crossed the room until I was standing right in front of Magnolia, looking down into her angry face. "We are together, Magnolia."

"We aren't!" She raised her hands to push me away. Catching her fingers in mine, I tugged, pulling her to my chest.

"Vance!" Magnolia went to step back, but it was too late. I dropped her hands and wound my arms around her back, bringing her body flush to mine.

"Don't even think about it," I warned.

She opened her mouth to say God only knows what, and I kissed her. She wasn't drunk, and she wasn't half-asleep. If she really didn't want me, I'd know in a few seconds.

It would kill me to do it, but if she really didn't want me, I'd walk away.

Her mouth was soft under mine, her lips full and sweet. I ran my tongue along the inside of her lower lip, and she moaned. Tilting my head, I closed my mouth over hers, tasting her, her breath mingling with mine, swallowing the tiny, needy sounds she made.

Fuck, just a kiss and I was hard as stone.

The way her heart pounded in her chest, I would've bet Magnolia was just as turned on as I was. I wanted to strip her clothes off and fuck her right there in the kitchen, but I wasn't going to.

Twice, I'd rushed her and twice, she'd frozen me out. This time, I was in control. If I let her call the shots, we'd still be dancing around each other on our deathbeds.

I dropped my arms and took a step back, leaving her standing there, wobbling a little, her eyes dazed, her pupils dilated. Her tongue licked her bottom lip, lingered, as if tasting me there. I thought I was going to lose it.

Reminding myself that I had a plan, I shoved my hands in the back pockets of my jeans and said, "We aren't together?"

Magnolia shook her head as if trying to wake up from a daze. "Vance, we can't."

"Why not?" I folded my arms over my chest and stared her down. "Why not? And don't tell me you're on the rebound or that I can't do commitment. Those are copouts. You've known me for years. You know by now whether you have feelings for me. If you really don't, if we're just friends, then fine, I'll let it go."

"I really don't. We're just friends," Magnolia shot back.

"Liar," I said. She looked away. "You're lying," I said again. "Look me in the eyes and tell me you don't have any feelings for me beyond friendship. Make me believe you."

"Fine," she snapped. She crossed her arms over her chest, mimicking my own posture, probably not realizing the position plumped her tits up until my mouth watered. Her eyes skittered around the room, glancing off mine twice before settling somewhere around my shoulder.

"Magnolia, you have to look me in the eyes. My shoulder doesn't count."

"I know." Her eyes traveled up, slowly, meandering over my features until they met my gaze dead on. My gut clenched at the raw emotion swimming there.

She was scared.

Underneath all the lust, so was I.

For me, lust was winning out over the fear of fucking up our friendship.

That was the difference between Magnolia and me. She was a lot better at self-denial.

I waited for her to say something. Anything. She opened her mouth and drew in a breath, then closed it, biting down on her lower lip so hard the soft flesh turned white.

"You can't do it, can you?" I asked softly. "You can't tell me you don't want me."

"I do," she finally admitted. "You know I do. But I don't want to."

"I want to enough for the both of us," I said.

"That's what I'm afraid of. You want to, but what happens when you get bored? This is going to change everything."

"And you don't like change," I said. "Just trust me, and stop thinking so much. This doesn't have to be complicated unless you make it complicated."

The fear in her eyes turned to doubt, and she looked away, still chewing on her lip.

Unable to stand it anymore, I framed her face in my hands and kissed her again, stroking the side of her jaw with my thumb until she opened her mouth to me.

My cock strained against my jeans as she melted into

me, her arms wrapping around my back, one hand sneaking beneath my T-shirt to lie against my skin.

That was what I wanted.

Her skin on mine. All of it.

All of her soft, smooth, creamy skin rubbing against me. I had the hem of her T-shirt in my hands when a cry sounded through the monitor, fretful and muffled.

We jumped apart as if Rosie had toddled in the room and caught us red-handed.

"I've got her," Magnolia said, stepping out of my arms. She high-tailed it out of the living room and up the stairs before I could stop her.

"Coward," I called after her.

She didn't slow down or say a word, just shot me the finger and disappeared upstairs. I'd let her go for now. She wouldn't escape me so easily the next time.

CHAPTER SIXTEEN
MAGNOLIA

Vance was right. I was a coward. A big, giant wimp. I couldn't think straight when he kissed me. That was why I always ran away afterward. The second he touched me, my brain melted out of my ears and all I wanted was more.

One of us had to think straight. I adored Vance. I respected him. And I'm not discounting how hard he'd worked on his sobriety when I say that he was impulsive and used to getting what he wants, when he wants it—a side effect of being raised in a wealthy, powerful family.

When it came to business, Vance analyzed every angle for potential repercussions.

Not so much in his personal life.

Rosie had bought me some time, and as I escaped up the stairs, I planned to use it to think about how to handle Vance. That plan didn't work. Rosie had other ideas. She was squirming restlessly in her crib, her cheeks hot and snot running down her face.

Poor baby girl. It took me a while to get her cleaned up, and then she couldn't settle down. The next twelve hours were a blur of pacing and rocking and pleading for her to get some sleep.

I don't know how single parents do it. A lot of the time, I was fine when it was just Rosie and me. Most of the time, she was a good baby, sweet and easy to please.

Then there were the times when she was fussy and feverish, and she sneezed so hard she managed to get snot and vomit in my hair. At times like that, it was a blessing to hand her to Vance and take a break.

We passed her back and forth all night, sneaking in cat naps in between worrying and walking. Her fever cycled up and down until sometime just before dawn, when it broke, leaving her covered in a light sweat but finally able to sleep.

Together, we gave her a sponge bath and settled her in her crib. Vance sent me to bed first, and I was mostly asleep when I felt the mattress dip beside me and the covers shift.

I cracked an eye just in time to see Vance lay his head on the pillow beside mine.

"Go to sleep," he whispered. "You can yell at me in the morning."

I would. He had his own bed. What was he doing in mine? I was totally going to yell at him in the morning. Or maybe in the afternoon, because it was already morning and I just wanted to sleep.

I was vaguely aware of sounds from the crib, pale sunlight leaking into my bedroom and movement beside me. Then it was quiet again, and I drifted back to sleep.

I dreamed of heat and Vance. I came awake slowly to find myself draped across his body, my cheek pressed to his chest, one leg hooked over his hips, and the insistent jut of his erection against my thigh.

He'd wrapped one arm around my back, his fingers possessively gripping my ass. With his free hand, he stroked my arm, his fingertips light on my skin, barely there, moving from my shoulder to my elbow, to my wrist and back again.

It was an innocent touch. Almost nothing. I was the one draped all over him. That didn't matter. I was seduced and I wasn't even awake. I tried to get my mind in gear. What was I going to do?

Vance was half naked. I wore a thin nightshirt. We were in bed. It wasn't going to take much to escalate this. I had two choices—run away, or make a move.

So, what would it be? Was I going to keep running? I thought about it, thought about what that had gotten me so far. I wanted Vance. He was right about that. I'd been lusting over him since the first day we'd met.

This was my chance to find out what had all those women coming back for more.

But he was my best friend. Having sex with him was a bad idea. A really bad idea. So bad that I still don't know why I lifted my head and stared into Vance's blue eyes. They were hot with arousal and very much awake.

"Do you want me to go?" he asked, and I knew if I said I did, he would go. I told him the truth.

"No, I don't want you to go."

To my surprise, he hesitated. Maybe if he'd pounced on me, it would've shaken my resolve, but that hesitation, that hint that he might be as worried about this as I was, convinced me.

I kissed him. Now that I'd decided to stop running, I didn't want to wait anymore.

Vance's hand on my ass tightened, and he hauled me on top of him, my legs spreading over his hips, cradling his erection between my thighs.

His mouth on mine, he fisted his hands in my cotton nightshirt and swept it up my torso and over my head, leaving me straddling him, naked except for a pair of plain white cotton panties.

"If you could stay right there for the rest of my life, I think I'd be in heaven," Vance said, his hot, hungry eyes taking in every inch of my bare skin. I started to flush with self-conscious embarrassment.

Vance was perfect, his body all silky skin and steely muscle, without any flaws I could see. I was in better shape since we'd started jogging together, but I wasn't taut or lithe, and my abs didn't have a hint of definition aside from my belly button.

Vance learned my body with his hands, stroking from my knees to my hips and up my waist to close around the sides of my breasts, pressing them together for a moment before stroking his thumbs over my nipples.

"Fucking beautiful, Magnolia. You're fucking beautiful. I've been imagining you naked for two years, but reality doesn't even come close."

I opened my mouth to protest. His eyes flicked to my face and he scowled. "Don't say a fucking word, Sugar."

I wanted to tell him not to call me Sugar, but his fingertips squeezed my hard nipples and thought fled from my mind. He could call me whatever he wanted if he did that again.

"Nothing I say is going to get through to you." He sat up in a surge of muscle, taking me with him and flipping me to my back. "I'm going to have to show you how much I love your body. Maybe then, you'll get it."

He did. Whatever Brayden and I had been doing in bed, whatever it was that we called sex... clearly, we'd been doing it wrong.

Vance settled himself between my thighs and cupped

my breasts in his palms, pressing them together, bringing first one nipple, then the other to his mouth.

He started gently, trailing his tongue over my breasts, teasing, waking every nerve, his fingers as busy as his mouth until my breasts were swollen, my nipples hard red beads.

I couldn't remember ever being so aroused, so needy, and his hands had stayed above my waist.

Just when I thought I would go mad, he lifted his head from my breasts and said, "I closed the door to the sitting room, but try to be quiet for this next part. We don't want to wake Rosie up."

What next part?

Before I could think through what he'd said, he was moving down my body, his lips trailing across my ribs, his tongue dipping into my bellybutton, making me squirm, before he settled between my legs, lifting first one, then the other, over his shoulders.

Braced on his elbows, he set his palms on my inner thighs, holding me open to his gaze.

I couldn't move, frozen in lust and embarrassment. No one had ever seen me so exposed. Not outside of a medical office.

I wanted to snap my legs shut and scramble off the bed.

I wanted to press my hot, slick flesh to Vance's mouth.

His tongue flicked out, tasting my inner thigh. I shuddered with pleasure and need. I had no idea what to expect.

No one had ever done this to me before.

I'd read about it, but that wasn't the same. My hands went to his, I don't know why. Not to stop him.

Maybe I just needed something to hold onto. His fingers tangled with mine, our wrists braced on my inner thighs and pinning my legs wide.

I had the random thought that I was glad I'd gone back

to yoga. Flexibility was good. Then I stopped thinking altogether.

Vance's tongue, his lips, were everywhere. Tasting me, teasing me. Embarrassment fled under the wave of hot, desperate arousal.

When he wrapped his lips around my clit and sucked the first time, orgasm hit me like a slap—fast and hard and shocking.

I'd never come like that with a partner. I wasn't expecting to, wasn't thinking about an orgasm. I'd never even come like that by myself.

I was still gasping and making a low, keening sound in my throat when Vance rubbed his stubbled cheek against my inner thigh and said, "I'm going to keep calling you Sugar. You taste so sweet."

He licked me again, giving a hum of satisfaction. I had no frame of reference for what this was. This wasn't sex. Not how I knew it.

I should've expected the second orgasm, but it built so slowly, I didn't see it coming.

Vance took his time, his tongue teasing and flicking and sucking and dipping inside over and over until I was squirming and mindless, caught in the gradually building wave of pleasure, so absorbed in him that the flash of bliss took me by surprise when it broke and crashed through me.

He cut off my moans with his mouth, kissing me, tasting of me—salty and musky and sweet—before he was there, filling me with that thick, hard cock. I think it might have hurt if I hadn't already come twice.

I knew he was big, but seeing him across the room and feeling him inside me were two very different things.

He pressed in slowly, making room for himself in my

body, his passage eased by how wet I was, how much I needed him.

When he was in to the hilt, filling me completely, he let out a short gasp of breath and moaned, "Fuck, baby. Fuck, so—"

His head dropped to my shoulder, his cheek brushing mine, his breath hitching in his chest as he started to move, his hips jerking in an uneven rhythm as if his body had escaped his control.

Following instinct, I tilted my hips and wrapped my legs around him, drawing him closer, deeper.

As if he'd been waiting for permission, he started to move, thrusting harder, faster. I would've told you there was no way I could come again. I would've been wrong.

Vance's breathing was shallow and harsh, his eyes squeezed shut. When he reached down and sank his fingers into my ass, tilting my hips further and thrusting even deeper, he hit something inside me and I exploded in sharp, almost painful pleasure, gasping for air and calling out his name, over and over.

His mouth took mine, silencing my cries as his body stiffened in orgasm. I didn't pass out afterward, but it kind of felt like it.

My brain was completely offline. All I could do was lie there and try to catch my breath. I let out a hitch when Vance pulled himself from my body, still half-hard.

Then he was gone, and I was cold, but still too over-whelmed to do anything about it. Water ran in the bath-room, and he was back, the condom gone and a warm, wet washcloth in his hand.

If I'd been thinking, I would've been embarrassed to have him stroke the cloth between my legs gently twice before tossing it on the floor. By the time I registered what he was doing, he was already done, sliding under the sheet, pulling the blankets over us, and drawing me into his arms.

I thought we were going to talk about it. Wasn't that what people did after they had sex for the first time? Maybe we were supposed to, but we didn't. I was back the way I'd woken up, my cheek on Vance's chest, my legs tangled with his, the soothing stroke of his fingers on my arm and tugging on my hair.

I listened to the thump of his heartbeat beneath my ear and thought about what I should say until I fell asleep.

Rosie woke us a few hours later. We shifted from our leisurely nap straight into panic mode when we heard her coughing and sneezing. Vance got to her first.

"No fever," he called into the bedroom. "I'll clean her up and feed her, and you can take the first shower."

I wasn't going to turn that offer down. Vance was still giving Rosie her bottle when I got out of the shower, so I took the time to dry my hair.

Maybe I was avoiding him, just a little. My body hummed with the aftermath of three unbelievable orgasms.

Literally unbelievable.

If I'd had any idea sex could be like that, I would've broken up with Brayden a long time ago. I didn't know.

I'd never understood how people said sex was better than chocolate.

Now I knew I'd just been having the wrong kind of sex.

I wasn't going to play the regret game with Vance. I wasn't that big of a liar, or a coward.

I wanted to have sex with him again.

And again.

Vance had been in control, and everything had been about me. The next time, I wanted to touch him, to explore every inch of that fucking fine body until he was just as desperate as I had been.

I wanted, needed, to make him feel as good as he'd made me feel. I wasn't going to start some crap about how we shouldn't have done it and it was a mistake. It probably was a mistake, but it wasn't one I wanted to take back.

Still, the analytical side of my brain couldn't stop asking me questions. What did this mean? How are things going to change?

The sex was amazing, I guess, but it didn't erase my original concerns. Just because the orgasms had blown my mind didn't mean they were anything different for Vance. For all I knew, that had been just average sex to him.

It was too late for me. I wasn't in danger of falling in love with Vance. I wasn't one of those people who could separate sex and emotion.

I already loved him.

Now this?

Eventually, he was going to move on. Right now, with Rosie on his hands, he needed me. He needed my help, he needed my support, and he wanted me in bed. It was the perfect arrangement for him.

For me, the amazing orgasms aside, it was a recipe for a broken heart, and I was walking right into it, my eyes wide open.

I was an idiot.

An idiot who still had to get ready for work. Finished with my hair, I put on some makeup, wrapped the towel around me, and went to go find my clothes. Vance and Rosalie were nowhere to be seen.

I'll admit, that was a relief. Standing in front of my closet, I chose a shift dress in a deep plum. It was comfortable but well cut and polished enough for work.

I slipped into the matching tailored cardigan and went to look for the bracelet I always wore with that dress. It had been my grandmother's, a simple amethyst and diamond pattern my grandfather had given her as an anniversary gift.

It wasn't a terribly expensive piece—the stones were on the smaller side—but the design of faceted flowers was whimsical and sweet and it made me feel close to my grandmother.

I couldn't find it. My desk at work could get disorganized, but I was careful with my jewelry. I didn't have a lot, most of it handed down from my grandmother, and I treasured every piece she'd given me.

Each one had a story, was a piece of her life, a memory of her. There's no way I would've misplaced so much as an earring, but the bracelet was gone. I checked everywhere, even my bedside table and the bathroom drawers.

By the time Vance came to check on me, I was biting my lip to hold back tears.

"Babe, do you want breakfast?"

I turned to him, shaking my head.

"What's wrong? Magnolia, tell me what's wrong," he said, crowding into my space. His hands were full of Rosie, but he held her against one shoulder and wound his arm around me.

"It's nothing. I just . . . I lost my grandmother's bracelet. I can't find it anywhere. I'm always careful with it. I don't understand how I could've misplaced it."

"Could you have left it at the loft?"

"I don't think so. I haven't worn it in a few weeks—" I cut off, trying to remember the last time I'd worn the bracelet. Everything had been turned around since Vance and Rosie had moved in.

The bracelet wasn't the first thing I'd misplaced lately—

there were a few odds and ends that I must have rearranged when Vance and Rosie had moved in that I couldn't find.

Nothing big. A clock I'd kept in the sitting room. A small painting on a tabletop easel that had been in the guest room. But the bracelet mattered.

I could see moving the clock and forgetting what drawer I'd stashed it in. Not my grandmother's bracelet.

"Maybe you took it off and put it in your desk," he said. "We'll look for it. We'll find it. I'm sure you didn't lose it. You're too organized for that."

A tear trickled down my cheek and I brushed it away, annoyed with myself. I was overreacting. Vance was probably right. I wouldn't have lost the bracelet. It would turn up.

He kissed the top of my head. I looked across his chest to meet Rosie's eyes, the exact shade of blue as Vance's.

She met my gaze with a solemn expression, her dark wisps of hair mostly covered by a pink cap that matched her rosebud mouth. I couldn't help but smile at her.

Her feet kicked against Vance's chest, and I caught one in my hand, stroking my fingers over her soft, tiny toes.

"Are you having second thoughts?" Vance murmured into my hair.

I nodded against his chest.

"You gonna run out on me?"

I shook my head.

I knew I was making a mistake, knew I had no business getting involved with Vance, but I wasn't going to run anymore.

"You promise?" he asked.

I nodded again. "I'm just . . . I don't . . ." I didn't know what to say, didn't have the words to explain in a way that wouldn't sound mean and accusing and bitchy.

"You're freaked out and you don't trust me," Vance said in a patient, resigned tone.

"Pretty much, yeah," I murmured.

"Not much I can do about that, Sugar, except prove you wrong."

I shrugged and kissed Rosalie's toes, unwilling to meet his eyes or contribute further to the conversation. He'd summed it up. He was either going to prove me right or prove me wrong. Time would tell.

"Do you have anything pressing for the afternoon? We already slept the morning away."

I straightened and stepped out of his arms, more comfortable now that we were on familiar ground.

"No. Everything is caught up. Why?"

"Why don't you take the afternoon off? Go see if you can get Charlie to play hooky, take her out to lunch. You've been stuck with Rosie and me for weeks. You need some time on your own."

"But what about Rosie? She's still sick," I objected.

"You have your phone if anything changes, but she doesn't have a fever, just a stuffy nose. That jogging stroller I ordered came in yesterday. We're going to put it together, maybe get some fresh air."

"You're sure?" I asked. He was right. I hadn't had any time to myself since Rosie had shown up in our lives. Maybe that was my problem. Maybe I just needed some girl time, some time away from Vance and his brain-clouding sexual magnetism to get my head on straight.

"Okay, if you're sure. I'll call Charlie."

"Go have some fun. We'll be here when you get home."

CHAPTER SEVENTEEN
MAGNOLIA

Charlotte Winters never played hooky from work. She worked late every night. She worked on weekends. I'd heard through the Winters grapevine—they were terrible gossips—that even Aiden, who had a reputation as a workaholic, worked less than she did.

The only time I'd known her to cut out on her job was when Brayden dumped me, so I didn't expect her to take me up on my offer of lunch, especially when I made it clear it would be a long lunch.

I hadn't driven my car in a while. It seemed like Vance was always driving, and he was right—I hadn't gone anywhere on my own in weeks.

I pulled up in front of the Winters Inc. building in Buckhead feeling giddy with freedom and oddly nervous, as if I'd left my purse at home.

But Rosalie wasn't a purse, and she was safe with her father. It was just odd to be so suddenly unencumbered. Charlotte appeared on the sidewalk shortly after I pulled up and slid into the car.

"You look like hell," I said.

Charlie let out a sigh. "I know. Can we not talk about it?"

"I don't know. That depends. Is it work?"

"If I say it is, will you drop it?"

"Maybe," I said.

"I don't want to talk about me," she said.

"You never want to talk about you." She didn't. Charlotte could be nosy as hell when it came to the people she cared about, but she hated talking about herself.

Ignoring me, she said, "I want to talk about you and Vance."

I turned bright red. I could feel it in my cheeks, the prickly heat of a fierce blush.

"I knew it," she shouted, practically bouncing in her seat. My eyes widened. I don't think I'd ever seen Charlotte this animated.

"You knew what?" I asked, trying to play dumb.

"You slept with him, didn't you? I know you did. Your face is bright red."

"Where do you want to go to lunch?" I asked, trying to derail the conversation.

"That new burger place in the Highlands," she shot back, refusing to be diverted.

I knew the place she was talking about. The food was amazing, and it was warm enough that we could sit outside. There was also an excellent pastry and ice cream shop across the street.

"Spill. I want to know everything. Well, almost everything. He *is* my cousin. You can leave out the really graphic details."

"Charlie," I protested, torn. I needed to talk to someone about Vance, and I trusted Charlotte, but he was her family. Wouldn't she automatically be on his side? Making a decision, I said, "Fine, I'll talk to you about Vance if you talk to me about whatever's going on at work."

Charlie narrowed her eyes at me and let out a light growl. One thing I'd learned about Charlie Winters—she could be stubborn.

"Fine," she ground out. "But there's some stuff going on I can't tell you. Client confidentiality stuff."

"I don't care about clients, Charlotte. I care about you. And every time I've seen you in the last few months, you look exhausted and unhappy. I know it's work because that's all you do, and you need to talk about it with someone."

"I said I'd talk about it. Geez, back off."

"Cranky," I commented under my breath.

"I'll talk. After you."

I had a feeling that was the best deal I was going to get. This time of day, the drive from Buckhead to the Highlands didn't take long. We got lucky with a parking spot on a side street not far from the restaurant.

While I loved living in my family home in Buckhead, I shared Charlotte's enthusiasm for the Highlands. Between the funky shops, excellent restaurants and cafés, and the combination of Victorian and Craftsman architecture, it always reminded me of a small town dropped in the middle of Atlanta.

It didn't surprise me that I liked the Highlands, but Charlotte's interest in the area always struck me as a little odd. Charlotte was buttoned up tight. With her perfect hair and her formal business suit, she looked like big business and old money.

The Highlands neighborhood wasn't low rent by any means. Houses here were pretty expensive, and our burger and fries lunch would be both local and artisanal—i.e. also not cheap.

From where I was standing, I could see two coffee shops, one of which doubled as an art gallery, a casual wear boutique, the sports gear shop where Vance had bought my running clothes, and a tattoo parlor.

Charlotte looked like Phipps Plaza—Tiffany, Prada, and Versace. So why did I think, in her heart, she was so much more the Highlands than Buckhead?

Ordering didn't take long since we both already knew what we wanted. I got a lemonade and grabbed a table. Charlotte sat down across from me and leaned forward, bracing herself on her elbows. "Okay, talk," she said.

"What do you want me to say?"

"Are you two together now? Like together, together?"

"I don't even know what that means, Charlie," I said, taking a sip of my lemonade to stall.

"You know what it means. You're just being difficult."

I made a face at her and admitted, "Okay, yes. I think. At least, we're going to try. I'm not . . . I'm not sure what I'm doing."

Charlie took my hand in hers and squeezed. "You can talk to me, honey. I'm on your side, I promise."

"Vance is your cousin, and I know you guys are close." Charlie shook her head and squeezed my hand again. "We are, and he is. I want him to be happy, and I've never seen him as happy as he is with you. So yeah, I like the idea that the two of you are together. But I care about you, Maggie. You're my closest friend, the only close friend I'm not related to, and I want you to be happy, too. It would be nice if you could be happy together."

I sat back and thought about what to say as a waiter delivered our food. I was tired of measuring my words and second-guessing. I opened my mouth and everything spilled out.

How I was afraid I was in love with him, how I didn't trust him, and how I was sure I was going to end up with my heart broken.

Charlotte ate her burger and listened patiently until I ran out of words. When I was finally silent, she swallowed the last bite, washing it down with a sip of her own lemonade, her eyes fixed on a spot somewhere over my shoulder, apparently thinking.

"I want to promise you everything's going to work out, but if I did, I'd be lying," she said. "No one can promise you that. Shit happens, even when people really love each other."

I was reminded, again, of everything the Winters family had been through. From all reports, both sets of parents had been deeply in love and it had still ended in tragedy. Even a happy ending didn't guarantee a happy ending.

"I know," I said. "It's just that this seems so convenient. Rosie shows up, his whole life changes, and all of a sudden, he wants to be in a relationship with me? He knows I've always wanted a family. He's even given me a hard time for dating Brayden because I want that family so badly, and then as soon as he has one—when he's overwhelmed and needs me—he offers me everything he thinks I want."

"Is it everything you want?" Charlotte asked.

I rubbed my thumb against a spot on the distressed wooden table top and thought about her question. I shook my head. "I don't know anymore. When I looked at Brayden, that's what I saw. A husband and children. A family. But then I found out he'd been cheating on me, and I realized a husband and children didn't necessarily make a family. If I'd married him, if we'd had kids . . . he probably still would've cheated on me.

"I don't mean that I changed my mind about wanting a family, but I guess I realized it's not as cut and dried as I always thought it would be. As I wanted it to be. And Vance has never given any sign that he has any interest in a relationship, much less a family."

"That's the tricky part, isn't it?" Charlotte said. "The funny thing is when we were kids, little kids, he was always so good with us—the younger ones, I mean. Aiden and Gage never had any time for us, busy with their big kid stuff, but Vance—and Jacob too—they were patient. They'd play with us. I always figured Vance would get married young. I always saw him with a house full of kids."

She took another sip of lemonade and looked away, letting out a sigh. "Then everything changed. Vance changed. Aiden told me once that he was really close to his mom when he was a kid and that after she died, he kind of transferred that to my mom, and when *she* died . . ." Charlotte swallowed and shook her head.

"We don't have to talk about this, Charlie," I said.

Charlotte shook her head again. "But I want you to understand. He changed after my mom died. We all did. Losing my parents was . . . none of us knew what to do, how to go on from that. And Vance did a total 180 from a sweet, chilled out guy who was into his art and girls and his family to this man-whore, heavy drinker we barely recognized.

"But that guy—the guy who's nailed half the women in town when he wasn't drinking everything he could get his hands on—that guy isn't Vance. The guy he's been since he stopped drinking, that's the Vance I remember. And that guy? That guy has some serious feelings for you.

"I can't promise you he's not going to fuck it up. You're

right. He has a shitty track record with women. And he's an alcoholic, which is tough. You're coming off a breakup with a total asshole who took you for granted and cheated on you, so you're not exactly in a great mindset to start a relationship either. Plus, all of a sudden, there's a baby. Who the hell saw that coming? There are about a million reasons why the two of you should not start a relationship right now."

"Too late for that," I interrupted.

"True enough. But, on the other hand, I think Vance has been planning this since you broke up with Brayden. Maybe even before. And I'm not sure you would've taken the risk on him if you weren't all shaken up from the breakup and Rosie showing up out of the blue. So maybe he saw his opportunity, and he took it. I don't know, honey. I wish I could give you a guarantee. I'm just saying that Vance is a good guy, and he cares about you."

"I know he is," I said. Even at his worst, I never doubted that Vance was a good guy. "And I know he cares about me. He's one of my best friends."

"But you have to take care of you," Charlie said, surprising me. She went on. "In my very humble opinion, you did a crappy job of that when you were with Brayden. This time around, you have to look out for yourself. I don't think Vance has had a relationship since he was a teenager. He was dating a sweet girl his senior year when my parents died. He broke up with her right after, and he never had another girlfriend until now. I'm sure he's great in bed, but he's probably a terrible boyfriend. I mean, he wouldn't cheat on you, but—"

"But there are a lot of ways this could go wrong that have nothing to do with him cheating," I finished for her.

"Yeah. Still, all the warning signs aside, I don't think he's willing to fuck this up. Not with you."

"I hope not," I said. I don't know that Charlotte's words were reassuring, except that they reminded me of two important things.

One, I had to remember to look out for myself. And two, she was a really good friend. No matter what, Charlie would have my back. As uncertain as everything was, that meant a lot. Now it was my turn to be a good friend, even though she'd get annoyed with me for it.

Chapter Eighteen

Magnolia

"Thanks," I said. "Now you go. I'm going to eat my burger, and you're going to tell me what the hell is going on at work."

Getting Charlie to talk was like pulling teeth, but I was determined. I took a huge bite of my burger and pinned her with my eyes.

She let out a gust of air and said, "Okay, I can't really say that much, but we have a client—kind of a client and kind of a business partner—and he's breaking a few laws. Intentionally and repeatedly. I'm working with Aiden on it, and we're easing out of the relationship between his company and Winters Inc., but that's not enough."

I swallowed and asked in a hushed voice, "Are you going to turn him in?"

"I think I have to." Charlie cut off and let out a breath. "No, I know I have to. I've got evidence. I'm almost ready, it's just . . ." Charlie's shoulders slumped, and she studied a nonexistent spot on the table. "I hate this. I hate being in this position. I hate this business, and I hate my job."

My heart squeezed at the sound of her voice. I'd never

heard Charlotte sound so small and defeated. I put down my burger and wiped my hands. "You're allowed to hate your job, Charlie," I said. "You don't have to keep doing this if you don't like it, if it's not what you want."

She shook her head and forced a bright smile on her face. Vance said I ran away from difficult situations, but in her own way, Charlotte was worse.

"I can't quit my job, Maggie. I can't. Aiden needs me. I'm the only other Winters at the company right now. Vance has his art and his investing, Annalise is off with her camera, photographing the world, and both Holden and Tate are busy with WGC and their club. Gage is off the map doing something he can't talk about with the military, and who knows if he'll ever come home. He used to love the business, and then he just bailed. Aiden has everything on his shoulders. I can't abandon him."

"What does Aiden say?" I asked.

All pretense dropped away, and Charlotte sat up straight. When she spoke, her voice was deadly serious. "I'm not talking about this with Aiden. No one is talking about this with Aiden, do you understand? Not you, not Vance, no one. Okay?"

"I swear," I said, holding my hand over my heart. "I swear I won't say anything to anyone." I thought she should talk to her brother, but it was her life and her decision.

"Anyway, we have another situation, and I need to ask for a favor," she said, picking up her lemonade and taking a last sip, clearly finished talking about her job and the family company.

I wasn't quite ready to drop the subject, but I didn't want to get in a fight with Charlie over it.

"What's up?" I asked, curious.

"Do you remember my Aunt Amelia?" Charlie asked.

"Of course I remember Aunt Amelia," I said. "I haven't seen her since my grandmother died, though. I should have visited. I just . . . it's been hard seeing her friends, and I didn't. I'm sorry. How is she? Is she okay?"

Charlotte's Aunt Amelia had been a friend of my grandmother's. Amelia was quirky and had a biting sense of humor. She used to make my refined grandmother laugh out loud and blush at the same time.

"She's okay," Charlotte said. "But she's getting to the point where she can't really live on her own anymore. Aiden is the best about spending time with her, and he asked her if she wanted to go live in some kind of home situation or move into Winters House with him, and they'd get a live-in nurse to help her out."

"Aiden offered to take her in?" I asked, kind of surprised.

"Of course. She's family. And they've always gotten along well. Plus, it's not like he doesn't have the room. He only offered the home because he didn't want her to be lonely, rattling around in that huge house with just him and a nurse."

Her words put me on alert. "What do you mean just him and a nurse?" I asked. "You live there, don't you? Did you move and you didn't tell anyone?"

"No, I still live there. We'll talk about that in a minute, but first, Aiden asked me to do the interviews for the nurse. He said he doesn't have the patience, the time, or the temperament. He's right. He'd probably hire some termagant with a clipboard. And you know Amelia. She's sweet and kind of flighty. She needs someone patient, with a sense of humor. Anyway, I told him I'd do the interviews, but will you help me? You know Amelia and you're good with people. I know you're busy right now with Vance's show and Rosie, but—"

"Of course I'll help," I said. Now that I was thinking of Amelia Winters, I realized how much I'd missed her. When my grandmother had died, I'd stopped seeing all of her friends, the pain too raw for me to handle reminders of the life we'd had. I shouldn't have done that. In a way, they'd been my friends too. "Just let me know when the interviews are, and I'll work it out. I—"

My phone rang, and I grabbed for it, worried it was Vance and Rosie was feeling worse. When I saw who it was, I stabbed a finger at the *Decline Call* button.

"Who was that?" Charlie asked, reaching for my phone. I slid it out of reach.

"Brayden," I said.

"What does he want?"

"No clue, but I have nothing to say to him." Changing the subject, I said, "Tell me what you meant about you living at Winters House."

Charlotte stood and pushed back her chair. "Come for a walk with me," she said, obliquely. "I want to show you something."

"After ice cream," I said, eyeballing the shop across the street.

Charlotte raised an eyebrow at me. "Of course, after ice cream," she said, hooking her arm through mine.

"So, tell me—what are you up to?" I asked.

"I'm not quite sure," she said.

My phone rang a second time. After a quick check, I declined the call and shoved it in my pocket.

"Again?" she asked.

I shook my head. "I'm ignoring him."

"Give me your phone," she demanded, holding out her hand.

I eyed her, suspicious. "Why? You're not going to call

him and tell him off, are you? I don't want to encourage him."

"No, I promise. Just give me the phone."

"Fine," I said, unlocking the screen and handing it over. She tapped at the screen as we walked, arm in arm, letting me watch for cars and other pedestrians. I wondered what she was doing with my phone, but she kept it angled away from my curious gaze.

As we stood in line at the cafe, she handed it back, saying only, "Now you'll know when he calls." We got ice cream and strolled down the street, passing shops, cafés, and restaurants.

A moment later, my phone buzzed to life again, this time with a mechanical voice saying, "Warning, the Loser is calling. Warning, the Loser is calling." I dissolved into giggles, almost dropping my ice cream. This time, I didn't bother to silence the call.

"Much better," Charlie said with relish.

"I agree." Brayden was a loser, and the sooner I erased him from my life, the better.

Charlotte led me around the corner and down a residential street filled with a mix of Victorian and Craftsman homes, some exquisitely restored and some in need of a little TLC.

She stopped in front of a two-story Craftsman with a wraparound front porch and faded, peeling paint in shades of gray. I think it was gray. It could have been purple or blue before time had leached out the tint. The yard was a mess of weeds and brambles, overgrown in some places and bare in others.

A prime example of the kind of homes in the neighborhood that needed some love. When it was fixed up, it would be adorable. At the moment, it was a little scary. A *For Sale* sign sat in the front yard.

"What you think?" Charlie asked. I looked from her to the house and back again.

"For you?" I asked doubtfully, eyeing the deep bow in the front porch and the loose shingles on the roof.

She shrugged one shoulder, staring at the peeling paint with a look I could only describe as wistful yearning. Charlotte didn't just like the house. She *wanted* it.

On the surface, they were a terrible match. Charlotte's polish, her starkly tailored business suit and her sleek hair, did not fit this house with its welcoming architecture and general air of neglect.

I watched her eyes devour the house, and I knew that this sad structure was more Charlotte than Charlotte was. At a loss, I said, "It's a little smaller than what you're used to, but anything would be small compared to Winters House."

An understatement. Winters House was bigger than some hotels.

"I know," she said. "It needs a lot of work, and I never have time. And actually, it's a lot bigger than you'd think. Too big for just me. But I saw it on the website, and it looked—"

"Like home?" I asked.

"Yes," she said. "It looks like home." I didn't bother to ask if she could afford it. She was Charlotte Winters. She probably had enough money to buy the whole street.

"You should—" My words were drowned out by the sound of a lawnmower roaring to life at the house next door. Both of us turned to look, and my jaw dropped.

The man pushing the lawnmower was well over six feet tall, with broad shoulders and long legs, every inch of his body chiseled with muscle. He had on a pair of faded khaki cargo shorts and no shirt, displaying tanned skin heavily decorated with tattoos.

The only one I could see clearly was the bird on his back—maybe a hawk—its talons extended, dripping blood. The tattoo was a little intimidating, but when he turned around, all thought fled my mind.

Cut cheekbones, light green eyes, a lush lower lip, and shaggy black hair. Holy crap. If *he* lived next door, I was having second thoughts about Charlie buying that house.

Leaning into Charlotte so she could hear me over the roar of the lawnmower, I said, "I was going to say you should put in an offer, but if he'd be your neighbor, let's go to the real estate office right now. Good Lord, he's hot."

As if he'd heard me, which was impossible, the hot neighbor looked up and winked.

Not at me. At Charlie. Her cheeks flushed, and she looked away.

"Let's go," she said, looping her arm through mine again and dragging me up the street, away from her dream house and the gorgeous guy next door. I tried to resist, but she was relentless.

"Are we going to the real estate office?" I asked. "We should at least get more information about the house, don't you think?"

"No," she said mulishly. "I'm going back to work. I don't know what I'm thinking. I have a place to live. It's stupid to think about moving out. And I don't want to leave Aiden on his own."

"I don't know. He's going to have Aunt Amelia and the nurse. I think you should move in next door to lawnmower hottie. You don't even have to talk to him. Just watching him mow the lawn is entertainment enough."

"That is true," Charlotte agreed, but she dropped the

subject of the house and asked me about Rosie. I knew her well enough to know when she was done talking about something. I let it go.

I was more than happy to talk about Rosalie. How was it that I'd been away from her only two hours and it felt like I'd left a limb behind? Not to mention Vance.

Lunch with Charlie was fun, but I was ready to get home to my family, even if they were only mine temporarily.

Chapter Nineteen
Magnolia

My mind was racing as I drove home from lunch with Charlie, thinking about everything she'd said about Vance, wondering if she was going to work up the nerve to put an offer in on that house, and if she did, if she'd ever talk to lawnmower hottie next door.

On the surface, lawnmower hottie was the polar opposite of the kind of guy I would've imagined for Charlotte, but then again, so was that house. And she wanted the house.

My mental wanderings ground to a halt as I pulled into the end of my driveway and saw a familiar car. Brayden had purchased the luxury sedan a few weeks before he'd officially finished his internship.

He couldn't afford to buy me an engagement ring, or help with the bills, but he had no problem coming up with the down payment for a $70,000 car. Asshole.

What was he doing here? What could he possibly want from me?

I parked my car at the front door and jumped out. I

could hear voices at the side of the house by the back gate, and Scout barking.

I rounded the corner to see Vance, shirtless and wearing a pair of athletic shorts, his fingers gripping the handlebar of the stroller, his shoulders set.

I couldn't see Brayden's face, but I knew that tone of voice. Neither of them had noticed my arrival. I stopped for a second, curious to know what they were arguing about.

"You're just a fucking opportunist, aren't you?" Brayden said. "You've wanted Magnolia for years, and the second I'm out of the way, you just fucking move in?"

"Are you calling *me* an opportunist? You? You, who let her take care of you for years while treating her like shit and cheating on her? Get the fuck off her property before I call the police," Vance growled.

"Nobody's calling the police," I said from behind them.

Vance didn't take his eyes off Brayden when he said, "Magnolia, go in the house. I'll take care of this."

"Brayden, what are you doing here?" I asked, ignoring Vance. Brayden stepped to the side, away from the gate and toward me, allowing me to see his face. All signs of temper were gone, replaced by a smooth, almost smarmy, smile.

How had I ever fallen for this guy? With his perfectly pressed chinos and his starched button-down shirt, he was bland and dull.

Vance's golden skin glowed from a light layer of sweat, the lines of his tattoos stark and bold, his muscles tight with anger. Vance was so much more alive, more compelling, more *everything* than Brayden.

"Do you want to go put a shirt on, guy?" Brayden said to Vance, and I giggled. He gestured at Vance and muttered, "Ridiculous, running around without a shirt on."

Letting my eyes skim Vance's six-pack as he turned to

face me, I winked and said, "Don't get dressed on my account."

"Wasn't planning on it, Sugar," Vance said with an exaggerated leer that prompted another giggle for me and a sneer from Brayden.

"Are you two together now? Is that what this is?" Brayden demanded.

Still ignoring him, I said to Vance, "Why does everyone keep asking us that? Why do these people think it's their business?"

"Because they're nosy and their lives are boring," Vance said, grinning at me.

"Charlotte's life isn't boring," I said.

"Yes, it is," Vance said. "Her life is beyond boring. Is that what you were talking about at lunch? You and me?"

"It's none of your business what we were talking about at lunch," I said, coming around the side of the stroller so I could check on Rosie.

I barely got a chance to see that she was fast asleep when Vance's hand closed over my upper arm and he hauled me back, away from Brayden.

I realized Brayden's presence was bothering him a lot more than he was willing to let on. Then I realized it wasn't bothering me that much at all.

Weird. Maybe all I needed to get over Brayden was to see him in the same space as Vance, to realize how little he meant in the big picture of my life.

He'd been a mistake, a waste of my time, and that was sad. But it was over, and I'd moved on.

Which begged the question, "Why are you here, Brayden?"

"I need to talk to you, sweetheart. There are things to say."

"She doesn't have anything to say to you," Vance shot out. I elbowed him in the side.

"There's nothing to say, Brayden. You cheated on me, then you broke up with me. It turns out that was the best thing you ever did. You got all your stuff out of the house. I checked after you left. Why don't you just get in your car and leave? If you come back, I'm calling the police."

"Sweetheart," Brayden said, his eyes heavy with false remorse. He held a hand out to me as if beseeching me to listen. Unfortunately for him, and for me, I knew him too well to fall for it. He kept going. "I made mistakes. I can admit that. But I want you back."

"Did you lose your job?" I asked evenly.

"No, but—"

"Did your girlfriend break up with you?" I went on.

"She doesn't have anything to do with—"

"You're right. She doesn't have anything to do with this. And I don't care if she kicked you out. All I care about is that you cheated on me with her while we were engaged. I care that you're a liar. But I'm done with you, so I don't care that much."

I turned to face Vance, giving Brayden my back, dismissing him. "Should we go put Rosie down? How long has she been asleep?"

"She'll probably wake up as soon as I unsnap her, but it's worth a try," he said, his smile warm and gentle.

"Did she like jogging?" I asked, smiling a little at the site of Rosie sleeping, not a snot bubble in sight, and at the sound of Brayden grinding his teeth behind me. He'd never liked being ignored.

"Maggie, just a few minutes. I just want to talk to you for a few minutes."

"No," I said, without looking over my shoulder. "I'm done with you. I have nothing to say."

His face hard, jaw set, Vance said, "If you're not in your car by the time we get in the house, we're calling the police."

"Maggie won't call the police on me," Brayden protested.

"Yes, I will," I said. I stepped to the side to give Vance room to turn the stroller around and said, "Scout, backdoor!"

My dog was not the brightest bulb in the box, but he knew what that meant, and he whirled from the gate and took off for the back of the house.

I concentrated on getting the door open for Vance to push the stroller through, hoping Brayden was leaving. I'd meant it. I would call the police. I just didn't want to.

To my relief, Brayden got in his car and drove away. I had no idea why he wanted to talk to me. I didn't believe for a second that he wanted to apologize. I don't think Brayden had apologized to me in the four years we'd been together.

The only reason he would've wanted to talk to me was if he needed me to do something for him. I was done doing anything for Brayden Michaels.

I had something much more intriguing on my mind, something he'd said. Charlie had said it too, only I hadn't believed her.

Before I could ask Vance anything, he said, "Can you get Rosie? I'm going to jump in the shower."

"I've got her," I said. She didn't wake as I carefully unsnapped her from the jogging stroller and lifted her into my arms.

The stroller was designed to carry a much larger child, but Vance had bought an infant insert to support Rosie's head and spine in the big seat. It must've been comfortable because she looked like she'd been asleep for a while.

I had her tucked into the swing in the kitchen when

Vance came back, wearing an old pair of jeans and a white button-down, untucked and unbuttoned.

I licked my lips. My brain couldn't quite register that we'd had sex that morning. It still seemed impossible. My body, on the other hand, had not only accepted the reality, but it was ready to relive it. First, I had a question.

"Is it true?" I asked. "What Brayden said, that you wanted to sleep with me when he and I were together?"

"You have to ask?" Vance came toward me, intent clear in his eyes.

It looked like his mind was in the gutter, right along with mine, but I wanted an answer before I stripped off his clothes and had my way with him. I sent a quick look at the swing, rocking the sleeping baby, before shaking my head at Vance and tilting it toward the living room.

He followed me out of the kitchen, through the sitting room, and into the formal living room. We rarely used it. It had a beautiful view of the grounds behind the house, but the furniture was stiff and a little too formal. My grandmother's style, not mine.

"What do you mean, *I have to ask*? You say that like it was obvious."

"It *was* obvious," he said. "It was obvious to everyone except for you, apparently."

"I didn't know," I protested. "You slept with so many women, and you never said anything."

Vance shoved his hands in the back pockets of his jeans and looked a little sheepish. "Yeah, well, I knew I didn't have a shot with you while I was drinking, and you were with Brayden then anyway."

"And after you stopped drinking?" I asked, cautious but curious.

"Just because I wasn't drinking, it didn't mean I had my shit together," he said, stating the obvious.

"You were still sleeping around a lot," I said, sounding exactly like a jealous girlfriend. I didn't care.

"Not as much as before, but yeah. You were engaged to someone else," he said, defensive.

"I didn't know," I said. "You sometimes made comments about my ass, but you never said anything real."

"And if I had? Would you have left him? Or would you have quit working for me and shut me out?"

I thought about that for a minute. From where I was standing just then, after a night in Vance's bed, the thought that I would've quit my job and cut him out of my life was insane. We'd been friends.

But for a long time, I'd been determined to make things work with Brayden and I'd been positive there was no chance of anything with Vance. Would I have dumped my fiancé to find out?

"I don't know," I admitted. "I don't know. But I'm a lot happier with you than I ever was with him."

"Obviously," Vance said, rolling his eyes at me. "For one thing, my dick is way bigger than his. And for another, I actually know what to do with mine."

I burst out laughing at his arrogance. He was kidding, but only kind of. That's because while his words were funny, they were also accurate.

"You were really thinking about me that way, all this time?" I asked, crossing the room to him.

"For years," he said. "I've wanted you for years."

I stopped in front of him and reached for my zipper.

Lowering it slowly, I shrugged my dress off my shoulders and let it fall to my waist, exposing my breasts in a lacy black bra. I hadn't had time to go shopping lately, not in a store, but I could do a lot of damage on the Internet with a credit card.

Vance's pupils dilated, his eyes fixed on my bare skin.

"Did you know I'd been thinking about you too?" I asked, reaching for the open collar of his shirt. "Pretty much since the day we met."

"Really?" Vance's voice was thick and slow. "What've you been thinking?"

"Why don't you let me show you?" I said, peeling his shirt off his shoulders and down his arms.

CHAPTER TWENTY
MAGNOLIA

Vance's shirt dropped to the floor. I'd have to act fast if I didn't want him to take charge. Not that I didn't like it when he took charge. The night before had been a lesson in everything Vance knew about making a woman come, but this time, I wanted more than that.

I wasn't ready to tell him how I felt about him. As much as I wanted to have confidence in what was happening between us, the truth was I just didn't. But I wanted him.

I wanted Vance and I loved him, and I needed a way to show it to him, to tell him what this meant to me without having to actually tell him.

Knowing Vance, he'd probably understand me better if I said it with sex anyway. I rested my hands on his chest and pushed, urging him backward until his legs hit the wide sofa.

My hands went to the snap of his jeans. I flicked it open with my thumb and lowered the zipper.

He stood there, his hands at his sides, watching me, the faintest tremble to his fingers telling me he wasn't nearly as relaxed as he seemed.

Good, because I was nervous.

Turned on, desperate to touch him, but nervous.

Most of my sexual experience was limited to Brayden, and he hadn't been adventurous in bed. Neither had I.

That was behind me. I had Vance, right here, waiting to see what I was going to do with him. I lowered the zipper on his jeans, tugging a little to get it down, his erection pressing into the fabric, waiting for me.

I hooked my thumbs in the belt loops and pulled, dropping to my knees.

His jeans fell to pool around his ankles, leaving me face to face with his cock. Vance had a beautiful cock. No question. Seeing it in broad daylight, I was a little shocked something that big had fit inside me.

At the time, it had felt like heaven, but now, I wasn't so sure. He was long and thick and very hard. I didn't have any techniques or tricks.

I could probably count on one hand the number of times I'd participated in oral sex. My experience was mostly limited to missionary in the dark. But what I lacked in knowledge I made up for with raw need.

I needed to suck his cock. I needed to taste him, to lick him, to sink my fingers into that perfect ass as I pulled him into my mouth. I wanted to show him what I'd been thinking of all those years we'd kept our hands off each other.

Putting my mouth on his cock was at the top of that list.

I didn't know where to start, so I dove right in, parting my lips and closing them around the head of his shaft, licking and sucking before dropping down as far as I could.

I didn't get further than halfway. Maybe with practice, and in a different position, I could take more of him. Based on Vance's groan, halfway was good enough.

My hands trailed up his legs, my fingertips absorbing the striations in his muscles, the silky skin, the rough rasp of his leg hair before rising to palm his tight ass.

I stroked my lips over his length, pulling at him with slick pressure, and touching every inch of him I could reach.

I loved everything about having him in my mouth—his taste, the way he smelled, musky and male, the sounds he made, the way his fingers threaded through my hair.

I don't know how long I was on my knees when Vance's grip in my hair tightened and he urged me back. I looked up at him in confusion. I know he liked what I was doing. His moans and his grip on my hair told me he did.

His eyes were midnight, lashes half lowered, red flags of color high on his cheekbones. He sat back on the couch, pulling me between his legs, then leaned forward to snag his jeans off the floor.

Vance pulled something from the back pocket. A condom.

"I have to fuck you now," he said. I had no argument with that. I would've happily sucked his cock until he came in my mouth. I'd wanted to. He'd barely touched me and I was so wet.

Every cell in my body strained toward Vance, wanting to be filled with him. Not just with his cock, but everything. Fingers. Mouth. Tongue.

His heart.

His soul.

All of him.

I wanted all of him.

I watched him roll on the condom, scrambling to get rid of my black lace panties and bra. They'd felt like a sexy tease when I put them on that morning, but now, I just wanted Vance's skin against mine.

The second I was naked, he pulled me onto the couch, straddling him. Two long fingers dipped between my legs.

"Fuck, Sugar. You're ready for me."

I was beyond speech. I rocked my hips into his fingers, taking more. He lined himself up and pulled me down, his hands on my hips slowing my descent, making sure I didn't take him too fast and that the stretch, the invasion of his body into mine, wasn't too much.

When he was in me to the hilt, I let out a breath, leaning forward, resting my temple against his cheek. It was so good. So right. His arms came around me, holding me to his chest, his heart thumping in a mad pace. I never wanted to move again.

Vance kept me there, pressed to his body, his breath warm against my cheek. I don't think I'd ever felt so safe, so wanted by anyone.

"I need to feel you come on my cock," he said, sliding his hand between our bodies, his fingers splayed across my abdomen, his thumb on my clit.

His other hand dropped to my lower back, holding me in place. In a slow, lazy circle, he moved his thumb, pressing and rolling my clit until I squirmed, moaning low in my throat.

"Shh," he warned. "Don't wake Rosalie up."

I squeezed my eyes shut. I didn't know if I could make that promise. It felt so good. I wanted to move, to ride him, but his arm around my hips held me still.

I was so full of him, stretched wide, my clit tight against the base of his cock, trapped between his hard shaft and his thumb.

I stretched up, trying to move just a little, putting my breasts even with his face. Vance took advantage, closing his lips around one nipple and sucking hard.

A gasp escaped before I bit my lip. I'd never thought about being quiet before. Not like this. It had never been an issue.

I loved Rosie to pieces, but I had to come. I was going to explode if I didn't come. And if I woke her up . . . that didn't bear thinking about.

Vance switched breasts, licking then nipping, changing the pattern of pressure of his thumb on my clit, speeding it up, pressing harder.

Everything in my body tightened, the muscles in my pussy clenching down, pleasure gathering, coalescing into a knot of need and desperation that grew bigger with every twist of his thumb.

"Vance," I whispered, "please let me. I have to move."

"You want to come? Then come. Come for me, right now."

He turned his hand and caught my clit between his thumb and one finger, squeezing hard. A white-hot bolt of pleasure slashed through the knot of tension between my legs.

I cried out, something between a gasp and a scream. I couldn't help it. The wave of bliss hit me just as Vance tumbled us both to the carpet and finally began to move.

He fucked me hard. My orgasm, finally set free, grew in waves that had me crying out, wrapping my legs around his hips and arching my back as he pounded inside me.

Vance groaned out, "Magnolia" as he came, his breath harsh rasps in my ear.

I wasn't surprised to hear noise coming from the kitchen when my brain settled back into my skull. My cheeks flushed hot. We'd woken Rosie up having sex. We were the worst parents ever.

Vance had rolled to his back, taking me with him. I

splayed across his long body, every muscle in mine limp. I didn't think I could move. I didn't want to move, except I could tell from Rosie's plaintive sounds that while she wasn't crying yet, she would be soon.

"I have to get up," I said. "I don't think I can look her in the eyes."

A rumble of laughter sounded from beneath me. "Who, Rosie? Magnolia, she's a baby, and she was in the other room. She doesn't know what we were doing."

"But *I* know."

"I'll get her. I'm not ashamed," he said, laughing. "I'm proud. If I didn't think you'd get pissed, I'd hire a sky writer to say, *Magnolia Henry is the best lay in the universe.*"

"Classy," I commented wryly. "Please restrain yourself."

"Hey, I said I wasn't going to do it. Doesn't mean it's not the truth."

I peeled myself off Vance and grabbed his discarded button-down from the floor. When we were having sex, I'd felt like a goddess, but now that it was over, I was back to being a mere mortal.

This mortal woman was not walking around naked in front of Vance. Not in broad daylight.

Still a little embarrassed, I escaped upstairs for a quick shower while I let Vance handle feeding Rosie. On my way back down, I checked the mail at the front door, idly thinking about the contents of the fridge and wondering what we should have for dinner.

The mail was the usual junk, a few bills, and an 8.5 x 11 manila envelope with nothing on the front, no address and no postage. Weird.

I carried it into the kitchen, where Vance was feeding Rosie. Dumping everything else on the center island, I opened the envelope, only half-listening as

Vance said, "You dodged a bullet when you ran upstairs. You don't even want to know what was in her diaper."

I drew the contents from the envelope and froze. I heard Vance say my name, but the power of speech had been ripped from my mind by the sight of the photograph in the unmarked envelope.

Vance's parents, their dead bodies lying on the carpet in his childhood home. I wanted to shove the obscene thing away and throw it in the trash. I racked my brain for an excuse, any reason I could avoid showing it to Vance.

I knew what had been happening, about the picture of their bodies that had been delivered to Jacob. I knew this was important, and I couldn't just make it go away, but I couldn't bear for Vance to look.

"Magnolia. Magnolia, what is it?"

His voice filtered to my ears as if he was at the end of a long hallway. I pushed the photograph back in the envelope and closed it, laying it on the counter.

"I'll finish feeding Rosie," I said. "You need to bring that to the Sinclairs or the police."

Vance's eyes went dark, and I knew that he knew what was in the envelope on the countertop.

"Is it the same as before?" he asked, his voice low.

"I don't know," I said, leaning down to ease Rosie from his arms. "I didn't see the other picture, so I can't say it's exactly the same, but it looks like a crime scene photo of your parents."

The second I had Rosie, Vance stood in a surge and moved to grab the picture.

"Don't look at it," I said, suddenly desperate that he not see what was inside. "Don't. It's probably exactly the same as Jacob's. Why don't you let me drive it over to Sinclair

Security? You stay here with Rosie. They can take care of it."

"It's okay, Magnolia. I've seen it before."

"It doesn't mean you need to see it again. Let me bring it to the Sinclairs, okay?"

"Everything's fine, Magnolia," Vance said, his voice distant, restrained. All his attention was on the plain, unmarked manila envelope in front of him. I didn't want to watch as he opened it and slid the picture out.

The first look had been more than enough, but I couldn't tear my eyes away. Two bodies, obviously dead, lay sprawled on a Persian carpet.

The man wore a suit and had a bullet hole in the center of his forehead. She wore a red dress, torn in the center of her chest by another bullet hole.

Her long, white blonde hair was spread around her, shockingly pale against the dark carpet, her legs at an odd angle, knees to the side and feet askew as if she'd crumpled to the floor.

Vance stared at the picture in silence, his body stiff, his breath shallow and tight. Finally, he put the picture back in the envelope and said, "I'm going to take this in, then go for a run. I'll be back later."

I didn't remind him that he'd already gone for a run that morning, or that I could take a picture to the Sinclairs for him. I didn't say anything except, "We'll be here, Vance."

I wanted to wrap my arms around him and tell him I loved him, but I didn't. Now wasn't the time. I just stood there, holding Rosie in my arms, and watched him stalk out the door, alone and hurting.

CHAPTER TWENTY-ONE
MAGNOLIA

Vance was gone for hours. I was in the kitchen when he got back, putting together a simple dinner of spaghetti with meat sauce, figuring he could reheat it when he turned up.

He came through the front door wearing the same jeans and a different shirt, his hair wet from a recent shower. He'd either gone for another run or worked out.

I didn't ask. His eyes were shuttered, his jaw stiff. I didn't want to push. Instead, I said, "Hungry? Dinner's almost ready."

"Yeah, starved. Do you want me to take the dog out?" I looked at Scout, whose head had popped up from his paws when Vance walked in the room. "Sure, it's been a while and he needs to get a little exercise."

Vance disappeared through the back door, Scout trotting behind him. I watched them for a few minutes as I stirred the sauce.

Vance threw the ball again and again, patient, not minding the slobber or the way Scout would drop it just a few feet away, never into his hand. I always thought Scout had the idea his humans should run for the ball, too.

I was plating dinner when they came back in. For the first time, we ate in the kitchen sitting room with the television on, barely speaking.

Vance was locked up tight, and I had no idea what to say to break him free. I didn't even know if I should try.

Seeing that picture earlier, the violent end of his parents' lives, I couldn't imagine how hard it must have been. We went to bed early. I tucked Rosie in, and by the time I was finished changing and feeding her, Vance was asleep.

I stood at the side of the bed watching him, his mouth tight even as he slept, creases at the corners of his eyes.

He should've looked restful. It made me nervous to see him under this much strain. He hadn't had a drink in over a year. But, I knew it wasn't that simple. And losing his family was at the root of the demons that had driven him to alcohol in the first place.

It was a triumph that, when faced with that picture, he went for a workout instead of to a bar.

It couldn't have been easy. None of this was easy. I just wished I knew how to help. I climbed in bed beside him, rolling my body into his and draping my arm across his chest.

In his sleep, he held me close. Fingers tangled in my hair, he let out a sigh. I drifted off, lulled by the beat of his heart, holding him as if my touch could heal him while he slept.

I jolted awake in the dark of night and froze, not sure what had pulled me from sleep.

Rosie?

There was no sound from the sitting room. The bed

jerked beside me, the mattress shaking as the headboard smacked the wall.

Vance. Vance had woken me.

I sat up, pushing my hair out of my eyes. The moon was full, bathing the room in translucent light, just enough to show me Vance's wet cheeks, the sight of his mouth open in a soundless cry.

His breath came in pants, and his legs shifted restlessly beneath the sheets. He made a sound of agony, low and guttural, that was almost a word.

"Vance. Vance, wake up." I framed his face with my palms, running my thumbs over his cheekbones to wipe away the tears.

Asleep, trapped in his nightmare, he looked young and defenseless. He made another sound, a moaning protest, but I couldn't decipher the words.

Whatever he was saying, only he could hear it. I sat up and pulled his head and one shoulder into my lap, stroking my fingers through his hair, scratching my nails against his scalp, making soothing sounds and saying, "Vance, wake up. It's okay. Wake up."

His restless movements calmed as I stroked his head, the tears on his cheeks drying under my touch. "Baby, please," I whispered.

I didn't want him to drift back into sleep. I wanted him to wake up, to see his eyes clear of the nightmare, for him to know he was safe and loved.

When his breathing calmed, I shifted to the side, lifting his head out of my lap and sliding down to lie beside him, twining my legs with his and pulling him into my arms, trying to surround him with comfort and affection.

Finally, he let out a long breath and his eyes opened.

"Vance, you awake?" He nodded, raising one hand and brushing his palm across his eyes.

"You had a bad dream," I said. "Do you remember what it was?"

Knowing Vance, he probably didn't want to talk about it. I didn't want to push, but I was afraid to let the nightmare fester inside him. He nodded again.

"Will you tell me?" I asked gently, expecting him to deny me.

"I was there," he said. At first, I didn't understand. Then, thinking of the picture, I was terribly afraid that I did.

"When? Not when it happened," I said, positive he hadn't seen his parents murdered. I knew, everyone knew, that the police had ruled their deaths a murder-suicide, but many believed the real killer was still out there. If Vance had seen them die, the truth wouldn't be a secret.

"Right after," he said, his voice so low I could barely hear him, his eyes fixed on the ceiling, seeing something other than white plaster. "We were supposed to be at Aunt Olivia and Uncle Hugh's house for a sleepover. Annalise was with Charlie and Aunt Olivia. Charlie was just a baby. Tate and Holden were only five. Annalise liked helping with them. Aiden was at a friend's house. Maybe if he'd been home, he would've kept the rest of us out of trouble. Aiden's always had an overdeveloped sense of responsibility."

Vance fell silent.

"He kept you guys out of trouble?" I prompted.

Vance let out a humorless laugh. "Most of the time. But some of the worst shit we did was his idea. That night, we were bored, couldn't sleep. It was spring break, just getting warm out. Uncle Hugh wasn't home, at the club I think, and Aunt Olivia had stayed home because Charlie wasn't feeling well and she didn't want to leave her with the nanny. Not with all the kids staying at their house.

"My mom and dad weren't even supposed to be home. Gage and Jacob and I wanted to play Sega, but the cartridge we needed was at my house. I was the youngest, and Gage and Jacob dared me to go home and get it by myself."

"In the dark?" I asked. "How far away was your house?"

"It was close. Less than a quarter-mile through the trees. I didn't have to leave the estate. It was dark and the woods were kind of creepy, but there was no way I was going to tell Gage and Jacob I was chicken. Not when I'd been bragging that I could crush them at Rayman. I ran the whole way. Something spooked me, probably just a bird or my imagination, and I booked it down the path.

"When I saw the lights of the house through the trees, I was relieved. It didn't occur to me that it should have been dark. My parents were supposed to be at the club with Uncle Hugh. They always turned the lights off when they left. But the whole house was lit up, and the door to my dad's office was wide open. I was afraid I was going to get in trouble, but it was so quiet, I decided no one was home. I went to turn off the lights in my dad's office and I saw them."

"Oh God, Vance. I'm so sorry."

Tears leaked from my eyes. I wrapped my arm tighter around his chest and squeezed, wishing I could take the memory from him.

He'd only been eight or nine. A little boy.

I'd found my grandmother, and the sight of her dead body, looking like she was asleep in her bed, had torn my heart out, but I'd been an adult and she'd been in her eighties.

His parents' bodies, the bullet wounds and the blood—

Vance never should have seen any of it. Not in a photograph and never in real life.

"I probably fucked up the scene," he went on. "Nobody said anything to me about it, but I was just a kid and I didn't think about evidence. I ran in and went straight to my mom, trying to wake her up before I realized it was too late. Then I did the second stupid thing of the night and called the police."

"Oh, Vance, that wasn't stupid. You were eight years old. And what you saw? You should've called the police."

"I should've called Maxwell Sinclair. He could've gotten the police without the media, could've kept the whole thing quiet. If I'd called Maxwell, everything would've been different."

"Vance, you're not being reasonable. You were a child. I'm impressed you had the self-possession to think to call the police at all. You can't blame yourself. And I'm sorry to tell you, but that kind of crime in *your* family? Even if you'd handled it perfectly, the media would've been all over you. You know that."

When Hugh and Olivia had died in an almost identical murder, they'd been adults and they'd been careful—so very careful—and it hadn't helped at all. Vance let out a sigh of resignation.

"Maybe not. My mother was still warm when I touched her. If I had been a few minutes earlier, I could've saved them," he said.

A chill stabbed through my gut.

"Or you would've been killed, too," I said.

Vance rolled on his side to face me. "You don't think my father killed her and then killed himself? That's what the police report says."

"No," I said, meeting his eyes, their color almost black in

208

the dark room. "My grandmother knew your parents well. She always said the investigation missed something, had to have, because there was no way your father would've ever hurt your mom. She remembered their wedding and said they were so in love that even after four kids and two busy careers, she'd see them having dinner at the club together and they looked like they were on a first date, your dad pulling out your mom's chair, your mom blushing and holding his hand. She said there was no way, that there must've been someone else there."

"Then why didn't they find anyone?" Vance asked.

"I don't know," I said. "My grandmother always said she thought the police were afraid to push too hard, that they were scared of what they'd find and they just wanted it to go away. But Vance, if she's right—and my grandmother is not the only person I've heard talk about this—you probably would've been killed too if you'd been home any earlier. Your parents loved you. They would not have wanted that. Would you? If it was the same situation, would you want Rosie to come in and try to save your life at risk to her own?"

"No. No, of course not," he said immediately.

The words settled into the quiet room, and Vance's muscles relaxed.

"I wish I could take those memories away," I said. "I wish you hadn't seen that. And if I ever find out who's sending those pictures . . ." I trailed off.

"You have to get in line for that," Vance said. "If we ever find out who's behind the pictures . . . probably better if the Sinclairs find them first."

"I just don't understand why they're sending them in the first place," I said. "Is it about your family? Is someone just trying to make you miserable?"

Vance shook his head, his eyes tired and frustrated. "If

that's their plan, it's fucking twisted. When I saw Jacob's picture, the way they'd colored in the tie, I thought it might be a clue. But none of us could figure out what it meant, and if somebody knows who killed my parents, why send us the pictures? Why not just tell the police? It doesn't make any goddamn sense."

"Was there anything weird about this picture?" I hadn't wanted to look closely enough to find out.

"Yeah," Vance said, "My father's cufflinks weren't his cufflinks. We're trying to figure out what it means. Aiden thought they looked familiar, but he couldn't place them. The whole thing is just fucked up, and I don't like the idea that someone is watching us closely enough to know that I'm living with you and felt safe enough to come to your house."

I hadn't even thought about that part of it. I'd been so worried about Vance that it hadn't occurred to me that a stranger who possibly meant us harm had been at the front door. I opened my mouth to ask Vance about it when he said,

"Evers is setting up all new security on the house. Please don't argue with me about it. Your grandmother barely has workable locks, the wiring for the old system is shot, and you never use it anyway. It's not safe. You're too isolated from your neighbors here."

"I'm right in the middle of Buckhead," I protested.

The second the words left my mouth, I realized how stupid they were. This was one of the safest neighborhoods in the country. And Vance had lost his parents and his aunt and uncle less than a mile from where we were sleeping.

A stranger had been at the front door earlier today, someone who possibly had a grudge against the Winters family. If Vance wanted to update the security, if it would help him sleep at night, I wasn't going to fight him.

"I'm sorry," I said. "Whatever you want to do is fine. Just have Evers send me the bill."

Vance's finger pressed to my lips, stopping my words. "Shut it, Magnolia. I'm not sending you the fucking bill."

"Whatever you want, Vance," I said against his finger, just before I bit him. He yanked his finger back and sucked on it, giving me an exaggerated wounded look. "Do you have a lot of nightmares?" I asked carefully.

"More often in the last year," he said, his eyes avoiding mine, fixed on my mouth.

Since he'd stopped drinking, he meant. I guessed that when he'd been drinking, there'd been no dreams.

"What do you do when you have a nightmare?" I asked.

"Usually, I go for a run or up on the roof to work out, sweat it out of my system."

"You already went for a run today," I said.

"Twice," he agreed, skimming his hand down my side and over my ass to hook behind my knee. He pulled my leg up over his hip.

I was wearing a stretchy, spaghetti strap nightgown— more online shopping—but I hadn't worn any underwear to bed.

Vance's fingers dipped between my legs, stroking me, lingering on my clit before sliding back up to pull the strap of my nightgown off my shoulder and down my arm.

"I don't want to go running again."

"No, I don't think you should," I said, trying not to smile as he traced a circle around my nipple, the flesh tightening into a point at his touch. I reached between our bodies and wrapped my fingers around his erection. He was mostly hard, and he surged in my grip.

"You might pull a muscle if you get too much more exercise today," I said seriously. "You should let me do all the work."

"You did all the work last time," he said, flipping me onto my back and rising over me after grabbing a condom.

"That's not how I remember it," I said, wrapping my legs around his hips. He kissed me, his mouth gentle, seeking, the kiss so much more than a prelude to sex.

I hooked my feet behind his ass and tightened my legs, pulling him into me, urging his cock against my pussy. He rocked into me, spreading the gathering moisture until we were both slick with it and he could press inside with slow, delicious pressure.

So slow. He filled me with deep, deliberate thrusts, kissing me the same way. Deliberately. Carefully.

Dragging out the pleasure of it until I was shaking, tears spilling down my cheeks, the intensity of our connection overwhelming.

The orgasm took me in one long wave, pulling me under until I was gasping with pleasure, my arms wound around his shoulders holding him tightly.

I couldn't tell Vance what was in my heart. Not yet. Maybe not ever. But I held him to me, my body trembling beneath his, hoping that he knew, hoping that some hidden part of him knew how much he was loved.

CHAPTER
TWENTY-TWO
VANCE

F amily meeting tonight. 7pm. Bring Maggie and Rosalie.

Aiden. I'd talked to him the day before when he'd met me at the Sinclair offices to look at the photograph. I assumed he was calling the meeting to discuss it with everyone else.

Fine with me. We didn't have plans for the night, and I'd take any chance to hang with my family and show off my girls.

Magnolia was at home, supervising the installation of the security system. She was getting the works—motion triggered video, panic buttons, driveway sensor—anything the Sinclairs could think of that would keep her safe.

I had Rosie with me, though she was currently fast asleep, giving me some much-needed quiet time.

We'd been slacking at work. Most of the prep for the show was finished, and we didn't have any investments that needed direct input.

If Rosie hadn't entered our lives, we would have jumped into a new project as soon as the show was set up, but for the past few weeks, we'd been enjoying a looser schedule.

Still, shit piled up. A few days of ignoring my email, and my inbox was clogged—fires to put out, calls to return. I'd been making good progress when Aiden's text had popped up on my phone. I took a second to text Magnolia before getting back to work.

Dinner at W House? 7pm? Everyone will be there.

She answered back immediately. *Sure. Pick me up?*

I'll be back before that. Almost done here.

K. How's Rosie?

I sent her a picture of Rosie in the floor gym, passed out on her back, one little hand still in the ring she'd been tugging when sleep had gotten the better of her.

Magnolia sent back an emoji of a ribboned heart, then, *Better get back to work before she wakes up.*

Slave driver.

Don't make me crack the whip :)

Yes, Ma'am.

I put my phone down and tried to get back to my to-do list, but now I was distracted by the image of Magnolia in black leather, cracking a whip.

She wasn't the dominatrix type, but she would sure as shit be hot in black leather. She'd almost made me come in my pants with that black lace lingerie the day before. Jesus.

Lately, it seemed like fucking Magnolia Henry was the cure for everything that had ever gone wrong in my life. Seeing that picture of my parents had been enough to leave me desperate for a drink, every beat of my heart, every breath tasting of raw pain.

I'd never shake that memory. It was burned into my brain. But the picture made it real in a way it hadn't been in years. Alcohol was my friend. Alcohol would chase off the memories. The guilt.

If Magnolia hadn't been there, I might have done it. I'd like to think Rosie would have been enough to make me stop and think. I could lie and say my daughter was the reason I hadn't gone straight to a bar.

She was part of it. Sure, she was. But Magnolia was the rest. She was the real reason. I had to stay sober if I wanted Magnolia.

Rosie would never remember if I fucked up and got wasted. She wasn't even five months old. But Magnolia would. She'd be my friend no matter what. I didn't doubt that.

But she'd never let me back in her bed if I started drinking again. I couldn't think of many things worse than being kicked out of Magnolia's bed. Not now that I'd had a taste of her.

The thing was, with her there, my body freshly sated with hers, her gentle smile and open heart, I knew I could handle the memories. That certainty settled in my bones when she woke me from the nightmare.

It was a familiar hell, the dream of finding them, lifeless in our home, still warm, blood leaking from bullet wounds in a slow drip.

I was used to coming out of the nightmare alone, used to heading straight for the bottle, or more recently, the gym, to burn the pain from my body and to sweat out the memories.

Magnolia petting me, soothing me with her low voice while she stroked my hair, her nails gently scratching my scalp—that was way fucking better.

Her touch, her body, was more home to me than any place or person had been since I was eight years old.

I picked up my phone and prepared to make yet another

call. I wanted to get this business over with so Rosie and I could go home to Magnolia. I had the number on the screen when the security system beeped to let me know someone was at the door.

Fuck. Switching apps on my phone, I pulled up the camera.

Fuck.

Fuck.

Sloane.

Of all the people I didn't feel like talking to, Sloane was at the top of the list. She was annoying on a good day. Since she'd discovered Magnolia and I were together, she'd been a royal bitch.

Unfortunately, we had a show in two days. I couldn't ignore her, as much as I wanted to.

I tapped the microphone button on the app and said, "Come on up, Sloane." Another tap, and I unlocked the door. I heard the whir of the elevator a few seconds later.

Rising from my desk, I met her at the door. I wanted to head her off so she didn't wake Rosie.

"Sloane, Rosie's sleeping. Let's stay in the kitchen."

"Fine," she snapped, her dark eyebrows drawn together. "Why isn't Maggie watching her?"

"Because Rosie's my daughter, and Magnolia had other business to take care of today."

"You need to get a nanny, Vance. You have better things to do than take care of an infant."

"No, I don't," I said. "The most important thing I have to do right now is spend time with my daughter. Everything else comes second."

"Even Maggie?" Sloane asked, a sly smile on her face.

"Magnolia is none of your business," I said.

"I never would have sent her to you if I thought you'd

end up fucking her. She held you off long enough, but I guess you got to her eventually. I shouldn't be surprised. I've heard you can talk a nun into spreading her legs."

"Sloane," I warned. She shrugged.

"Aren't you going to offer me coffee?" she asked.

"No. I'm slammed, and I want to get home. I thought everything was ready for the show. What do you want?"

"You don't need to get home, Vance. You *are* home. Don't let the baby and Maggie delude you. You're an artist. Playing house is fun for a while, but you can't sustain it long-term. You don't have it in you. It's not who you are."

I was rapidly losing patience. "You don't know anything about who I am, Sloane. Magnolia and Rosie aren't your concern."

"Wrong," she said, her eyes hard. "I couldn't care less about the baby, but when you fuck over Maggie, you're going to lose your business manager, which is going to disrupt your production. That *is* my concern."

"I'm not going to fuck over Magnolia," I said. Sloane rolled her eyes.

"Of course you are," she said, laughing a little. "When was the last time you slept with the same woman twice in a row? I've never known you to have a girlfriend. Now you move in with Maggie and think you're what, husband material? Be serious."

"Sloane, you have no clue what you're talking about. I'm not looking to be 'husband material'. I'm still trying to figure out how to be a father. We've got enough going on right now without you trying to complicate it."

"I'm not trying to complicate it, Vance," she said, and the sympathy in her eyes almost seemed genuine. "I'm trying to simplify it. All you should be worrying about is your art and your business. Fucking with Magnolia is going to fuck with your business. It's that simple. End it with her. Get a nanny. Or make her the nanny. I don't care. She's pretty much your nanny as it is now, anyway."

"She's not the nanny," I snapped, wondering for the first time if this was how everyone else saw it.

Did the whole world assume I was just fucking Magnolia to get her to help me with Rosie? Is that why they were so curious about whether we were dating?

I shook my head. No way. Maybe Sloane thought that, and Brayden. But if my family thought I was using Magnolia, they would've kicked my ass already. And I knew Magnolia didn't believe that.

I thought about the night before, the way she'd wiped tears from my face and welcomed me into her body. No, Magnolia knew this was about so much more than sex. And so did I.

Sloane could go fuck herself.

"If you need to get laid . . ." Sloane said.

Suggestion dripped from her words as she sauntered across the kitchen, not coming to a stop until she was so close her hips bumped mine.

Too close.

From a distance, Sloane was gorgeous. Shiny black hair, green eyes, cheekbones that could cut glass, long legs, and round, high tits.

She knew how to dress, with class and style, even if her hemlines were a little short and she showed too much cleavage. But up close?

Up close, the illusion fell apart.

Her tits were fake, she was bony, and she wore way too much makeup. Not that I was tempted, but I'd always suspected she'd be a shitty fuck. Way too selfish and self-involved to relax and have fun.

"What are you doing Sloane?" I asked, taking a step to the side to put some space between us. I'd gotten used to the feel of Magnolia's soft, round body pressed to mine. Sloane was a gnawed-on bone in comparison.

"Like I said, I'm trying to simplify things." She took a step to the side herself and laid her palms on my chest, smoothing them up to grip my shoulders, trying to pull me down for a kiss. Not going to happen.

"You think fucking me would simplify things? You're insane."

I grabbed her wrists and peeled her hands off my shoulders, trying to push her back. For someone so skinny, she was strong.

Sloane was shorter than me, the top of her head barely reaching my chin, but she planted her toes on the top of my foot and lunged up, pressing her mouth to mine.

That was it. I was trying to be careful, hadn't wanted to hurt her, but I was done. Fucking done. I pushed her back and stepped away, putting the island between us while she got her balance on her spike heels.

"What?" she said, her over-plucked eyebrows raised in surprise.

"What are you doing? Are you crazy?" At that moment, I was kind of thinking that she was. As if she were a rabid animal who might lunge at any moment, I took another step back.

"It never seemed worth jeopardizing our working arrangement, but I've always wanted you. I thought if you were willing to lower yourself to fuck Maggie Henry, you probably weren't that worried about mixing sex and business, so I thought I'd take a shot."

"You're. Fucking. Fired," I said.

Few words had ever given me such satisfaction.

I'd stayed with Sloane out of apathy. She was a bitch, but she was good at her job. Finding another manager and gallery would be a pain in the ass, but she'd gone way too far.

"What?" she screeched. "You can't fire me. We have a contract."

She was right, we did have a contract. Fortunately for me, I knew the terms of that contract in detail.

"You can expect a letter from me detailing the severance of our business relationship per the terms of the contract," I said. "Thirty days from receipt of that letter, we will no longer have a business relationship. Whatever doesn't sell at the show on Friday, you have those thirty days to sell, and then I'll take the work back."

"Vance, don't overreact. I'm sorry if I was out of line." Sloane took a few hesitant steps toward me, but the look on my face must've stopped her, because she met my eyes and ground to a halt.

"You were way more than out of line, Sloane. I'm done with the way you talk about Magnolia, I'm done with the way you talk about my daughter, and I'm done with your attitude. We'll get through the show together, and then I don't want to see you again. Do you understand?"

She shook her head, dismissing me. "Once you calm down, Vance, you'll change your mind. I won't even hold it against you. I understand you've been under a lot of pressure. We'll just forget we had this conversation."

Not meeting my eyes, she walked around the other side of the island and headed for the door. I let her go without comment.

I wasn't going to change my mind. The hassle of finding a new agent seemed so much less important than never having to see Sloane again.

I pulled up the number of a courier service I'd used a few times and requested that someone come by immediately to pick up and deliver a letter.

Once that was arranged, I headed straight for my laptop and the printer. I wasn't going to waste any time getting out the letter severing our business relationship.

The show was in two days, and I knew well enough that I was going to get distracted. I wanted Sloane taken care of before she could cause any more trouble.

Chapter Twenty-Three

Magnolia

"You okay, Babe?" Vance asked, shooting me a look when we pulled up to a stop sign.

"Just tired," I lied. It wasn't completely a lie. I *was* tired. Rosie wanted her formula every few hours, never mind if it was the middle of the night.

We switched off night-time feedings, but it was still exhausting. I liked my sleep, preferably a solid eight hours of it. At this point, eight hours of uninterrupted sleep was a distant memory.

Lack of sleep wasn't why I was so quiet. It was the phone calls.

First, Brayden's. Six of them, each with increasingly desperate messages. He needed to talk to me, wanted to meet, didn't understand why I was ignoring him.

I didn't pick up. I should have erased the messages without listening.

Brayden's calls weren't as bad as the one from Sloane. That one, I did answer. I had to. We had a show in two days, and I still had a job to do.

I knew she was just causing trouble, and I knew she was

a bitch. That didn't make it any easier to hear her shrill voice telling me about her 'intimate tête-à-tête' with Vance.

I didn't believe for a second that he'd touched her, despite her insinuations. Vance didn't find Sloane attractive, a point he'd made clear more than once.

That didn't mean I liked hearing her say, "I see why you fell for him, darling. His mouth is delicious."

It was, but there was no way Vance had kissed Sloane. No way. He wasn't a cheater.

But the other part? When she'd said, " I don't know how to tell you this, but I thought you should know. We were talking about things, and he said straight out, *'I'm not looking to be husband material. I'm still trying to figure out how to be a father. I've got enough going on without making it complicated.'* His words exactly, Maggie. I just didn't want you to get your hopes up. You two work so well together, and I know how mixing sex with business can lead to disappointments."

There had been catty triumph in her voice, which was—oddly enough—the reason I believed she'd quoted him accurately. When she talked about his mouth, her voice had been high-pitched, with a barely discernible thread of anxiety. But when she quoted him, she sounded nothing but smug.

I could hear those words coming out of his mouth. Easily imagine him saying them. We'd never talked about what our relationship meant or where it was going.

If it was going anywhere. Rosie had shown up, they'd moved in with me, and then Vance and I had fallen into bed together. It was all so very convenient for him, wasn't it? I was just along for the ride.

Vance hadn't made any promises. He had never given me the impression he was thinking long-term. The best I'd gotten from him was that this wasn't 'casual'. But that didn't tell me anything at all.

Dwelling on it wasn't going to do me any good. We were in the car on the way to Winters House, would be there any second, and if I looked mopey and upset, Charlie would pick up on it. The others might too, but Charlie knew me best. I didn't want to talk about it with her.

Charlie loved me, but Vance was her cousin, close as a brother, and I knew she'd just tell me to hang in there. Maybe she was right, but I'd spent years 'hanging in there' for Brayden only to get dumped. Waiting for Vance to figure out what he wanted was feeling less appealing by the day.

Aiden met us at the door, looking as casual as I'd ever seen him in an untucked button down and jeans.

Before I could think to stop him, he took the baby carrier from me, deftly unsnapped Rosie, and gave her a smacking kiss on the nose. She pressed her palms to his cheeks and drooled in delight.

Aiden noticed us staring and said, "What?"

"I never thought of you as being good with babies," I said. Most of my interactions with Aiden were business related. He was a shark in a suit, not a guy you pictured tickling babies under their chins. With comfortable ease, he held Rosie against his chest.

"I'm the oldest of the eight of us. I was nine when Charlotte was born. Trust me, I've changed my share of diapers."

He didn't wait for a response, but turned and led us into the house. I'd been to Winters House a few times before, but never when it was so full of family. The house was formal, designed in a grand Mediterranean style, but the sound of voices softened it, made it welcoming.

It looked like the entire Winters clan was gathered in

the parlor. The room, with its high ceilings, Persian rugs, and polished woodwork, demanded cocktail dresses and suits. Everyone wore jeans except for Tate's girlfriend, Emily, and Jacob's girlfriend, Abigail.

Emily had a sense of style I envied. Even casually dressed, her look had flair. I loved her cropped lime pants and fitted cream lace top. I needed to get her to take me shopping. I tended toward the boring at work, and lately, my wardrobe was whatever I threw on that I didn't mind Rosie destroying.

But maybe when she stopped throwing up on me, I could talk Emily into giving me some pointers. I was never going to be as polished as Charlie or Abigail, but I could use a little more style.

Abigail headed for us, her heels clicking on the wood floors. She was never anything less than elegant. I wasn't sure she even owned jeans. Tonight, she wore a pale pink sheath dress with black spike heel sandals. She looked gorgeous, but the sight of her shoes made my toes hurt.

She made a beeline straight for Aiden and plucked Rosie from his arms. Turning to us, she said accusingly, "You've been keeping all the baby goodness to yourselves. Unfair. You *do* know I'm available to babysit."

Vance grinned at her and put his arm around me. "No, we didn't. But now that we do, I can promise we'll take you up on it."

"See that you do. She's adorable." Abigail dropped her head and breathed in the scent of Rosie. I had to admit, except when she needed a diaper change, Rosie always had that deliciously sweet baby smell. Like lavender and baby powder and love.

"She looks so much like you," Abigail said.

"If you mean devastatingly attractive, then yes, she

does," Vance said, winking at Abigail, who looked at me and shook her head.

"Vance Winters is a rogue," she stated. "But I'm sure you already know that."

I laughed. "I'm not going to argue," I said. "But he has his good points."

"I'm standing right here," he protested. Abigail looked up at him, a gleam in her eye, and said, "You are standing right here. And while I've got your attention, and your daughter, I wanted to know—are you aware that the Winters Foundation is doing a benefit next month for ACFB? It's a silent auction—"

Vance cut her off with a grin. "I'm always good to support the food bank," he said. "You can have whatever you want."

"Whatever I want? What if I want a Vance Winters piece for the auction? Do you have anything you're willing to donate?"

Vance shook his head. "Anything that's not sold would work. Why don't you hook up with Magnolia, and she can take you through what's available? Pick what you want before the show this weekend, and we'll mark it as sold."

"I'll have to talk to Sloane about it," I said, "but we can put together a plaque stating that it's available at the silent auction and maybe drum up some interest for the benefit at Vance's show."

Abigail beamed. "Wonderful, wonderful. Thank you so much." In a lower voice, she said, "This is my first big event for the Foundation, and I want it to be perfect. I got thrown into this last-minute and I'm a little nervous."

"I'm sure it'll be a success," I reassured her. "If you have time tomorrow, we can get together and I can take you through what we have. We can talk to Sloane—"

"Oh, yeah, by the way—I fired Sloane," Vance said, looking a little uncomfortable.

"What?" I asked, shocked. "When?"

"This afternoon," he said. "I don't want to get into it. We can talk later, but we're not working with her any longer. After the show is over, she'll have another thirty days before the contract officially terminates, but she might give you some trouble tomorrow. I'll take Abigail to the gallery."

"Why don't you want me to go?" I asked, suspicious.

What had happened with Sloane? She hadn't said anything about Vance firing her when she'd called earlier. Vance shook his head.

"We can talk about it later. Just stay away from her."

I shrugged. This wasn't the time to grill him about Sloane.

"Call me tomorrow morning," Vance said to Abigail, "and we'll set something up. Now, are you going to give me my kid back?"

"Not yet," Jacob said, interrupting. He slid an arm around Abigail's waist, pulling her against his chest, looking down to study her face as she cuddled Rosalie.

If Aiden was a shark in a suit, Jacob had a reputation for being even worse. He was cold, hard, and uncompromising.

He'd always been kind to me, but I didn't doubt the rumors. Seeing the look on his face as he watched Abigail with Rosie, I also believed the rumors that Jacob Winters was deeply in love.

There was something in his eyes, more than affection, more than warmth. He looked at her like she was everything to him. Like she was his world.

Abigail tilted her face toward Jacob, but didn't take her eyes off Rosie's. "Do you want to hold her?" she asked. Jacob took Rosie with the same ease Aiden had displayed.

At Abigail's look of surprise, he said, "Aiden wasn't the only one with a herd of younger cousins and siblings. By the time Charlie was five, I swore I never wanted to see another baby again. But this one looks okay."

He nuzzled the top of his Rosie's head, the tender gesture surprising.

We were interrupted by the sound of metal striking glass and turned to see Holden grinning, his arm around Emily, the fork he'd struck against his glass dangling in his hand.

Wait, what? Emily was Tate's girlfriend. Why did Holden have his arm around her like that? Jo, Holden's girl, was watching with a half-smile.

"We have an announcement," he said, the wide grin on his face matching the one on Tate's, in contrast to the semi-amused scowl Emily wore.

"We don't have to do this now," she said. "We haven't actually decided."

"Yes we have. I heard it. Tate heard it. Josephine heard it. Aiden heard it. You agreed. Deal's done."

"Fine," Emily muttered. "Go ahead."

"Tate and I are very pleased to announce," Holden said, "that Emily has finally agreed to join us at WGC after she graduates."

Tate let out a whoop and tugged Emily out of Holden's grasp, lifting her in the air and spinning her around. "She also agreed to move in with me," Tate said.

Emily laughed and protested, "Tate, shut up."

"No fucking way," he said, setting her back on her feet and kissing her. When he was done, he said, "Do you know how stubborn you are?"

"Apparently, not as stubborn as you," she shot back.

"Damn straight," he said. Vance turned to Holden, now standing beside us, one arm around Josephine.

"Why didn't Tate make the announcement?" Vance asked.

Jo laughed. "Because Emily refused to negotiate with Tate. She said he was devious and he knew how to talk her into anything."

"Smart," I said. "How long did it take you to talk her into signing on?"

Holden shook his head in exasperation. "Too long. We've been trying to get her on board since we found out she designed a game we both like. But she said it was a conflict of interest. She's very stubborn. But she's also a huge fan of *Syndrome* and crazy in love with Tate, so we had an edge."

Syndrome was Winters Gaming Group's flagship game and a massive hit. Both Emily and Josephine were computer science grad students at Georgia Tech.

Josephine was doing work I didn't really understand with some kind of device meant to help the blind navigate. Word was they'd made good progress with it, and Josephine would have her pick of employers when she graduated.

But Emily's specialty was game design, making her a perfect fit not just for Tate, but for his company. I wasn't surprised they'd talked her into working for them, even though the last time the subject had come up, she'd been adamant about not taking any handouts.

From what Tate and Holden said about her talents, offering her a job was no handout. They were lucky to have her.

"You're not going to make another announcement, are you?" Josephine asked Holden in an undertone.

"Do you want me to?" he asked, dropping a kiss on her

temple. She shook her head. "Not really, but you can tell Vance and Magnolia."

Curious, I waited. Vance interrupted to say, "Josephine's moving in with you."

"Did you tell him already?" Jo asked Holden.

"He didn't have to. He wouldn't let Tate get one up on him like that."

Holden sent Vance a glare that was only partly in jest. "Jo moving in with me has nothing to do with Tate. I've been trying to get her to move in with me since our first date. But she didn't want to stick Emily with their lease, and Emily refused to do the same to her, so Tate and I had to gang up on them to get our way."

He looked so pleased with himself, I had to laugh. I knew Holden well before Josephine had shown up, and I would have put him at the top of my list of guys who were never going to settle down.

He'd met Jo at Mana, the club he owned with Tate, while she was on a date with another guy. One look at her, and he'd fallen hard.

It was cute because while Jo was pretty, with her dark blonde hair and intelligent blue eyes, she was not the girl I would have thought would capture Holden's attention. She was a geek, in the coolest way possible, and was more often to be found in old jeans and a hoodie than in club wear.

I guess while Holden had been happy to hook up with the girls he met at the club, that wasn't what he wanted long-term. He looked completely satisfied with his life, his arm around Jo and a smile in his dark eyes.

Charlotte poked her head in the living room, still wearing the suit she'd worn to work. She gave us a wave and said, "I'll be right back."

She returned five minutes later in jeans and an Emory

T-shirt, her hair in a messy ponytail, her face cleaned of makeup.

Like that, she looked about fifteen, except for the circles under her eyes and the pallor to her skin. Heading straight for Abigail and Jacob, she scooped up Rosie before Abigail could protest.

Jacob leaned down to whisper something in Abigail's ear that brought a pretty pink flush to her cheeks. It was both sweet and bizarre to see him so gentle and affectionate with Abigail.

I'd sat in on investor meetings with Jacob, and while I liked him, he was a little scary. Not with Abigail. With her, he was a completely different man.

Charlotte only got a few minutes to blow kisses on Rosie's cheek before Mrs. Williamson, the Winters family housekeeper, announced that dinner was served.

Now in her forties, Mrs. Williamson had come to the house as a maid when she was only eighteen, not long before Vance's parents had died.

With the house mostly empty these days, Aiden and Charlotte didn't need much staff, but Mrs. Williamson was more than staff. She was family. And even with fewer residents, the house and grounds still needed full-time management.

We were all casual, but the only place a group this large would fit was the formal dining room, and we followed Mrs. Williamson down the hall. The table was long enough to fit twice our number. She'd seated us at one end, close to the fireplace. Despite its size, the fire and the polished wood furnishings made the room cozy.

I started to look for the baby carrier, thinking I'd give Rosie a bottle and hopefully she'd fall asleep while we ate, but Mrs. Williamson appeared at my side, took Rosie from

Charlie, and said, "Don't worry, I've got this one. It's been way too long since we've had a baby in the house."

Charlotte sat beside me, Vance on the other side. I scooted my chair closer to Charlie's and whispered, "You look tired. Are you okay?"

"Yes, and ditto. Rosie keeping you up? Or something else?"

Charlotte could see right through me, but I wasn't going to talk about any of the doubts plaguing my mind at the Winters family dining table. Not with Vance sitting beside me. I had to work this out on my own.

"I'm fine," I said. "I just couldn't fall asleep last night after I got up to feed Rosie, and I'm worn out, that's all. What's going on with you?"

"Nothing," Charlie whispered back. I didn't call her a liar out loud, but I knew she could see it in my eyes. She let out a sigh and said, "That house I showed you? It's under contract."

"Oh, that stinks. Is that what's bothering you?" I asked.

Charlie shrugged one shoulder and didn't meet my eyes. "Not all of it," she said. "But a lot of it, yeah. I guess I didn't realize how much I wanted the house until it was gone."

"The house or the lawnmower hottie next door?" I teased, nudging the side of her chair. A light flush brought color to her cheeks, and she shook her head, her ponytail swinging from side to side. I said, "I think it's the hottie as much as the house."

Charlotte's cheeks turned even pinker. "It's not the hottie," she protested. "I really liked that house."

"Then call the agent," I said. "Just because it's under contract, it doesn't mean it's sold. A lot of stuff could go wrong. You never know."

"Maybe," Charlotte said.

"Do it," I urged. "Just in case. Now that you know, really know, that you want it, it'll make you feel better if you at least make a phone call."

"I'll do it tomorrow," she promised. The cook, who I'd never met personally but who Charlotte said was amazing, served us himself.

I had to agree with Charlotte's assessment. His food was spectacular. Herb roasted chicken, mashed potatoes, green beans, and chocolate cake for dessert.

It was comfort food, not gourmet, but every bite was perfection. I'd forgotten what it was like to eat a dinner I hadn't cooked without rushing to finish before Rosie needed one of us.

By the time I took the last bite of chocolate cake, I was stuffed full, almost woozy with satiation.

I drank a glass of wine with dinner, and the wine combined with the food had me almost asleep on the short drive home. Vance's aggravated voice brought me back to full consciousness.

"What the fuck is he doing here?" Vance said, smacking his hand on the steering wheel for emphasis. I looked up and noticed with dismay that Brayden's luxury sedan was parked in front of the door. What the hell did he want with me?

"He's been calling me all day," I said without thinking. At the dark expression on Vance's face, I wished I'd kept my mouth shut. He looked like he wanted to beat Brayden to a pulp, and Brayden was absolutely the kind of guy who would press charges.

"Stay in the car," Vance ordered.

"No way," I said, undoing my seatbelt and jumping out as soon as the car came to a halt.

I was around the hood and facing off with Brayden a

second later, Vance right behind me. He put one hand on my shoulder, but he didn't try to move me.

"Do you want me to call the police?" I said to Brayden. "Because I think I was very clear the last time you came to my house that if I saw you here again, I would call the police."

"Magnolia—" Brayden started. I was in no mood to listen.

"You don't have any right to be here. There's nothing of yours in the house, and you don't live here anymore. Go. Away."

"If you'd answer your phone or return one of my calls, I wouldn't have to come by," Brayden said with exaggerated patience.

Just the sound of his voice put my teeth on edge.

"I didn't get everything of mine out of the house. I need to come back in and go through some of the closets. I lived here for three years, and my stuff was spread all over. Unless you've been through every single room, you don't know that I didn't leave anything, and I know that I did, so stop being such a bitch about it."

"I will call you tomorrow," I said, slowly and deliberately. "I'm not letting you in the house tonight. We're tired, Rosie's tired, and I just want to go to bed."

"Why not just let me in now?" Brayden said.

His refusal to leave was irritating the hell out of me. I didn't think this was about me, about us, but the next thing he said made me wonder.

"You think you've got it all figured out now, don't you? Shacked up with Winters and his kid? You think I'm the asshole for breaking up with you and cheating on you. Maybe I am. But you're the stupid one.

"You're a fucking doormat. You let me get away with

murder for years—I let you pay the bills, I was cheating on you, and I strung you along with an engagement when I had no intention of marrying you. So yeah, I'm an asshole, but here you are letting this guy do the same fucking thing. He gets a kid all of a sudden, and now you're what? His girlfriend or his nanny? Just remember that while you're blowing me off, thinking he's got your back. He's doing the same thing to you that I did. At least I'm willing to admit it."

Brayden got into his car and slammed the door. Vance's hand tightened on my shoulder and he jerked me backward, out of the way, as Brayden hit the gas, tires spinning, and flew past us down the driveway.

I stood there, frozen, Brayden's words ping-ponging back and forth inside my head. There was something vindicating about his admission that he was an asshole.

I hated having it laid out that way, how he'd intentionally used me. It was humiliating that he'd admitted it so easily. It was also liberating, in a way.

Yes, I'd been an idiot. I knew that. But it reminded me that the real failure in our relationship had nothing to do with me. It was him.

Brayden was an enormous flaming jerk.

The only thing I'd done wrong was put up with him.

Which left me with Vance. That part of Brayden's little speech stung. Vance was not Brayden. He wasn't. I knew he wasn't. I wanted to believe that I'd learned my lesson. I wasn't a doormat.

Not anymore.

But what Brayden had said was so close to Sloane's accusations. Vance himself had admitted to Sloane that he wasn't looking to be anyone's husband.

I wasn't expecting a ring. We'd only been together a few weeks, but I had to be honest with myself. He and his daughter were living in my house. If he wasn't thinking that we were a family, didn't see himself as a husband, then what were we doing?

I felt a little sick. I was in love with Vance. He was my closest friend, and I'd fallen in love with him. My whole life was wrapped up in him.

I shook my head, trying to banish my uncertainty. Vance was not Brayden. It might look the same from the outside, but I was not making the same mistakes with Vance I'd made with Brayden. I wasn't.

"You okay, Babe?" Vance asked. "If he shows up again, don't say a word to him. Just get back in your car and call the police. I don't like that he's so insistent about getting into the house."

I nodded numbly, saying only, "Do you need help with Rosie?"

"I've got her," Vance said, studying my face in the dim light outside the front door. "You sure you're okay? You're not letting him get inside your head, are you?"

"No, I'm fine. I'm just tired," I said.

I was saying that a lot tonight. I was tired. Everything would look better in the morning. I took the keys from Vance and unlocked the front door.

I didn't want to talk anymore, and with everything tumbling around in my head, for the first time, I didn't want to have sex with Vance. I couldn't think when he touched me.

My body trusted him, wanted him, and my brain didn't trust my body.

I washed my face and changed into a nightshirt while Vance was busy with Rosie. When he came to bed, I pretended to be asleep.

CHAPTER TWENTY-FOUR
MAGNOLIA

I woke up to the sound of the baby wailing, my eyes sticky with sleep, my head aching.

I'd fallen asleep as soon as my head hit the pillow the night before, but I felt as though I'd cried myself to sleep. Rosie was moving around in her crib, fretful and unhappy. Vance was nowhere to be seen.

I sat up and pushed the covers back, shaking my hair out of my eyes. I had to get to Rosie. I stumbled into the bathroom to brush my hair and splash water on my face before I pulled on a pair of jeans and a T-shirt.

Rosie's diaper was wet and worse. I loved that baby to death, but good God, her diapers were horrible.

I got her cleaned up and made her a bottle, which stopped her crying and left me desperate for coffee. Both Vance and Scout were missing when I went downstairs, a note leaning against the coffee maker telling me they were out for a run.

At least the coffee maker was full, but it would've been nice of Vance to ask if I wanted to go for a run instead of leaving me with the cranky baby and that toxic waste dump of a diaper.

I put Rosie in the floor gym as soon as she finished her bottle and I'd burped her—mercifully, without her throwing up in my hair—and sat at the island to finish my coffee.

I'd told myself that everything would seem better in the morning. I'd been wrong.

I was just as confused as I'd been when I'd fallen asleep. I was frustrated with Vance and more frustrated with myself. The mess I was in wasn't really his fault.

It was mine. It was me. I was the one who let him in—into my house, into my bed. He never made me any promises, never declared any intentions other than wanting to have sex with me.

I knew Vance cared about me, but I didn't think he was in love with me. And I sure as hell wasn't going to ask him. I was tired of feeling like I was begging for love.

I was head over heels for him, and head over heels for Rosie. I was putting myself out there, my heart on the line, and I was going to end up shattered. When it happened, it wouldn't be anyone's fault but my own.

I stood in the kitchen, looking out the bay window to the backyard, missing my grandmother with every fiber of my being. She was the only time I'd ever known real love. Unconditional love.

The night before, at Winters House, love had been everywhere. Those couples glowed with it. Love was the backbone of the Winters family. They'd been through so much and they would fight to the death for each other.

The only person I'd ever had who loved me was my grandmother, and she was gone.

Was I going to spend the rest of my life satisfied with

crumbs? I realized, too late, that the reason I'd been okay with Brayden's lack of devotion was that I'd had Vance.

By the time things had started going wrong with Brayden, I'd already been working for Vance and we'd grown close. Nothing had ever happened between us. It wasn't a romance, but his friendship had turned into my main source of emotional support.

I hadn't needed Brayden to be perfect, because I'd had Vance. When things eventually fell apart with Vance, I would be alone.

Truly alone.

As if my mind had conjured him up, Vance appeared in the backyard, Scout at his side. He was shirtless, his golden skin gleaming with sweat. Scout followed him through the yard to the carriage house in the rear of the property.

A lot of carriage houses from this era had been turned into guest houses. This one was really no more than a glorified garage that no one used because my grandfather had added an attached garage in the 80s.

The building was in good structural shape and had been freshly painted, but the inside was a disaster of disorganization. Decades of the Henry family's junk—stuff we were attached to or too lazy to throw away.

When Vance opened the door, I was half curious as to where he'd gotten the key and half worried the interior would collapse on his head in a wave of boxes and papers and broken bicycle parts.

He disappeared into the carriage house. It was at least ten minutes and half a cup of coffee before he reappeared, a determined expression on his face, and headed to the back door.

"What's with the carriage house?" he said as soon as I opened the door.

"What do you mean? It's a carriage house. No one uses it, as I'm sure you could tell. Where did you get the key?" I asked.

"It was in the kitchen drawer," he said, shrugging. "I think we should empty it out and turn it into a studio. Then I could work there instead of going in to the loft every day."

I stared at him, speechless. Converting the carriage house to be used as a studio would be a major renovation. Vance's work was a fire hazard. The first floor of his loft had been specifically designed to accommodate his welding equipment.

If he wanted to use the carriage house as a studio, we'd have to gut the building and redesign it from the inside. That was a big deal. A huge commitment.

This house, the property, were the only things I had of my grandparents. I hadn't even redecorated, even though a lot of the furniture didn't suit my style.

Tearing out the inside of one of the buildings to give Vance a studio?

I struggled to find words.

"Magnolia? What? Don't you think it would work?"

"I don't . . . I think . . ." An awful realization washed through me, and words tumbled out. "I think you need to move out." I snapped my mouth shut in horror.

Had I just said that? Vance's eyes widened and his face went pale. I guess I had. I hadn't even been thinking it. I'd just opened my mouth and heard myself speak with no input from my brain.

"You want me to move out? Babe, we don't have to do anything with the carriage house. It was just an idea," he said, turning to grab a coffee cup and filling it.

My stomach rolled with nerves and dismay. I could take

it back. I wasn't sure Vance had really heard me. I opened my mouth again, planning to apologize.

"I think you need to move out," I repeated. I spoke as if on autopilot, my voice flat. "I don't think I can do this with you anymore."

"Do what with me?" he asked, eyeing me warily.

"You and me. I can't do this. Everything changed so fast after you found Rosie. You both moved in, and then we were sleeping together, and now you want me to remodel my house so you can work here . . ."

My voice trailed off, and I wished desperately for the words to explain how I felt, but everything that popped into my head made me sound too vulnerable. Needy.

I was tired of feeling needy.

"Magnolia—" he started, and I interrupted.

"My whole life is about you and Rosie," I said. "Now you want a studio here, and I don't even know what we're doing together. I can't keep playing house with you. I love Rosie. I—"

I almost said it. *I love you.* I bit my tongue hard. I was not going to tell him I loved him. I was not putting myself out there like that. He stared at me, incomprehension all over his face. Did he really not get it?

Apparently, he didn't because he said, "We're not playing house, Magnolia. That's not what this is."

"Then what is it, Vance? If we're not playing house, then what are we doing?"

"We're together," he said in an exasperated tone that implied I should know what that meant.

My frustration exploded out of me in a tirade of words. "What does that mean, we're together? Together, like we're friends who sleep together? Together, like I'm your girlfriend?"

"Like you're my girlfriend, for fuck's sake." He shoved a hand through his hair. "Magnolia, tell me what's wrong."

"I don't know what you want from this," I said, unable to meet his eyes. I didn't want to see annoyance, or worse, pity.

"I don't want anything," he said.

Disappointment speared through me, followed by dull, numbing resignation. I'd hoped. I'd hoped so hard that I was wrong.

"That's what I thought you'd say," I whispered, my voice stuck in my throat.

"That's not what I meant," he said, setting his mug on the counter with a sharp clank. "I want us to be together. That's what I want."

I stared at my bare feet on the hardwood floor. I could still end this whole conversation, shrug and say I was having a bad morning and everything was fine. Was that what I wanted?

With a sick, sinking feeling in my stomach, I knew it wasn't. I didn't want to go on like this, always feeling at a disadvantage, loving Vance and waiting for him to leave me.

Talking around the problem and waiting for him to make his feelings clear wasn't getting me anywhere. I either needed to act like an adult and have the guts to be honest with Vance or I was never going to know where I stood. I'd been protecting myself, but if I wanted the truth, I had to take a risk.

I was going to get burned. I knew it. But I had to know.

Gathering my courage, I raised my eyes to his and asked, "Are you in love with me? Do you want to get married? Have kids with me?"

His face went blank, his lips pressed together. Not the resounding yes I was looking for. My shoulders slumped in defeat.

In a voice that was almost too quiet to hear, I said, "I deserve that, Vance. I deserve to be with someone who loves me, who wants a life with me. I'm tired of going with the flow, hoping things will work out. We've known each other for years. If you don't love me now, you never will."

"Magnolia," Vance said. "Don't do this. Give me a chance. Everything is upside down right now. I'm still getting used to Rosie. I haven't thought about anything long-term. I just need time."

"No, you don't. You've had years of me by your side, every day. Now we're sleeping together. More time isn't going to change anything."

I crossed the room and shoved my feet into a discarded pair of flip-flops I kept by the back door. Picking up my purse from the counter, I took in his perplexed expression and said, "I don't trust my own judgement anymore, Vance. I love you. I love Rosie. But I don't want to be convenient. I don't want to wait and see how it works out. You and Rosie are my whole world. And I'm not yours."

I turned to leave the kitchen. Vance called out behind me, "Magnolia, we can talk about this."

Without looking back, I said, "I'm going out for a while. I don't want you here when I come home."

He said something else, but I didn't stick around to listen. I grabbed my keys and headed out the door, tears streaming down my cheeks. I'd put everything I had on the line and I'd lost.

Again.

I had my self-respect back, but it was cold comfort without Vance.

CHAPTER TWENTY-FIVE

VANCE

"M r. Winters, he's in a meeting. It might be better if you waited—"

I waved a hand at Aiden's PA and strode past her, ignoring her protests. I needed to talk to my cousin. I pushed open the door to Aiden's office to see him sitting behind his desk, a man and a woman in dark suits sitting on the other side, both of them taking notes as Aiden spoke, one on a tablet and the other on a legal pad.

Aiden looked up as I entered, his familiar dark eyes assessing me. When Aiden looked at me like that, I always felt like he had x-ray vision. He saw everything, and he knew me better than anyone except Magnolia.

Fuck. *Magnolia.*

What the fuck had happened? I was drinking a cup of coffee, thinking about the logistics of turning the carriage house into a studio, and then she asked me to move out.

I was still reeling. I'd called her over and over for the first hour after she left. She ignored me at first, then texted to say, *I'm coming home in 30 minutes. Don't be there.*

I packed up some of our stuff, and Rosie, and I left. It wasn't like Magnolia to overreact or lose her temper. I was good at convincing her to agree with me. All I had to do was get her to talk to me. But since she'd kicked me out and wouldn't answer her phone, that wasn't looking likely.

"We'll continue this later," Aiden said to the two people in his office. They stood and left, eyeing me but saying nothing.

I took one of the seats opposite Aiden, setting Rosie's baby carrier in the other. She was awake, but was happily occupied by the travel mobile on the handle of the carrier.

"What's up?" Aiden asked. It was the definition of a loaded question. Everything was up. And down. And fucking sideways. I started with the easy part.

"I need you to watch Rosie for a few hours. I have to meet Abigail at the gallery to make arrangements for a donation and take care of some things for the show. And I have a meeting with an investor I completely forgot about. I can't take Rosie with me."

Aiden studied me for a long moment before he said, "What about Magnolia? She can't watch Rosie for a few hours?"

I looked out the window of Aiden's office, unable to meet his eyes as I said, "Magnolia kicked me out. She won't answer my calls."

"What did you do?" Aiden asked evenly.

"Why do you assume I did something?" I demanded, glaring at him.

Fighting with Aiden was always a waste of time. He never lost his temper. That steely look in his eyes only got colder, sharper.

I looked away and said, "I didn't do anything. She

flipped out on me, wanting to know what our relationship meant and where it was going and how I felt about her before I even had a cup of coffee, and then when she didn't like my answer, she threw me out."

I was working up a good sense of righteous indignation when Aiden shook his head and let out a laugh. "I love you, Vance, and I'm proud of you. You've been successful in almost every area of your life, but you are a total idiot when it comes to women."

"What the fuck are you talking about?" I said, suddenly at sea. I was fantastic with women. "Women love me," I protested.

"*Women* love you," Aiden said slowly. "But this isn't about *women*. This is about one woman. This is about Magnolia. And she's been in love with you for years. What did you tell her when she asked you how you felt?"

"I said I didn't know," I answered, my throat tight. Even angry with Magnolia and feeling wronged, I knew that was a shitty answer to her question.

"You're kidding, right?" Aiden said. "Please tell me you said anything other than that."

"She blindsided me," I said defensively.

"And now that you've had time to think about it?" Aiden asked.

I started to speak, not quite sure what I was going to say, when the door slammed open. Charlie stood there, her sleek chignon falling down and her cheeks pink with rage.

"What did you do to Maggie?" she demanded, storming into the room and slamming the door behind her. I shot to my feet, worry stabbing through my gut.

"What do you mean? Is she okay? What happened?"

"That's what I want to know. She just called me and

asked me to take care of the dog. She won't tell me where she is, she said she's not coming home today, and she was crying. What the hell, Vance? If something's wrong with Maggie, why are you here?"

"She kicked him out," Aiden supplied helpfully.

"What did you do?" Charlie screeched.

"Why does everyone assume this is my fault?" I yelled back, my temper flaring out of control.

This was my family. Mine. Shouldn't they be on my side? Why couldn't this be Magnolia's fault?

She was the one who wouldn't listen.

She was the one who wouldn't talk to me about it.

Aiden just shook his head at me.

"Playing the odds," he said. Looking at Charlie, he explained, "She asked him if he loved her and he told her he didn't know."

Charlie's face fell, her anger sliding away, replaced by a look of immeasurable sadness. She moved Rosie's carrier out of the other chair and unsnapped her, cuddling Rosie in her lap and studying her face for a moment before she looked at me.

"Vance, you're an asshole. When the woman you love asks you how you feel about her, you don't tell her you don't know. As if Maggie hasn't been through enough, you have to stomp all over her heart? How could you do that?"

"She took me by surprise," I mumbled. That excuse was starting to wear thin, even to me. "And how do *you* know I'm in love with her?"

Charlie rolled her eyes at me. "I can't believe you're really this dumb. This is what happens when you spend your entire adult life sleeping around and never even attempt to have a normal relationship with a woman. Of course you're in love with Maggie. Can you look me in the eyes and tell me that you're not? Because if you've just been using her—"

Charlie looked down at Rosie and said in a low voice, "That would be pretty much the worst thing you could do to your best friend. Her parents dumped her when she was eight, she lost her only family when her grandmother died, and her fiancé cheated on her then broke up with her a month ago.

"I've never known anyone who needs a family as much as Maggie. She stuck with Brayden for years because she wanted to get married and have kids. If you moved into her house with Rosie to make your own life easier, and you aren't in love with her and don't want a life with her, then you just became the biggest bastard I've ever met."

When Charlie put it like that . . . I really was a bastard.

"Fuck," I muttered, unable to look at either of my cousins.

"You really didn't think this through, did you?" Aiden asked. I scrubbed my palms over my face, my stomach turning over.

"I had a plan," I said. "After she and Brayden split up, I was going to give her some time to get over him and then I was going to ask her out. But Stephanie showed up with Rosie and . . . I've been a little distracted, okay?"

Aiden let out a puff of breath and leaned back in his chair. "Okay. I can see how the sudden appearance of a daughter you didn't know existed would shake things up. But Vance, Maggie's been hurt enough, don't you think?"

"She said she wanted to be my world," I said, mostly to myself.

"If that's not who she is to you," Charlie said, "then just let her go. I'll track her down. I'll make sure she's okay. But don't go after her if you can't give her what she wants. She loves you. If you don't love her back, really love her, then let her go."

I pushed out of my chair and went to the window, staring blindly out at the panoramic view of downtown Atlanta.

Fucking hell. There was no way I was going to let Magnolia Henry out of my life. The problem was, love had always seemed like a trite word. A Valentine's Day, greeting card kind of thing. People threw it around all the time, as an excuse or a promise.

I couldn't tell you how many times some woman who barely knew me had said, *But Vance, I love you.*

What I had with Magnolia was so much bigger than that. It was more. She was everything. My closest friend. My partner.

She was home.

She was my heart.

Fuck.

They were right. I'd been a dick. I was distracted by Rosie, and everything with Magnolia was so easy. I was happy, she seemed happy, and Rosie was happy. In my world, everything was good.

No, fuck that, everything hadn't been *good*. Everything had been fucking amazing.

Spending my days with Magnolia, working with her, hanging out with her, taking her to bed at night, and waking up next to her in the morning.

Fucking perfection.

And it killed to know that the whole time, she'd been feeling scared and unloved. God dammit. I'd just assumed we were fine. Assumed we had time to figure out the hard stuff later. This was completely new territory for me. My problem was usually how to get rid of a woman, not how to win one back.

Aiden had called it. I had no idea what I was doing. My years of experience with women might serve me well when I took Magnolia to bed, but when it came to her heart, I was as clumsy as a child.

"Why didn't I just tell her I loved her?" I asked no one in particular. It appeared that my cousins were done giving me shit because neither of them said anything.

Not until Aiden commented, "It certainly would've solved a lot of problems if you had."

I ignored him. To Charlotte, I said, "Do you know where she is?"

"No. She wouldn't tell me. She said she doesn't want to see anyone."

"Do you think you can get her to the show tomorrow?" I asked.

Charlotte eyed me warily.

"That depends," she said. "Are you going to fix this?"

"I'm going to try," I said. "Will you help me?"

"I'll watch Rosie," Aiden offered, standing up from behind his desk and taking Rosie from Charlotte's arms. "I'll bring her home to Mrs. Williamson and work from my office there. I have a light afternoon, and Mrs. Williamson would love an excuse to watch Rosalie."

Charlotte stood and brushed her hands down her skirt. "Let me fix my hair and make a couple of calls. Then we'll get out of here. Whatever you've got in mind, Vance, it had better be good."

I didn't have much of a plan. I hadn't had time to come up with one. All I had was determination and love. They would have to be enough.

I was going to get Magnolia back. Rosie and I needed her.

I was crap at relationships, but I knew Magnolia. No one could make her happy like I could. Now that I'd pried my head out of my ass, I just had to find a way to prove it to her.

Chapter Twenty-Six

Magnolia

I was hiding. Hiding and feeling sorry for myself. After storming out of the house, I'd jumped in my car and taken off, headed nowhere. A few minutes later, I'd pulled over into the parking lot of Starbucks. I was crying too hard to drive safely.

I'd told Vance I didn't trust my judgment anymore. It was the most honest thing I'd said in a long time.

I didn't trust my judgment. On anything. I would have sworn that Vance had feelings for me. I truly thought he loved me, at least a little.

The blank look on his face when I'd asked him—I couldn't remember it without wanting to throw up. My life was a mess. I sat there for almost an hour, staring through the windshield of my car at the front window of Starbucks with no idea what to do.

Vance called. I ignored him. He called again. And again. I didn't answer. There was nothing to say. His silence when I'd asked him if he loved me had been brutal.

I couldn't bear to listen to his excuses. I was terrified he'd talk me into coming back, into settling for affection when I wanted love. It wasn't his fault if he didn't love me, but it would be mine if I accepted anything less than everything.

That had been my mistake with Brayden. Settling.

I finally texted him to make sure he was gone when I got back. Then I couldn't bring myself to go home. I ended up calling Charlie, dodging her questions and begging her to take care of Scout. I felt bad for abandoning him, but I just couldn't stand the idea of sitting alone in my house.

When my grandmother had died, it had been so lonely. Letting Brayden move in had helped, but I knew it would be so much worse now that Vance and Rosie were gone. I couldn't face it yet.

I drove down the street to the AC Hotel at Phipps Plaza and checked into a room. Between room service and the mall downstairs, I could hole up there forever. I was curled up on the king size bed in my room, watching the television screen flicker when my phone rang again.

I was ready to ignore it, but the unfamiliar number caught my attention.

"Hello?"

"Maggie, it's Evers."

"Evers, if Vance put you up to calling, you can just tell him to leave me alone."

There was a long silence. "This has nothing to do with Vance," he said, and I realized his tone was all business. "I'm here at your house. The team finished with the system a few hours ago and left to get lunch. The system wasn't armed, but the motion activated video capture was turned on. They got an alert that someone was in the house, and when they pulled up the video to check the system, it wasn't you or Vance."

"Who was it?" I asked, afraid I already knew what Evers would say.

"It was your dickhead of an ex, Brayden. He has a key and claims you gave him permission to enter."

"I did not," I said, furious. "Did he get into the house?"

"He'd already entered by the time the team got back, but they caught him filling a backpack with small valuables. Have you had any trouble with things going missing?"

I let out a breath I hadn't realized I'd been holding. "I took his key when we broke up. He must have had another," I said, stating the obvious. "Things have been going missing. I thought I was crazy, that I was just misplacing stuff."

"Please tell me you want me to press charges," Evers said.

"He's still there?" I asked.

"We weren't going to let him walk after he broke into your house," Evers said. "You contracted with us to manage your security. We had permission to be in the house, and he's not on the list of residents. I'll call the police for you right now."

"Yes, please. Absolutely call the police. Do I need to come back there? I'm . . . out for the day. I can if I have to, but—"

"No, Maggie. You don't have to come back right now. I can handle everything for you."

"Is Scout okay?" I was sure Evers would've said something if my dog had been hurt, but I had to make sure.

"Your dog? He's a weird looking little guy, but he's fine. He was in the backyard. Not too crazy about having all of us in his space, and he *really* doesn't like your ex, but he's fine."

"Charlie's supposed to stop by at some point this afternoon and pick him up. She's keeping him overnight. Can you make sure anyone who's there knows it's okay for her to take him?"

"No problem, honey. We've got everything under control."

"Thanks, Evers. Is there any way to track down the things he might've taken?"

"Email me a description of what you know you're missing, and I'll get my guys on it."

"I'd appreciate it," I said. "The only thing I'm really worried about is my grandmother's bracelet."

"We'll find it. I promise." Softly, he said, "And Maggie?"

"Yeah?" I asked, wary at his change in tone.

"You had a fight with Vance?"

"I don't want to talk about it," I said. I'd known Evers a long time, and he was a good guy, but he was Vance's friend first.

He proved it by saying, "Yeah, I don't really want to talk about it either. Just listen. I know he can be a jackass, but be patient with him. He cares about you."

That wasn't good enough for me. Not anymore. I didn't say that to Evers.

I would love Evers forever if he could track down my grandmother's bracelet, and I was immensely grateful that he'd put in the security system that had caught Brayden stealing from me. But I was not talking to Evers about my disaster of a relationship with Vance.

"Call me if you need anything from me," I said and hung up the phone.

That was one problem solved. At least I knew I wasn't crazy. I hadn't lost my bracelet or the clock. I wondered if he'd been trying to get into the house the times he'd shown up claiming he wanted to talk to me. It was a great cover if he was caught lurking around. I was so stupid.

Great job, Magnolia. Boyfriend number one is a cheating thief, and boyfriend number two basically made you the nanny and then talked his way into your bed.

I was done with relationships. After emailing Evers a description of the things I thought were missing, I took a long bath and settled in on the bed to watch the *Die Hard* marathon that was currently playing on one of the hotel's movie channels.

The universe must have known I was going to be nursing a broken heart if it gave me hours of John McLane.

When I'd broken up with Brayden, watching action movies and eating ice cream had seemed like the best way to soothe my bruised heart. Explosions and Bruce Willis weren't doing the trick this time.

I found myself wiping my cheeks off and on as the time passed, tears leaking from my eyes as I tried to ignore the heavy weight on my chest.

I thought about ignoring Charlie when she called, but she had my dog. I didn't really want to talk to anyone, but she was doing me a favor by taking Scout for the night. I'd feel terrible if something was wrong and I didn't answer.

"Hey, Charlie. Is Scout okay?" I asked.

"He's fine. Aiden has him in the backyard, trying to wear him out with the tennis ball."

"That won't take long," I said. Before she could say anything, I went on. "I don't want to talk, Charlie. No offense."

"I'm not going to make you talk about my shithead cousin. Promise. I was only calling to see what you're going to do about the show tomorrow."

The show. Vance's show at Sloane's gallery. I'd completely forgotten it was the next day.

Crap.

I would rather be coated in honey and strapped to the top of a fire ant hill than go to that show.

"I'm not going to the show," I said.

"Maggie, you have to go to the show. You're responsible for setting it up."

"I am not. It's mostly Sloane's work. It's her gallery."

"You know what I mean. You've been working on this for six months. You can't stay home. And you can't spend the rest of your life hiding out."

"I know that," I snapped. "But can't I have a few goddamn days to wallow before I have to get out there and act like a human being again?"

"No," Charlie said. "If it weren't for the show, then I'd say sure. I'd tell you to pack a few bikinis, go on vacation, and suck back pretty drinks with umbrellas in them until you can't remember his name anymore. But if you don't go to that show tomorrow, every single person you know is going to be talking about it. Do you want them feeling sorry for you?"

"I don't care what those people think," I said.

I didn't.

Okay, I kind of did. I didn't want to be the sad-sack reject who got dumped by her fiancé and then was stupid enough to sleep with her boss. Not that Vance was my boss in the traditional sense, but still.

Missing the show would make me look sad and pathetic. Just because I *felt* sad and pathetic didn't mean the entire world had to know about it.

Reading my mind, Charlie said, "I know you don't care what they think, but you're going to regret it if you don't go. Here's what we're going to do. I'm going to pick you up tomorrow. I'm going to bring you something to wear, and I'll help you with your hair and makeup. You're going to look un-freaking-believable. We're going to sweep in, dazzle everyone, and then disappear. You only have to hold it together for an hour. We'll show everybody how fabulous you are and get out."

I could do that. Especially if Charlie was with me. I could absolutely hold it together for an hour.

"I love you, Charlie," I said. "You're the best."

"I know," she said. "Are you going to tell me where you are yet?"

"Nope," I answered. "Text me when you're ready to leave tomorrow. I'll tell you then."

"You don't trust me?" She asked with a smile I could hear over the phone.

"Nope," I said again. This time, she laughed out loud. "Probably a good call. I'll text you tomorrow afternoon. Try to get some sleep. You don't want circles under your eyes tomorrow."

I hung up and tossed the phone on the bedside table. Charlie really was a good friend. The best. I dreaded the idea of going to the show. I hadn't decided if I was going back to work for Vance.

Just then, with my chest hollow, my stomach queasy, and my cheeks scratchy with dried tears, it seemed impossible.

Curled under the covers of my hotel bed, the flash of explosions and gunfire on the TV reflecting in the plate glass window across the room, I decided I wasn't going to think about the future for the next twelve hours.

I was going to watch TV, eat room service, and hide from life until I was forced to get out there and show everyone that I was just fine.

Even if it was a big fat lie.

CHAPTER TWENTY-SEVEN

MAGNOLIA

"Sit still, Maggie. You're going to fidget yourself right out of the car," Charlie said, giving me the side-eye.

"I'm not fidgeting," I lied.

"I should have made you drink the third glass of wine," she said, merging into traffic.

She'd shown up at my hotel room a few hours before, carrying enough luggage to move in. Twenty minutes later, she had me sitting at the desk, a glass of wine in my hand, as she painstakingly curled my long, thick hair.

Charlotte usually wore her own hair in some variation of a chignon, but when she felt like it, she could be a hair genius.

A little product and her curling iron transformed my hair into a wild mass of loose curls that tumbled over my shoulders and down my back.

She'd pulled strands from the front, twisting them and pinning them up, framing my face and lending elegance to the curls. It was almost too much, but the dress she'd chosen for me was plain, almost stark in design, and the extravagant hair balanced it out.

I had a dress at home, but Charlie had taken one look and declared it 'boring'. She'd gone shopping for me, saying I was too conservative. Coming from a woman who lived in business suits, it was an ironic accusation.

At first, I'd refused to wear the dress she'd picked out. For one thing, it was short. I didn't do short. If I had to worry about bending over in it, I didn't wear it.

There would be no bending in this dress. If I dropped anything, it was gone forever while I had this thing on.

Also, it was black. I liked color. Still, I had to admit, the black wrap dress made my body look ten times better than it really was.

My legs weren't bad after months of running, and though the skirt was short, it covered the roundest part of my thighs. The fabric pulled together at my waist, making it look tiny. I wasn't showing much cleavage. The dress was tasteful, but something about the cut emphasized my breasts.

I was curvy to begin with. In this dress, I was a bombshell.

I'd tried to do my own makeup, but Charlie had brushed me aside, shoving another glass of wine in my hand and telling me to drink up. I had.

Despite her help with my dress and everything else, I didn't want to go to Vance's show. The idea of being anywhere near him made me ill.

He'd stopped calling. Not even a text. That was that. It hurt even more to know he'd given up on me so easily.

I knew I'd done the right thing in kicking him out. He didn't love me, and I wasn't going to waste another second of my life on a man who didn't want me more than his next breath.

I wanted it all. Love. Family. I was going to hold out for

someone I could love with everything I had, someone who loved me the same way.

That all sounded good in theory. Reality was a deep ache in my heart, a gaping hole that used to be filled with Vance.

And Rosie. How could I have fallen so hard for a person who wasn't old enough to sit up? I'd always wanted children, but I'd had no clue how one tiny, helpless human could claim me so completely.

Part of me was on constant alert for the sound of her crying, worried she needed something. I knew she was with her father, and Vance adored his little girl. The way he'd stepped up for her was one more thing to love about him.

My breath hitched in my chest as I smothered a sob. Charlie's head whipped around.

"Don't you dare cry and mess up my makeup job. You look gorgeous and we're almost there. Just hold it together a little longer, and this will all be over. We'll go in, have a drink, chat for a few minutes, and then sneak out the back. If you feel yourself getting weepy, bite the inside of your lip. Hard. Or pinch the skin between your thumb and pointer finger. They both work."

"What?" Her advice was so matter-of-fact, I knew it came from personal experience.

"Bite the inside of your lip or pinch the skin between your thumb and pointer finger. Hard enough to hurt. The pain will distract you long enough to keep yourself from crying. It doesn't do the trick for long, but it helps."

I didn't need to ask Charlie when she'd needed to keep herself from crying in public. I'd seen the pictures of her at her parents' funeral.

Every tear had been photographed and sold for entertainment. The Winters family had learned the hard way to keep their emotions to themselves.

I dug my nails into that tender strip of skin between my fingers and found that she was right. The flash of pain didn't do anything about the hole in my heart, but it shocked my nervous system enough to chase away the tears.

A few minutes later, we were pulling up in front of Sloane's gallery. A valet took Charlotte's keys, and she rounded the car to me, threading her arm through mine and tossing her sleek, auburn hair over her shoulder.

"Smile," she hissed at me. "Don't give the vultures anything."

I did, stretching my lips into a replica of a smile, pretending to look around the packed gallery as we entered.

After all the planning, I'll admit to a surge of triumph at the crowd. Half of the pieces already had red SOLD stickers pinned beside the descriptions. The last piece Vance had finished took center stage in the first room, towering above the elegantly dressed guests.

Twice my height, somehow both sinuous and muscular, the shades of grey metal gleamed beneath the strategic lighting.

I expected to see a SOLD sticker on that piece as well. It hadn't been a commission, but we already had a buyer in mind, and the last I'd heard, it had been a done deal.

Now, instead of a price, the information plaque stated that Vance had donated the sculpture to the Winters Foundation's silent auction. Abigail must have been thrilled. It was worth a ton.

I imagined Sloane's fury when she'd heard the news. For the first time that night, my smile was genuine.

Heart pounding in my chest, I scanned the room for Vance. He was nowhere to be seen. Vance was never the shy artist lurking in the corner at his own shows. He was usually himself—charming, cocky, amusing—and at the center of the crowd.

I was grateful that he was out of sight. It would be so much easier to get through this if I could avoid him completely.

Charlie towed me to the bar and shoved a drink in my hand. I took a sip and winced. "What is this?"

"A Moscow mule," she said.

"It's too strong," I complained.

"I know. That's the point. Drink up. There are people heading this way."

There were. Investors we were working with on a few projects. We did the cheek kiss, social hug thing and they jumped right in to business. I let out a breath of relief.

Business I could handle. I knew every detail of our projects. I could talk numbers in my sleep. Or while most of my attention was on the shifting mass of people in the room, hyper-alert for any sign of Vance.

So far, so good. The investors thanked me for the update I barely remembered giving and wandered off. I turned to scan the crowd from another angle when Charlie's fingers closed around my arm.

"She-bitch at three o'clock," she said in a low voice. Sure enough, Sloane was bearing down on us, her perfectly made up face screwed into a familiar look of annoyance.

"Where have you been?" she hissed. "You were supposed to be here to help me set up."

I shrugged, utterly without an answer. I *should* have been there to help. I hadn't even bothered to call. It was rude, thoughtless, and I couldn't bring myself to give a crap.

My heart had been smashed to pieces, and for once in my life, I was looking out for me.

It wasn't like Sloane didn't have gallery staff. She hip-checked Charlie out of the way, snatched the drink from my hand, and wrapped her arm around my shoulders, her fingers biting into my skin through the thin fabric of my dress.

Steering me at a quick pace through the crowded gallery, she said, "There's a major problem with the setup in the garden. Major. Why haven't you been answering your phone?"

I didn't know what she was talking about. I'd had my phone turned on all day and she hadn't called me once.

The hallway at the back of the gallery should have been lit, the door to the garden wide open to encourage the guests to wander outside and see the pieces that should've been placed in the gallery's outdoor space.

Instead, the hall was dark and the door was shut.

We'd been planning the show for months. How could a major part of it have gone wrong in the last twenty-four hours?

Sloane wrenched open the door, planted her palm in the middle of my back, and shoved, propelling me outside.

The door slammed shut behind me, the deadbolt clicking into place. I spun around and pulled on the handle. It turned, but the door remained closed. She'd locked me out.

What the hell?

Sloane could be a raging bitch. Most of the time, she *was* a raging bitch, but she usually made sense. The show was big business for her.

Why wasn't the garden set up? Why would she yell at me for being late and then throw me out?

I could only hope Charlie would realize I was missing and come find me. Resigned to waiting until someone rescued me—there was no way I was climbing the smooth concrete walls of the garden in four-inch heels and a cocktail dress—I turned to face the garden, intending to sit on one of the wrought iron benches.

Belatedly, I noticed that the garden was lit from above with fairy lights that had been artfully strung around the walls, through the tree in the back corner, and over the gazebo in the center.

When had Sloane installed a gazebo?

The whole effect was whimsical and romantic, the sparkling lights delicate and sweet. It didn't go with the modern aesthetic of Sloane's gallery, or the spare, almost aggressive metal sculptures we'd planned to display in the space.

I wandered deeper into the garden, curious and confused.

Fashioned of thin poles with a domed top, the gazebo had metal leaves and vines woven around the supports, perfectly fitting the fairy lights twined around the metal.

I'd seen one in a similar style at an antique show and had been talking about getting one for my back yard, but I had never gotten around to it.

A single Edison Bulb hung from the center of the domed top of the gazebo, illuminating the small café table in the center. On it sat an ice bucket with a bottle of champagne, two glasses, and a small metal sculpture of a house.

About as wide as a paperback book, no more than six inches tall, the little house was roughly made, but it reminded me of my own. I picked it up to study it more closely and found it unexpectedly heavy.

I knew from experience that metal sculpture could be like that. Sometimes, it was light as air though it looked dense, but often, it was the other way around. Something rattled as I turned the house in my hands.

I looked through the open front door and saw a small black box. What was this? I replaced the little house on the table and stepped away. This had been set up for someone. I was interrupting. I shouldn't be here.

"Do you like it?"

I looked up to see Vance standing in front of the gazebo, his hair loose around his face, wearing a navy suit with a deep blue button-down shirt.

I'd chosen his clothes myself a few days before. The tie I'd picked out, with narrow stripes the exact shade of his eyes, was nowhere to be seen. Instead, he wore the collar unbuttoned, the golden skin of his throat warm against the crisp shirt and dark suit.

I stared at him, my chest tight, the corners of my eyes prickling, my heart pounding, wondering what the hell was going on.

Chapter Twenty-Eight

Magnolia

Against my will, my knees went weak. Vance knew how to wear a suit, and with his hair loose, he had that whole debonair Viking thing going on.

I was not up for this. Speechless, I dug my teeth into the inside of my lip, biting down hard to fight back my tears.

I was not going to cry in front of him. I shook my head in answer to his question. I didn't know what he meant. Did I like what?

"The gazebo," he clarified, gesturing to the metal structure surrounding me. "I've been working on it for a while. Ever since you said you wanted one. You can paint it to match the house . . ."

He trailed off. I didn't know what to say. He'd made me a gazebo? Like I was going to want to put a gazebo Vance had made me in my backyard so I could look at it every day and be reminded of how much he didn't love me.

I shook my head again, still at a loss for words. Coming here tonight had been a mistake. If I'd been able to escape, I would have. I would've pushed past him and gone straight out the door. If only Sloane hadn't locked it.

"I made the house for you too," he said, watching me closely.

I looked down at the miniature metal house on the table beside the champagne. Maybe I'd had one too many glasses of wine, because I didn't get it. Vance swore under his breath.

"I'm fucking this all up. Again." He came into the gazebo, his big body crowding mine, and picked up the house. I expected him to hand it to me, but he held it close to his chest, looking nervous. "You said you deserve to be someone's whole world. And you're right. Magnolia, you deserve everything. Love. Family. Everything. I want that, too. But only if I can have it with you."

I bit my lip again, but I couldn't stop the tears that spilled down my cheeks. Vance swallowed hard and held up the little metal house.

"I didn't know how else to show you. But I realized, Magnolia, that you're my home. It's not a place, it's you. Since the day my parents died, I've felt like I was drifting, like home had been torn from me and I'd never find it again. And I didn't. Not until you. When I'm with you, I have everything I've ever wanted. I love you. I love you more than anything in the entire world. Except for Rosie. But I thought that, maybe, we could love Rosie together."

I was crying too hard to see clearly when he tipped the little house on its side and knocked the black box into his hand.

Opening it, he pulled something out and said, "Magnolia, I want to spend the rest of my life showing you how much I love you."

He dropped to one knee and looked up at me, his hand outstretched, something sparkling fire between his fingertips.

"Will you marry me?"

I'm pretty sure my jaw dropped. He'd bought a ring? I squeezed my eyes shut and wiped my tears away so I could get a better look.

Oh, my God. He'd bought me a ring. He was asking me to marry him. Not in an offhand, Brayden kind of way.

I remembered what he'd said years ago about a proposal. *You give the girl a ring, get down on one knee, and do it somewhere special she'll be able to remember her whole life.*

He'd sure as hell known what he was talking about.

I took in the garden with fresh eyes—the fairy lights, the gazebo, the flowers, the champagne. The locked door.

Ask her in a way she'll remember for the rest of her life.

"Magnolia?"

I'd never heard Vance sound so uncertain. "You're sure?" I asked.

I wanted this. I wanted him. More than anything I'd ever wanted, I wanted Vance. But not if he hadn't thought it through. Not if he wasn't sure. I didn't think I could take losing him again.

"I've never been more sure of anything in my entire life. I love you, Magnolia Henry. You're everything—you're my partner, my best friend. You're so fucking sexy you make my head spin. You make me laugh. I want to wake up next to you. I want to make babies with you. I want it all. Only with you."

I studied the ring in his hand. It shone in the sparkling lights, a square-cut diamond with a pavé surround, old-world and elegant. It was a statement of a ring, chosen by a man who wanted everyone to know he'd claimed his woman, and by a man who knew me inside and out.

"Are you going to say anything?" he asked. "Because I'm not letting you out of the garden until you say yes. I know you're pissed off, and you should be. I was an ass. But you love me, and—"

"Yes," I interrupted. "Yes. Yes, I'll marry you."

Vance was sliding the ring on my finger a second later. He stopped cold as the circle of gold settled into place and stared at my hand.

"We can wait," I said, as transfixed by the sight of the ring on my finger as he was. "We don't have to rush."

"I don't want to wait," he said. "If you want to plan something big, we can. I'll be patient. But I'd marry you tonight if I could. We can catch a plane to Vegas."

I shook my head, words caught in my throat. I didn't want to wait either, but I wasn't getting married in Vegas. "I want to get married at my house," I said. "At our house. In the garden. Out back. Only family and close friends."

Vance pulled me into his arms, wrapping them tightly around me, his lips brushing my temple. "That sounds perfect. How long will it take to pull something like that together? A few weeks?"

I hummed in the back of my throat. I had a feeling a few weeks was an optimistic schedule. I didn't even have a dress. "We'll figure it out," I said. Drawing back, I looked up into his impossibly handsome face. "Are you really sure?"

Vance laid a finger across my lips, stopping me from speaking. "Don't ever ask me that again. I was a fucking idiot before. I've been in love with you for years, okay? I just didn't know what to do about it. Aside from the obvious."

"The obvious?" I asked, grinning as his arms tightened around my waist.

Vance grinned back and kissed me, his lips teasing mine apart, taking control until I was bent back over his arm and gasping for breath.

"I had that part clear," he whispered, his lips moving against mine. "It was the rest I had to figure out."

The door to the gallery swung open, and Sloane's voice cut through the darkness. "Are you two done yet? I need to move the pieces in here and open it up. Are you sure you won't let me put a price on the gazebo?"

"It's an engagement gift for my fiancée, Sloane. It's not for sale."

"Fine. Then get your champagne and your fiancée out of my way so I can sell some art." She stormed back into the gallery, letting the door shut behind her, this time leaving it unlocked.

"Did she help you set this up?" I asked, having a hard time believing Sloane would help get us back together.

"She begged me not to dump her and the gallery. Since her attitude about you was the reason I fired her, I told her she could have a second chance if she helped me get you back. She's probably the only person who wanted you to say yes as much as I did."

"What about Charlie?" I asked as the lights in the garden flicked on.

With more illumination, I could see the stands for the garden sculptures, the information plaques and spotlights already arranged. The door opened again, and workers came through, carrying the sculptures that we'd planned to display in the garden. In a few minutes, we'd be surrounded by art lovers, no longer alone.

I asked again, "Did Charlie know?"

"Are you going to get mad at her if I say yes?" Vance asked, running his lips along my cheekbone. I glanced down and did a double-take at the huge rock on my ring finger.

"Of course not. Charlie's my best friend."

"Did she pick out that dress?" Vance asked, leaning just far enough away to run his eyes down the length of my body.

"She did. Why?"

"Because you look unbelievably hot, and if we weren't about to be surrounded by people, I'd be fucking you against the wall right now."

"Really?" He trailed a finger down across my collarbone to dip into the wrap neckline of the dress, his finger disappearing beneath the fabric to slide inside my lace bra. I shivered.

"Really. You look hot in anything. Even those men's pajamas you still had from college. But this dress is almost criminal. And those shoes. Fuck, Magnolia. I don't know whether to thank Charlie or yell at her for picking it out."

"Why would you yell at her?" I asked, enjoying our last few moments of privacy.

"You didn't see the way the men in there were looking at you. I don't care if you have my ring on your finger—you're not leaving my side for the rest of the night."

"I've always thought of you as a Viking," I said, "but right now, you remind me more of a caveman."

Voices filtered into the quiet night as people entered the garden, eager to see the work they'd been told had been 'held back' for a special viewing.

Charlie emerged from the crowd and rushed forward, her hand reaching for mine. She lifted my fingers to the light and turned them, first one way, then the other, examining my ring.

"I knew it would be gorgeous. Did he grovel?" she demanded. "I hope you made him grovel."

"Hey!" Vance said, taking my hand from Charlie and pressing it to his chest. He held it in place with his own, the strong beat of his heart thumping beneath my fingers. "Stop manhandling my fiancée. And stop encouraging her to mess with me."

"You deserve it," Charlie said, uncowed by Vance's dark expression. "You were an ass."

"I was," Vance admitted. "And I groveled a little."

"Did he?" She asked me.

"A little. Enough. He groveled exactly enough," I said. People milled around us, murmuring. One brave soul ventured close enough to ask, "Is the gazebo available?"

When Vance curtly answered, "No. It's a gift," she said,

"Will you make one on commission?"

Before he could offend the woman, I jumped in to say, "If you'll give Sloane your contact information, he'll let you know after the show. He's just a little tense tonight." I sent her a sympathetic smile. "You know how artists are. He gets jittery when he has a show."

She nodded sagely and promised she'd find Sloane. Charlie was stifling a giggle, and Vance gave my waist a hard squeeze. "The only time in my entire fucking life that I've ever had the jitters was when you wouldn't agree to marry me."

"You said no?" Charlie cut in.

"She turned him down?" I heard over my shoulder. I turned to see Aiden behind us, frowning at Vance. "You fucked it up, man? How?"

"I did not fuck it up," Vance growled, lifting my hand from where he had it tucked to his chest and showing Aiden my ring. "She said yes. She just made me wait first. I think she wanted to torture me."

"I wasn't trying to torture you," I protested. "I was in shock. I wasn't expecting a proposal."

"That's my fault," Vance whispered in my ear. "You

should have been expecting it. I should never have let you wonder about how much I love you."

I melted into him. How long did we have to stay at the show? My sensible side said we had to stay to the end. The newly engaged woman who'd spent the previous night crying into her pillow wanted to jump the wall and sneak off to have sex with her fiancée.

At the moment, I liked her much better than my sensible side. I nudged Vance with my elbow and said, "Hey, do you want to sneak out? What's Sloane going to do, fire you?"

Vance's blue eyes went electric and he lowered his mouth to mine. His tongue was tracing my lower lip when I heard from behind me, "Maggie! I need to talk to you, baby."

I turned to see Brayden, wearing a suit and sporting a black eye, stalking across the walled garden to the gazebo. Every person in earshot fell silent.

Wonderful.

Almost everyone here knew me, knew Brayden, and knew our sad drama of cheating and a broken engagement.

Atlanta was a big city, but my corner of it sometimes felt like a small town. Vance shifted to put himself between Brayden and me.

I stepped to the side. I wasn't afraid of Brayden, but I was curious to know what he wanted.

"Why aren't you in jail?" I asked.

A gasp went up from the crowd.

I couldn't say I didn't enjoy the heck out of that. I was tired of playing the rejected girlfriend. A stint in jail made being dumped the far lesser crime.

"Maggie, how could you have me arrested?" he asked, coming to a stop in front of me. "I need you to drop the charges, baby. This was all a misunderstanding. You just need to let me explain."

I laughed. I couldn't help it. He was completely insane if he thought there was any explanation for what he'd done. I told him so.

"You're crazy. You were stealing from me. You stole my grandmother's bracelet, her clock, and more. Your backpack was stuffed full when you were arrested. I'm not dropping anything. You can rot in jail for all I care. I hope you do."

"I'll lose my license," he pleaded. "I'm sorry. It was a mistake. I owed some money and I didn't have it."

"So you stole from me?" I asked, incredulous. "You took family heirlooms, things my grandparents expected me to hand down to my own children, and pawned them to pay your debts? Who did you owe money to?"

"Can you keep your voice down?" he asked, glancing around.

The crowd was listening with avid interest, not even pretending to look at the art. *We* were the show now, and if Brayden thought this entire conversation wasn't going to hit every ear in Atlanta by midnight, he was sadly mistaken.

"No," I said. "Who did you owe money to? And for what?"

"I can't tell you," he mumbled, looking at the ground. "Can't you just let it go?"

"No. Tell me what you wanted the money for and I'll drop the charges."

Vance squeezed my arm and said, "Magnolia."

"Do you promise?" Brayden asked.

"First tell me why you needed the money," I said.

"For Heather's engagement ring," he confessed in a low voice. "I was over-extended and I couldn't get credit. She wanted a ring, and I thought—"

"You thought you'd steal from your former fiancée to buy a ring for your new one? God, you're a dumbass," I said.

If I hadn't had Vance beside me, his ring on my finger and his declarations of love fresh in my ears, I might have murdered Brayden. As it was, I laughed.

"So will you drop the charges? I really am sorry," he said with a sheepish smile I'm sure he thought was charming.

"No," I said.

"But, you promised," he sputtered. "You said—"

"I lied," I cut in. "And you're an idiot."

"Come on, Maggie, don't be such a bitch. I'm sorry about everything, but you don't need to get back at me by doing this."

"Get back at you?" I laughed again. "I don't need to get back at you at all. I've moved on. I don't care about you anymore. But you were stealing from me. You knew I loved that bracelet, knew my grandmother gave it to me, and you pawned it for cash. You must have known I'd go crazy looking for it, but all you wanted was to make yourself happy. You'll have to hope your lawyer can work a miracle, because we have you on video at my house and they're tracking down the things you pawned. You're going to lose a lot more than your license."

"You fucking cunt—" Brayden swore.

He didn't get the chance to say more. Vance lunged forward and swung his fist, catching Brayden right on the jaw.

Brayden dropped like a sack of rocks. Vance stepped back and shook out his hand.

"Fuck. Forgot how much that hurts."

I caught his hand in mine and rubbed his fingers. "Careful with those hands, honey," I said. "You can't work if you get injured."

Vance kissed my forehead. "I've been dying to hit him for years. If he moves, I'll do it again."

"He's not worth it," I said.

"No, but you are." He rested his lips on my skin, and I leaned into him, twining my fingers with his.

"When you're not being an asshole, you're pretty sweet," I said.

"Charming, not sweet," he said, trailing his lips down my cheekbone to my mouth and kissing me slowly. I forgot everyone was watching us and kissed him back, my body melting into his.

"Uh, guys? The dickhead is getting up," Charlie said, staring down at Brayden as if he were something she'd stepped in.

I looked over my shoulder to see Brayden sneering at us, propped up on one hand, touching his cheek gingerly with the other. "I'm fucking pressing charges, asshole. You hit me!"

"No shit," Vance said with a laugh. "Did you just figure that out?"

"I'm going to fucking kick your ass," Brayden shouted.

Not likely. He was still wobbling to his feet when I pulled my hand free of Vance and stepped in front of him. Vance tried to pull me back, but I waved him off. Brayden couldn't even stand up straight. He wasn't a threat.

"Get out of my way, Maggie," he said. I took a step closer and set my hands on his shoulders. Behind me, I heard Charlie say, "Oh, shit."

"There's something I've been meaning to tell you, Brayden," I said.

He opened his mouth to speak, but he never got the words out. Before he had the chance to spew more bullshit, I lifted my knee and slammed it into his balls.

Brayden let out a high-pitched squeak and collapsed to the ground, jaw hanging loose, limbs splayed, gasping for air.

Vance took my hand and swung me around, dropping me over his arm in a low dip as if we'd been dancing.

He set his lips on my neck and said, "You're amazing. I fucking love you, Magnolia." In a whoosh of movement, he swung me back upright and held me tight to his body. "What do you say we get the hell out of here and celebrate our engagement?"

"Please," I said. Vance picked up the bottle of champagne by the neck, wrapped his arm around my waist, sent Aiden and Charlie a two-fingered salute, and led me through the murmuring crowd. He was parked in the tiny lot behind the gallery.

After helping me up into the Range Rover, he got in, started the engine, and said, "Home?"

"Yes. Let's go home."

He took my hand in his as he drove, stroking the ring on my finger as we passed through the hushed streets. "Is Rosie with Mrs. Williamson?" I asked.

"Yep."

"All night?" I asked.

Vance gave my hand a squeeze and turned his head to look at me. His eyes shone with love and sparked with lust.

"All night, Magnolia. All night."

"Mmm," I said, pressing my knees together at the wave of heat between my legs. I'd only been without him for one night, but it felt like a lifetime.

"You know what I want, Sugar?" Vance asked, his voice a low rumble in his chest.

"Tell me."

"I want you, in our bed, wearing nothing but my ring and those fucking shoes. That's what I want."

"I can do that," I said.

And I did. All night.

Epilogue: Part One
Magnolia

One Month Later

Bright spring sunshine bathed my skin as I lay on my side in the backyard. I'd spread a quilt on the freshly mown lawn, and Rosie and I were enjoying the beautiful weather after days of rain. The ground was a little damp beneath the quilt, but we didn't care.

Rosie was rolling over now, and keeping her on the quilt was more of a challenge than I'd expected. She couldn't crawl, but she'd figured out she could get almost anywhere by rolling.

Our sweet little girl had a spark of trouble in her.

Just like her daddy.

Vance was across the lawn, at the back of the property, supervising the renovations on the carriage house. Now that we were engaged, he and Rosie had officially moved in and we'd agreed to go ahead with the plan to turn the carriage house into his studio.

It would be ideal once it was rebuilt on the inside, right

down to the small gravel driveway to the door so he could receive delivery of materials.

Life was just about perfect.

Except for the wedding. I was partially regretting the decision not to elope. It would have been so much easier to fly to Vegas, grab a dress off the rack, and just get it done.

We even had connections out there—Evers's brother, Axel, ran the western division of Sinclair Security out of Las Vegas and was best friends with Dylan Kane, the owner of the Delecta Casino and Resort. Dylan had called Vance personally to offer anything we wanted.

Like a fool, I'd turned him down.

I wanted a small, romantic wedding in my backyard. And that's what I was getting, complete with exchanging our vows in the gazebo Vance had built for me.

Planning a wedding was much more involved than I'd guessed. I should have known. I'd helped Sloane plan enough shows at the gallery to understand that these things involved so many more details than they should have.

Abigail had taken charge. She was so sweet and refined, I hadn't realized she was also terrifyingly organized and very stubborn.

I was efficient and organized when it came to business. But party planning? Not so much.

I wanted to marry Vance. And I wanted it to be romantic. I just couldn't bring myself to care about flowers, or table settings, or music, or seating arrangements. Or anything aside from my dress, the guest list, and the cake.

It wasn't that Abigail didn't listen to me. She did. She was wonderful—patient and thoughtful and filled with creative ideas that gave away the close attention she'd paid to who Vance and I really were. And she was doing the whole thing for free.

Well, not entirely for free. She'd strong-armed Vance into making another donation to the foundation as her fee. Abigail was born to extort money out of wealthy people in the name of a good cause.

Her first benefit for the Winters Foundation had been a raging success, and the next one would be even better. She'd beamed when we'd decided to ask for donations to the food bank in lieu of gifts.

She was such a sweetheart, I felt terrible that I'd been dodging her calls. Only for one day. I needed a break from the wedding.

I looked up to see Vance loping across the lawn, a roguish grin on his handsome face. He reached the edge of the quilt and scooped up Rosie, who had rolled in his direction the second she'd seen movement.

Scout, who had been supervising the construction work with Vance, came around the quilt to collapse beside me, leaning his short, long body into mine. I rubbed his ears and lost myself in watching Vance swing Rosie in the air.

She loved it, babbling with glee and reaching for the sun.

He was *such* a good dad.

When Rosie was done, Vance dropped down to join Scout and me on the quilt, setting Rosie between us. She promptly rolled toward Scout and reached out to play with his paw.

Scout gave a harrumph and settled his head on his other paw, content to let Rosie play as long as he knew she was safe.

"She's rolling everywhere," Vance said, looking down at Rosie's drooping eyelids. She was napping less and sleeping longer at night, but she was also more active.

It was a good thing we were getting more sleep. We needed the energy to keep up with her.

"I know. She almost rolled herself to the top of the stairs this morning," I said.

"Do we need to get a gate already?" Vance asked, his eyebrows drawing together in concern.

"Probably. She'll be crawling in another month or two."

Vance rolled to his back and let out a groan. "I'm not ready for crawling. She's already a terror and she's only rolling."

"I know," I agreed. "But I don't think we get a say."

"Nope." Vance turned back to his side and looked at me from beneath his thick eyelashes. I knew that glint in his eye. I wasn't surprised when he said, "When do you think she'll fall asleep?"

Taking in Rosie's soft touch on Scout's paw and her glazed eyes, I said, "Not long. Why? Do you want to go try to get some work done?"

"Definitely. If by *work* you mean stripping off your clothes and making you come."

"Hmm. I could make room in my schedule for that," I said.

"I was thinking we should move Rosie from the sitting room to the other master bedroom. The one I was using. That way, she'll be close, but we'll have a little space."

It was a good idea. The day before, I'd put Rosie down for her nap, and then Vance had tucked me in. Naked.

It would have been heaven, but I'd ended up screaming his name and I'd woken Rosie. I'd learned the hard way that a wailing baby is a complete orgasm killer.

It wasn't my fault. Really. I'd never been a screamer during sex before. I tried to be quiet with Vance. Sometimes, I even managed it. But other times, I lost all control. He really was that good.

Remembering, I shifted to lie on my front before I gave in to the urge to peel off my clothes right there.

All I had to do was think about sex with Vance and my body came to life. Think about sex, see Vance with his shirt off, catch that glint in his eyes . . . it didn't take much.

"Let's take her up now," I said. "You can move her crib, and we'll put her down for her nap." I eyed Rosie's slow blink. A few more of those, and her lids would stay closed. "I don't want her to fall asleep out here. She might wake up when we bring her in."

Vance scooped Rosie up and nudged Scout off the quilt while I grabbed our things. Rosie snuggled her head into his shoulder and let out a huff of air.

She'd worn herself out with all that rolling. Maybe she'd take a nice long nap. I could only hope.

We were headed to the kitchen door when my phone rang. Charlotte. "Hey, Charlie, what's up?"

"Are you guys busy?"

"Just putting Rosie down for a nap, why?"

"What about after?"

"We don't have anything planned," I said, curious. Charlie wasn't usually this cagey. "What's going on?"

Vance caught my question and looked at me, his eyebrows raised. I shrugged.

"Can you meet me somewhere after Rosie wakes up?"

"Sure, where?" I asked.

"I'll tell you later. I don't want to talk to Vance about it over the phone. Just call me when you're ready."

"Okay, later." I hung up and shoved the phone in my pocket, wondering. What didn't she want to talk to Vance about?

"What's Charlie up to?" Vance asked as we climbed the stairs to the second level.

"I don't know. She wants us to meet her somewhere after Rosie's nap, but she wouldn't tell me where."

"She's been off lately," he said, handing me Rosie so he could drag her crib through the double doors that led to the bedroom that had been my grandfather's. We could move the changing table later.

As soon as Vance slid the crib into place, he returned to unplug the video monitor. I got busy changing her diaper. The sooner we got her settled in her crib, the sooner I could have Vance all to myself.

"She won't talk to me," I said, snapping Rosie back into cotton jammies and fastening the Velcro on her wearable blanket.

"Charlie likes to keep everything inside," Vance said.

"Yeah, like you can talk," I said, laying Rosie down in her crib and turning on the mobile she liked to watch while she fell asleep.

"Hey, I talk about my feelings all the time." He came up behind me and slid his hands beneath my t-shirt, his fingers nudging my bra out of the way. "I feel like fucking you. I love licking your pussy. It makes me really fucking happy when you come on my cock."

"Vance," I protested, my cheeks flaming red.

"Those are feelings. Important feelings."

He led me away from the crib, carefully shutting the door as we snuck across the sitting room to our bedroom. We shut that door as well. Better safe than sorry and all that. I stripped off my shirt, taking my bra with it.

"You smell like fresh cut grass and flowers," Vance said, running his lips over my shoulder.

I buried my nose in his hair and breathed. He smelled

like Vance, of heat, and the outdoors, and man. No other scent could fill my heart and set it racing. I dropped my hands to his jeans and pulled at the snap.

"Naked. Now," I said.

"Bossy," he murmured.

I didn't answer, just shoved his jeans to the floor and backed up, pulling him with me to the bed. His long, hard body came down on top of mine, his hips settling between my legs.

"Magnolia," he breathed, rocking his hips into mine. "I was watching you lying in the sun, and I wanted to fuck you there. I wanted to see you naked under the blue sky, all this smooth skin bare for me."

"Too bad the construction workers were there," I said, moaning as his cock rubbed against my pussy, the head teasing my clit.

"They're not here now." He slid one hand between my legs, his fingertips pressing inside. He brought them back up, gleaming with moisture, and sucked them into his mouth. "You taste so fucking good. I need more of that."

I wasn't going to argue. Vance moved down my body with slow deliberation, the silky slide of his skin against mine a tease, heightening my arousal before he'd really touched me.

His tongue flicked across my clit, and I gasped.

Vance lifted his head and met my eyes. "Feel free to scream all you want, Sugar."

I wasn't going to scream. I didn't mean to. A few minutes later, I forgot all about that. He licked, he tasted, he sucked my clit between his lips as he drove two fingers deep inside me.

I came in a rush of gasping breath and sounds that *might* have been screams.

It wasn't my fault. What Vance could do with his mouth and two fingers was a miracle. He surged up the bed and was filling me with his cock while I was still coming.

When he was in to the hilt, he froze. We'd decided to forgo condoms recently and neither of us was used to how different it felt.

How intimate. How real.

"Fuck," he groaned. "I can feel you squeezing my cock with your pussy."

His mouth took mine, his lips tasting of me and of the uniquely perfect flavor that was only Vance. He seemed content to stay where he was, buried inside me, kissing me senseless, pinning me to the bed.

His mouth moved, his lips tugging, teeth nipping, his tongue tasting me, twining with mine. All I could do was hold on and sink into his kiss. Every touch, every brush of his lips told me how he felt, showed me how much he loved me.

I could have kissed Vance forever. I would have. But I needed to move. My orgasm had ebbed into another slowly growing wave of need, tension coiling inside me.

Vance was all patience, kissing me over and over, the weight of his heavy body keeping me still.

I lifted my legs, wrapping them around his lean hips, trying to rock up into his cock. He filled me completely in this position, stretching me open. Propping himself up on his elbows, he looked down our bodies to where we were joined.

"Is this what you want?"

He didn't thrust. Nothing that overt. Instead, he made a tight circle with his hips. I sucked in a breath. He'd barely moved, his upper body completely still, but the flex of his hips ground his pelvis into my clit, sending a molten flare of pleasure through my pussy.

He did it again, the movement almost nothing, but so intense I didn't know if I could take it. I squeezed my eyes shut and let out a ragged moan.

"I'm going to fuck you just like this," he whispered, "until I feel you come so hard on my cock you take me with you."

He stopped talking and kissed me again, slanting his mouth into mine, swallowing my moans as he made another tight circle with his hips, driving a spike of pleasure straight up my spine and into my brain.

I clamped my knees to his sides, hanging on for dear life, kissing him, his mouth my anchor in the rising tide of pleasure.

My nipples rubbed the sparse hair on his chest. My heels dug into his muscled legs. My fingers gripped his shoulders as if I could keep myself from falling.

Without the distraction of thrusting, touching, fucking him back, I could feel every tiny change in position. His hips circled one last time, and my clit exploded.

Pinned beneath Vance, all I could do was kiss him harder, feeding from his mouth, giving him every gasp and cry.

I could feel the muscles in my pussy tighten on his cock in hard, sucking pulses, dragging him with me into bliss, just as he'd wanted. His own groans melded with mine, his breath short as he filled me.

I was still shaking when he rolled to his back, taking me with him, my limp body draped over his as he reached out to pull the quilt over our bodies.

His hand stroked through my hair, tugging gently at the strands in a way he knew was guaranteed to lull me to sleep.

"Are we taking a nap?" I asked, drowsy and replete.

"Just for a while. I want to lie here with you like this."

"Mmm," I agreed. I could stay here forever, skin to skin with Vance, his cock still inside me, his hands stroking me with reverent love. "I love you," I murmured.

"My Sugar Magnolia," Vance said. I gave a laughing growl at the hated nickname. He tugged a lock of hair and said, "You taste so sweet, I can't call you anything else."

"Mmm." I wasn't going to argue about it while he was playing with my hair and I was half-asleep. Secretly, I kind of liked the way he called me 'Sugar'. But don't tell Vance that.

"I love you too," he whispered against the top of my head. "And I'm going to spend the rest of our lives showing you exactly how much."

I pressed a kiss to the hollow of his throat and drifted into sleep, my heart full of Vance.

Epilogue: Part Two

Vance

What the fuck was Charlie thinking?

I stood on the sidewalk, looking at her on the front porch of a dilapidated house in the Highlands, and I shook my head.

"What did you just say?" I asked, sure I must have misheard her announcement.

"I bought it. It's mine," Charlie said, her chin set to stubborn.

Shit. I knew that look.

"Bought it for what? Kindling?"

"Vance!" Magnolia shoved her elbow into my side. "It's pretty."

"It's completely structurally sound," Charlie said. She looked down at the dip in the wood of the front porch, only feet from where she stood. "Mostly. It's mostly sound. The foundation is fine."

"And the roof?" I asked, looking up at the ragged shingles. Charlie followed my gaze and frowned.

"The roof needs some work," she admitted. "Come inside and look around."

"I'm not bringing my daughter in there. She'll sneeze, and the whole place will fall down on our heads."

"Vance, it's fine. I had it inspected. It's perfectly safe."

To prove her point, she opened the front door and disappeared inside. Magnolia, the traitor, followed her, saying, "Come on, Vance."

I went after them, Rosie strapped to my chest in her baby carrier. At the first sign the place was unstable, we were out of there.

I crossed the sagging porch with a light step, hearing Magnolia say, "I can't believe you didn't tell me you put in an offer, you sneak."

"I didn't want to get my hopes up since I was the backup contract. But the original buyers found out about the plumbing and pulled out."

"What about the plumbing?" I asked.

"It needs a lot of work," Charlie admitted, sending Magnolia a look I assumed was meant to express how annoying I was.

"What's going on, Charlie?" I demanded.

None of this made sense. Charlie didn't need a place to live. She had a whole suite at Winters House, with a cook and a housekeeper and Aiden to keep an eye on her.

She didn't need this place. And she didn't know anything about construction or renovations.

"Why would you buy a heap like this?"

"I'm moving in. I'm going to live here," she said.

"What do you mean, you're going to live here?" I asked. I may have shouted. Rosie squirmed against me. I kissed her temple and said, "Does Aiden know?"

Charlotte looked at Magnolia, guilt all over her face. "Not yet. I wanted to see what you said first."

I understood immediately. I was protective of Charlie.

We all were. She was the baby of the family. But I was still way more laid back than Aiden. He was going to go ballistic. I shook my head.

"You'd better show us around."

Magnolia and I followed as she led us through the house. The floor was sound, but the brick and tile on the fireplaces had been stripped.

The woodwork was fantastic, original and perfectly done, except some moron had painted it in thick layers that would have to be carefully stripped.

If Charlie put in the time and money, the house would be amazing.

It was going to be a lot of time and a ton of money. Charlie had the money. Not family money, but her own. She'd been working for Winters Inc. since she was eighteen, part-time all through college, and she had done her MBA while working for the company full-time.

She was a vice president at twenty-three, and as far as I knew, she'd spent very little of her salary.

She lived at Winters House, and there was no way Aiden would let her pay rent. She never took vacations. She drove a ten-year-old Audi Aiden gave her at sixteen, when he'd upgraded to a newer model.

If she'd been banking her salary all these years, it wasn't a stretch to imagine she had a small fortune in cash socked away.

But why would she blow it all on a money pit like this place?

"Lay it out for me," I asked after a quick swing through the second level. "What does it need? Other than new plumbing and a new roof?"

Charlotte wasn't easily intimidated, especially by her family. She met my glare and said, evenly, "All the woodwork needs to be restored. The floors need to be refinished. The kitchen and bathrooms are a gut. The upstairs needs to be redone. It has seven bedrooms, including the attic, but only one bath. I want to turn three of the bedrooms into a master suite and add another bath."

"That's all?" I asked, not trying to hide my sarcasm.

"No," Charlotte said evenly. "There are other issues, but those are the big ones."

"And when are you going to do all this work?" I asked. "Honey, you work seventy-hour weeks. Do you have a contractor? Please don't tell me you think you're going to do the work yourself."

"I'm figuring that out," she muttered, breaking eye contact, her gaze sweeping over the foyer of her disaster of a house.

There was a light in her ocean blue eyes I hadn't seen in years. Longing and excitement.

Shit. I didn't like this plan of hers for so many reasons. But if it was going to bring life back to Charlie, maybe even drag her out of the prison she'd made of her job, I was all for it.

"Magnolia and I are taking it easy right now. If you need a little help lining up work, let me know," I said.

Charlie's face lit with a smile. Yep, I'd do a lot to see my baby cousin look happy. I wish I could remember the last time I saw her smile like that.

Losing Aunt Olivia and Uncle Hugh had changed us all. Some of us, like Gage, Annalise, and me, had extreme reactions—me with my drinking, Gage joining the army and disappearing overnight, and Annalise taking off to roam the country with her camera.

We'd been the showboats in our grief. Charlie had just dried up and shut down. The vibrant, off-beat, funny, irreverent girl she'd been had faded away, and she'd become the Charlotte we knew now.

Perfect in every way, but not quite Charlie. I missed her. We all did.

"Do you want me to talk to Aiden for you?" I asked. She shook her head.

"I'll tell him. Just give me some time. I don't want to say anything until we get the new nurse hired and Aunt Amelia settled. And I have some work to do here before I can move in."

"Plumbing first?" Magnolia asked. Charlie nodded. "I'll get you the number of the guy we're using on the carriage house. He can at least get you a working bathroom while you figure out what to do with the upstairs."

Charlotte started to answer, but the roar of a lawn-mower outside the window had her swinging her head around.

Magnolia let out a giggle and strode to the window. Her hands on her hips, she gave a low hum of appreciation.

"Charlie," she hissed, as if whoever was outside the window could hear. "Come here."

Charlie did, joining Magnolia at the window. A faint blush rose on her cheeks as she stared at the neighboring backyard, and she bit her lower lip.

What the fuck?

I joined them just in time to see a giant of a man, every inch of him muscle and ink, pushing a lawnmower. Something about him was vaguely familiar, but at this distance, I couldn't place his face.

God damnit. Why was nothing ever easy?

"Stop ogling your neighbor, Charlotte," I said.

Her clear blue eyes slid to meet mine, a flash of embarrassment in them, before she and Magnolia dissolved into giggles.

"You sound like Maggie when she's being prissy," Charlie said, gasping for breath. "And a little ogling isn't hurting anyone. He doesn't even know."

"That's not the point," I said.

Shit, she was right. I did sound like Magnolia when she was being prissy. Fuck me.

Unable to stop myself, I went on, "I don't think a woman with four broken engagements is qualified to pick her own dates."

"Four?" Magnolia asked, turning wide eyes to Charlie.

Charlie shrugged, not the least bit ashamed of breaking up with any of her rejected suitors. She shouldn't be. They were all assholes.

"I'm slow to catch on, but I get there eventually," she said, turning her eyes back to the guy next door, a smile playing on her lips. "Anyway, I'm not looking for a boyfriend. Or a fiancé. All I want is this house."

"And you got that," Magnolia said, giving her a hug. "Congratulations. Anything we can do to help, just let us know."

"I'll keep you posted," Charlie murmured, still watching her dangerous looking neighbor.

If this house made her happy, we were with her all the way. But if that guy next door came within ten feet of Charlie, I was going to kill him. And Aiden, Jacob, Holden, and Tate would be in line right behind me.

Do you want to read Charlie and Lucas's story?
Keep reading for a sneak peek of
The Rebel Billionaire.

SNEAK PEEK
THE REBEL BILLIONAIRE

CHAPTER ONE
Charlie

"You're fired."

I laughed.

Why wouldn't I? Aiden was joking. He couldn't fire me. I was Charlotte Winters, and we were sitting in the executive offices of Winters Incorporated. I'd been working for the family company since I was eighteen. I belonged here. Sometimes it felt like this was the only place I belonged.

Aiden couldn't fire me. I waited for him to laugh along with me.

The laugh never came. He sat behind his desk, his usually warm brown eyes chilly and impenetrable. Aiden was the only man I knew who could loom while sitting down. I fought the urge to shrink into my chair.

I'd seen him aim that cold stare at plenty of people - employees, clients, his ex-wife. Never me.

"Aiden, you're not firing me," I said, trying to force

amusement into my voice. This was all a joke, right? Aiden held my gaze, unflinching. I sat up straight, feeling my own eyes go cold. "Is this about Hayward?"

Aiden paused for a split second before shaking his head. "This has nothing to do with Hayward," he said, meeting my eyes. He was lying. Wasn't he?

"You agreed that we had to turn him in. You went with me to the FBI. How can you fire me over it?"

Aiden's jaw was set as he said, "Charlotte, this has nothing to do with Bruce Hayward. You handled that situation perfectly and I'm proud of your courage."

"I don't understand."

"I already told you. You're fired. Security has cleared out your desk. When we're done here, they'll escort you from the building."

His words were a punch to the gut. Tears threatened. I knew that prickle in the back of my eyes. I bit down on the inside of my lip, my teeth cutting into the tender flesh so hard I tasted the copper of blood. I would not cry. I refused. Swallowing hard, I stood, planting my fisted hands on my hips. I knew I was in real trouble when Aiden stayed where he was.

If this was about a power play, he would have come to his feet and reestablished his dominance. If he was letting me take physical control of the room, it was only because he knew he'd already won. Fear was an icy wave cresting behind me. When it broke, I'd be lost. I *was* my job. If he kicked me out of Winters Inc, what would I do? Who was I without the company?

Steel bands wrapped my ribcage and I couldn't draw a breath. Turning my back on Aiden, I inhaled slowly, digging my nails into my palms and dragging my emotions under control. I'd learned the hard way to keep my feelings to myself. Always. Even with my family. No one saw my pain, my fears. No one saw me cry. Ever. Not since I was ten.

Aiden knew me better than almost anyone alive, and he gave me the time to pull myself together. Also not a good sign. When I thought I could keep my voice level, I said, "I'd like you to explain this to me. After years of giving everything I have to this company, I'd like to know why you think you can let me go."

There, I'd done it. I was calm. In control. I was not about to scream and burst into tears. I was not going to curl into a ball and sob. And I was not going to kill Aiden. Not yet.

In the same cool voice he used when he delivered bad news, he said, "Charlotte, keeping you on isn't what's best for you."

My voice as icy as his, I asked, "What's best for the company, or what's best for me?"

"For you. It's not what's best for you," he said.

A volcano of rage burned away the ice. What the fuck? Keeping a lid on it, just barely, I managed to grind out one word from between my clenched teeth. "Explain."

Aiden let out a sigh and leaned back in his chair, dropping the chilly CEO persona. His eyes on mine had all the warmth I was used to from my big brother. It only made me more furious.

"Charlie. You've been working here since you were eighteen. It was bad enough when you were in school. Now that you've graduated you work all the time."

"So do you," I said in a short burst of sound. He did. He worked every day. He was here first and was the last to leave. Except when I was here late. Or early.

He might have a point about me working too much, but I was no worse than Aiden and he knew it.

"But I love my job," Aiden said, his tone so gentle I had to fight back tears. "I love this company. I always have. And you don't."

"You can't fire me for not liking my job!" I shouted. "No one likes their job. That's why it's a job and not a hobby. This is ridiculous!" I felt myself losing control, my fury and terror spiraling up and spewing out of my mouth. "You can't fire me because I don't love my job. I'm an exemplary employee."

"You are," Aiden interrupted. "You're an excellent Vice President. If you weren't my sister, I'd be giving you a raise."

That little bit of complete illogic pushed me over the edge. I kicked my chair, sending it rolling to crash into Aiden's huge walnut desk. He didn't flinch. I pointed at him, stabbing my finger into the air to punctuate my rage.

"This is completely sexist. You're doing this because you want me to get married and start having babies like Maggie."

"That's absurd," Aiden said with a wince. "I do NOT want you to get married. Jesus. Not until you get better taste in men. And I'd rather not think about my baby sister having babies of her own."

"You wouldn't be doing this if I were a man," I said, sullen, my arms crossed over my chest.

"Charlie, how many senior executives do we have who are female?"

"Seven," I said, knowing the point he was going to make.

"Exactly. Just under half. And how many of those have families?"

"Five. So why me? Why are you firing me?"

I bit my lip to shut down the plaintive whine in my voice.

I knew Aiden wasn't sexist. I was grasping at straws. I knew it wasn't my performance. I was good at my job, even if I didn't like it. If it wasn't sexism, then what? Why was he doing this to me? Didn't Aiden understand that my job was all I had?

"It isn't about your gender, Charlotte," Aiden said in that same gentle tone. "I'd do the same if you were Holden, or Tate. Even Jacob."

"But not Gage?" I asked, half sarcastic and half trying to figure out what the hell was going through Aiden's oversized brain.

"Not Gage. Gage loves the company," Aiden said, his tone almost wistful.

"Then why isn't he here?" I said in exasperation, feeling my temper slipping its leash again.

"I never should have let you come on board, sweetheart. But you were so determined and I was selfish."

I sat in my chair abruptly, my anger down to a simmer. "Aiden, you're never selfish." He wasn't. Aiden was about two things - his family and the company. He'd open a vein for any one of us in a second.

"I was," he insisted. "I never pressured any of the others to join the company. I knew Holden and Tate would find their futures elsewhere. And Jacob loves business, but he needed to run his own shop. With Vance and Annalise it was clear they had no interest in a nine-to-five job. I was right with all of them. Except you."

"Aiden," I protested, "You always supported me. That's why I don't get this. You don't have to fire me. We can work something out. I'll cut back."

"I supported you, but I didn't look out for you. I was selfish. I always thought Gage would come home, and we'd do this together. But he's doing what he needs to. I understand that. When you wanted to come on board, I should have told you no."

"But why?" I begged. "Don't try to tell me I haven't done a good job."

"I can't. You're bright and you have a head for business. No one works harder. But your heart isn't in it."

I shoved to my feet. "I'm not the only one here who isn't in love with Winters Incorporated."

"No, Charlie. But you're the only one who's my sister. I love you. And you're not happy. I can't be a part of that anymore."

"You don't get to choose that for me."

"Maybe not. I can't tell you what to do now. You're going to have to figure that out on your own. But I can tell you what you aren't going to do. And that's come to work tomorrow."

"I'll go somewhere else. There are a hundred companies who would love to give me a job." I wasn't being cocky. It was true. I might not love my job, but I was good at it.

Aiden shook his head, looking almost sheepish before the expression dissolved into a grim look that made me nervous. "You won't find another job in Atlanta," he admitted. "You'll have to take some time off to think about what you want."

"What? You blackballed me? How could you do that?"

Everything I'd worked for since I was eighteen was slipping between my fingers and there was nothing I could do to stop it. Hot tears streamed down my cheeks. Horror congealed in my stomach. I never cried. Not in front of anyone. I wiped my cheeks with my palms, hurt and anger a hot, poisonous ball in my chest. I would have expected betrayal from anyone else before I would have looked to

Aiden. He was more than my older brother. He'd practically raised me after our parents had died.

Through the blur of my tears I saw him coming towards me. I put up a hand to stop him. If he tried to comfort me I was going to bash him in the head with the heavy Baccarat pen holder on his desk. All our family needed was for me to end up in jail for killing Aiden. After two suspected murder/suicides, we'd had all the scandal we could take.

I backed up, putting my chair between us. Biting hard on the inside of my lip to stop my tears, I said, "Back off. I hate you right now."

"I know you do, Charlie. I can live with that. But I miss you. I miss the Charlie you used to be. And I know you miss her too."

I held my breath, strangling my shout of rage. I stormed out of Aiden's office. No one commented on my red eyes as I rushed through the halls. Aiden had been thoughtful enough to have my desk packed into a box while we were in his office, the bastard. Security didn't exactly escort me out, but they were there, lurking.

Fucking Aiden. How could he do this to me? What did he mean, he missed me? He saw me every day!

At the memory of his face when I left, somehow both contrite and resolved, my vision flared with white hot rage, so fierce I was blinded by it. I was not going to think about Aiden. I was not going to think about the scope of his betrayal, or wonder how my beloved brother could have done this to me. If I did, I might swing the car around and go back to the office. If I laid eyes on him again, I'd kill him.

I barely noticed my family home as I sped up the drive. Located on eight wooded acres in the heart of Buckhead, Atlanta's most elite neighborhood, Winters House was a seventeen thousand square foot Mediterranean style mansion. At that size it could have been imposing, but the warm, creamy walls and red tile roof gave it the look of a historic Italian villa, both welcoming and impressive.

Built in a square around a central courtyard, the design made the big building intimate, as well as more secure. When I was a child, the inner gate had never been closed. After my parents died, we'd all been grateful our home could double as a fortress. With so much of our family gone, we'd wanted to protect what was left.

I pulled through the circular drive and came to a stop in front of the black iron gate that protected the courtyard. Stabbing my finger at the remote to open it, I waited, vibrating with anger and impatience, for the heavy gate to swing open. I pulled in front of the tall front doors and parked, taking my keys with me. I didn't want the staff to move the car as they usually did. I wouldn't be here long enough.

For once, I didn't give a thought to how things looked. I just wanted to get my things and get out. The home I'd always loved looked like a prison, complete with my brother as warden. I loved Winters House. We all did, but everyone else had eventually moved out. I'd stayed, not comfortable leaving Aiden to rattle around in the big house by himself, with only staff for company.

I was over it now. If I had to look at him at the dinner table, I'd stab him with a fork.

Lucky for me, I had some where to go. Funny how things worked out. A month before I'd bought a run down Craftsman style home in the Virginia Highlands neighborhood. I don't know why. Buying that house was the first irrational thing I'd done since I was a teenager. I didn't need a house. And while real estate could be a good investment that was more Jacob's thing than mine.

All I can say is that the first time I laid eyes on that house, I wanted it. Now it was mine, and it was a mess. The roof leaked, the plumbing was shot, and the electrical wasn't much better. At least I'd managed to get the single bathroom on the first floor working. A sleeping bag and a mini fridge and I could move in.

No one was home at Winters House. Another stroke of luck on this unbelievably shitty day. Mrs. Williamson , the family housekeeper, must have been out running errands. There was a gardener, some day maids and a cook, but they were nowhere to be seen. I raced to my suite and slammed the door behind me, catching a glimpse of my reflection in the full length mirror in my dressing room.

It was like looking at a familiar stranger, even after all these years. I had my mother's shiny auburn hair, but I wore mine pulled back into a restrained, professional chignon. I was her height and had the same curvy build. I could still remember the scent of her perfume and the warmth of her hugs. I'd never be my Mom, but she hadn't wanted me to be her. She'd wanted me to be me.

I had no idea who that was anymore.

For a second I had a flash of another me superimposed over the view of my charcoal suit and sensible heels. Me at fifteen, a little plump, wearing a Misfits t-shirt and a paint splattered pair of Converse, a blue streak in my long hair. Before my life changed for the second time. Before Elizabeth moved in. It was the last time I remembered being me. Really, truly me. But I couldn't go back. No one could.

If I didn't have Winters Incorporated, I had no idea how to go forward.

I stripped off the suit and pulled on jeans and a sweater. No reason to be dressed up if I was unemployed. Especially if I was going to my house. I loved every decrepit inch, but the place was a mess. Stuffing clothes and toiletries in a bag, I called Maggie. Magnolia Henry was my cousin's fiancée and my best friend. No answer.

Just before I could leave a message, I remembered she and Vance were out of town with Rosie, Vance's infant daughter. They'd said it was a business trip, but they'd brought along their new nanny and I'd teased Maggie that it was more a pre-honeymoon than a business trip. She'd blushed so pink I'd known I'd been right. If she had any idea what had happened, she'd rush home in a second. I wasn't going to ruin their mini-vacation. I'd just have to handle this on my own.

I slung the bag over my shoulder and stomped down the stairs, taking a perverse satisfaction in letting my temper out. No need to be professional now. What the hell did I care what anyone thought? It wasn't like I had a job. I didn't even have the prospect of one.

Aiden had blackballed me. My knees wobbled at the wave of fury. I couldn't seem to get my head around how thoroughly he'd destroyed my career. He knew I wouldn't leave Atlanta. I love my city. Gage and Annalise aside, my family was here. My friends were here. I could probably find something if I was willing to move, but I wasn't going to flee Atlanta because Aiden was a controlling asshole.

I ground to a halt at the door to his home office. I wasn't above a little petty revenge. Not in my current mood. What I had in mind wasn't petty. On the shelf behind his desk, sat a crystal decanter filled with brown liquid. Aiden's pride and joy. He wasn't much of a drinker, but he did like his whiskey.

I'd never seen him drunk, but I often joined him in his office for a glass after a long day. We drank whiskey together, but never what was in that decanter. I'd never seen him touch the contents, aside from a single glass the day it had arrived. Carefully, I picked up the decanter and one glass, taking them both with me. He'd be furious. Maybe as furious as I was at being fired. Served him right.

I didn't stop to think until I was pulling into the cracked and overgrown driveway at my house in the Highlands. I unloaded my bags, locked my car, and took the crystal decanter and glass to the back porch. The covered porch circled the house, and most of it was rotted and unstable. The section outside the back door was safe enough, I thought. I liked to sit out there, admiring my tangle of a yard and imagining what the house would look like when I was finished with it. I'd barely gotten started. Too many hours working and not enough free time.

I didn't have that problem now.

My stomach did an uneasy flip at the reminder that I was unemployed. It wasn't the money. Even accounting for the cost of the house, I had money. I'd been working for Winters Incorporated since my freshman year in college and I'd kept expenses to a minimum.

Hard to spend money when all I did was work. I still drove Aiden's car, the one he'd given me when I turned sixteen. I'd lived at home, so no rent, mortgage, or utilities. He didn't even let me pay for groceries. I never went on vacation and I rarely shopped except for work clothes. Since buying suits wasn't my idea of fun, I kept that to a minimum too.

I was twenty-four years old with a flush bank account, but no job and no life. A tiny voice whispered that maybe Aiden had a point. Screw that. It would be a long time before I'd be willing to talk to Aiden, much less admit he might have done the right thing. This was *my* life. I knew he could be controlling, but firing me was beyond insane.

Gritting my teeth, I poured myself a generous portion of whiskey into the crystal glass I'd stolen from Aiden's office. At the familiar burn of the liquor, I smiled for the first time since I'd walked into Aiden's office that morning. The whiskey was the best I'd ever had. At fifteen thousand dollars a bottle, it should be. Aiden had bought the Macallan Select Reserve Single Malt at an auction a few years before. He wasn't generally extravagant, but he loved this whiskey.

I took another sip and grinned, remembering the first time I'd stolen Aiden's whiskey. I'd been thirteen and gotten my backside tanned. Back then, the punishment had been worth it, though I'd thought the whiskey was disgusting. How things had changed.

Now I welcomed the smooth burn of the Macallan. Aiden had already delivered his punishment, so why not? If he could yank my entire life out from under me, I could drink his ridiculously expensive whiskey. Even the crystal decanter was valuable. A special anniversary edition, it was worth almost as much as the contents. Now all he had of the set was a single glass. I drained every drop of whiskey from the one I'd stolen and refilled it. I was going to get drunk on obscenely expensive whiskey and figure out the rest of my life later.

"Isn't it a little early for whiskey?"

The voice was smooth, dark and luscious with a husky bite. At first I thought it was the whiskey talking. Then I looked up.

Shit. Standing on the other side of the fence was my neighbor, the one Maggie and I called *Lawnmower Hottie*. The name was silly, but apt. At first I'd only seen him mowing his yard, always shirtless, his chiseled body on full display. He was tall, taller than my brothers and cousins. At least 6' 6". And solid. Broad shoulders, lean hips, and long legs. All of him covered in muscle and what seemed like acres of tattoos.

He should have scared me. My cousin Vance was big, had muscles and a bunch of tattoos. But not like this guy. Lawnmower Hottie was dark. Olive skin, black shaggy hair, apple green eyes. I'd never seen him smile. And I'd looked. I'm not going to admit how often I'd spied on him. I was Pavlov's dog. I heard that lawnmower start up, and I went straight to the window.

"How much of that have you had to drink?" he asked, nodding at the decanter beside me.

I looked from him to my half empty glass before I answered. We'd never spoken, never exchanged more than a vague half wave, but now was as good a time as any to get to know my new neighbor. For once, I was feeling reckless, my anger and the whiskey mixing in my blood, tugging at my memories of another time, when I'd been another girl.

"This is my second," I said, holding my glass up to the light. "Do you want some? I don't have another glass. You'll have to share with me."

Lawnmower Hottie was over the fence in one fluid leap, landing on the balls of his feet, moving far too quietly for his size. This man was a predator. Dangerous. Before I could regret my invitation, he was sitting beside me, his spicy male scent blending with the whiskey, going straight to my head.

Had I said I was feeling reckless? The heat of his body warming my side, he took the glass from my fingers, his skin brushing mine, electric sparks shooting down my nerve endings at the brief contact. My breath caught in my throat. His green eyes were as clear as glass as they studied the whiskey before he raised the tumbler and took a sip.

Up close, he was a study in contradictions - the clarity

of his green eyes gemlike, the line of his jaw aggressive, a perfect match for those bladed cheekbones. And his mouth. Lush and full, it was the mouth of a lover, a mouth made for kissing.

I found myself leaning into him, his lips a magnet. I started to pull back, to get myself under control. I was Charlotte Winters. Perfect Charlotte Winters. Perfect grades, perfect clothes, perfect job. Always perfect.

Not anymore. That Charlotte was gone. I was left with Charlie, and Charlie was unemployed, sitting on her back porch in the middle of the day drinking whiskey and thinking bad thoughts about kissing her neighbor. Charlotte would get up, politely excuse herself, wash out the glass and set it to dry beside the sink before she went off and did something sensible. But Charlotte wasn't here. And Charlie knew exactly what she wanted.

I didn't care if it was the whiskey, the crappy day, or just good old fashioned lust. I knew what I wanted. Maybe not in the big picture. My life was in a shambles and I had no clue what to do about that. But right there, whiskey and desire fizzing in my veins, Lawnmower Hottie close enough to touch, I knew exactly what I was going to do.

Before I could think twice, I closed the distance between us and pressed my lips to his. Fireworks exploded behind my eyelids. He let out a grunt of surprise before his hands closed over my shoulders. For a brief moment I was afraid he was going to push me away and disappointment stabbed through me.

Then I opened my mouth to his, my tongue stroking across his lower lip, and he pulled me closer, my breasts pressing to his broad chest, his mouth slanting over mine, taking control of the kiss. My blood sang and my body was molten. He tasted of whiskey and pleasure. Of danger and sex. I had to have more.

I was a mess, lost and without direction. I had no idea what I was doing with my life, but I knew one thing.

I wanted more of this man. And I'd do whatever I had to do to get him.

Also by Ivy Layne

Don't Miss Out on New Releases, Exclusive Giveaways, and More!!

Join Ivy's Readers Group @ ivylayne.com/readers

THE HEARTS OF SAWYERS BEND

Stolen Heart

Sweet Heart

Scheming Heart

Rebel Heart

Wicked Heart

THE UNTANGLED SERIES

Unraveled

Undone

Uncovered

THE WINTERS SAGA

The Billionaire's Secret Heart (Novella)

The Billionaire's Secret Love (Novella)

The Billionaire's Pet

The Billionaire's Promise

The Rebel Billionaire

The Billionaire's Secret Kiss (Novella)

The Billionaire's Angel

Engaging the Billionaire

Compromising the Billionaire

The Counterfeit Billionaire

THE BILLIONAIRE CLUB

The Wedding Rescue

The Courtship Maneuver

The Temptation Trap

ABOUT IVY LAYNE

Ivy Layne has had her nose stuck in a book since she first learned to decipher the English language. Sometime in her early teens, she stumbled across her first Romance, and the die was cast. Though she pretended to pay attention to her creative writing professors, she dreamed of writing steamy romance instead of literary fiction. These days, she's neck deep in alpha heroes and the smart, sexy women who love them.

Married to her very own alpha hero (who rubs her back after a long day of typing, but also leaves his socks on the floor). Ivy lives in the mountains of North Carolina where she and her other half are having a blast raising two energetic little boys. Aside from her family, Ivy's greatest loves are coffee and chocolate, preferably together.

VISIT IVY
Facebook.com/AuthorIvyLayne
Instagram.com/authorivylayne/
www.ivylayne.com
books@ivylayne.com

Made in United States
North Haven, CT
09 February 2024

48501416R00183